KETURAH THE II

Book One

Vickie L. Mosley

All Contents: Written by the Author
Published By: Irish Writing & Publishing IWP
Editing: Wendy Bray
Book Cover Design: Vickie Mosley
Book Cover Model: iStock Images
Biblical Scriptures throughout this book are found in King James Versions

ISBN: 10: 0692965823
ISBN: 13: 9780692965825

DEDICATION

This book is dedicated to my wonderful mother Betty Jane Hendricks Mosley who in the process of raising me passed on to me her love for fried chicken, singing in harmony, reading and storytelling. Mom has always been an amazing storyteller and could come up with a what-would-you-do- scenarios at the drop of a dime. In Sunday school class she had an amazing way of making the Word of God come alive without even trying. People use to say that I was my mom's shadow because where ever she was, I wasn't that far behind. I praise God for that title today and for catching the mantle that was on her life. Mom was quick witted, and the original comeback queen. My first counselor, confidant, mentor, personal coach, cheer leader, and closest friend. I love and miss you mom, and will one day see you again in Heaven.

ACKNOWLEDGMENTS

First and foremost, all praise, glory and honor go to the Lover of my soul King Jesus, without Him there would be no Keturah the II. He saw a writer in me when I didn't. Thank you, Jesus, for trusting me to tell a biblical story in modern times about a woman you walked with in antiquity.

To my family, I thank God for you all. To my sister Laurie Phillips who original designed my first book cover and was able to see the vision I saw. Thank you for the words of encouragement just by saying get to writing. To Ashley Byrd, the first face of Keturah for the last three years. To my brother Steve and sister in law Lynette Mosley thanks for believing that I could do this. To my dad Herbert Mosley, thank you for leaving me be when you saw me banging away on my keypad. To Wendy Bray for doing the second edit on Keturah and encouraging me to continue to write. Finally, to other extended family and friends who said a kind word or just prayed, thank you and I love you all.

To my bestie, Dr. Lanise Rosemond. Lanise you have been such a blessing and a friend; I cannot tell you how much your prayers and support have meant to me over the years. Even when we'd go on vacation together and I normally had my laptop with me, you never bothered me knowing that writing was my thing. Thank you for allowing me to be me in your presence. Love you much.

To my home-girl Ronanda Palmer. You are an amazing preacher and teacher, song writer and such a gifted writer yourself I love to hear your work thank you for being willing to read and correct mine.

PROLOGUE

He had a soft side. He wasn't the territorial no nonsense business tycoon most people believed him to be. No, that wasn't the only side to Abraham Taylor. Looking down at his wife Sarah, he smiled. She knew the truth; she knew him better than anyone. Hugging her gently to his chest, he kissed the top of her head allowing his cheek to rest in her silky hair. A knock on the door caused him to jerk his head towards the sound.

"Dad, are you still in there? I would like to come in now, if that's alright?"

"Isaac." He whispered; his son was out there, as a matter of fact, everyone was out there waiting, he thought, while turning his attention back to the beautiful sunset. "Let them wait." Only a sliver of the enormous fireball was visible as it settled below the mountain peaks, bidding the day farewell. Breathing out a resolute sigh, he knew it was time to say goodbye.

"I'm leaving now, sweetheart." He whispered, as a lump formed in the back of his throat. Carrying her back to the bed, he laid her down, fixed her hair and brought the covers up to where her hands rested. "You fought the good fight, sweetheart, now take your rest, I'll see you again...in paradise." His voice cracked, as he leaned in and brushed his lips over hers one last time. They were cold! He quickly withdrew. Yes, she was really gone. As anguish and despair overwhelmed his soul, he remembered her last words.

"Don't let this change you Abraham, there's more to you than most people know; please let people see the other side of you."

Isaac's persistent knock on the door continued. "Dad, please open the door!"

His son's frantic voice shook him out of his stupor. "Get it together man." Straightening up from her bed and walking over to the chair. He picked up his outer coat and suit jacket. He looked back at her body one last time.

"Where is death's sting?"

This familiar Bible verse surfaced in his mind as he rubbed his chest. Death's sting was right there settling in the center of his heart. A mournful groan escaped his lips. Jerking his eyes away from the painful sight, he made it to the door in three easy strides. Unlocking the door, he swung it open and was confronted with the mournful gazes of his loved ones. A hush filled the waiting area. As usual, his family always looked to him for the answers, only this time, he didn't have any. This time they were on their own.

"Avery, have the car b r o u g h t around." He barked the order at his right-hand man and friend. He needed air. His lungs burned with the stench of death lingering in his nostrils.

"Sure, Abraham." Avery Jaymes promptly obeyed, walking ahead of him toward the exit.

"Dad, what about the funeral arrangements?" Isaac asked in a choked voice.

It nearly undid him to hear his beloved son so heartbroken, but still he kept moving. "Avery, make sure the pilot is ready to leave, as soon as we get to the airport."

"Sure thing, Abraham."

"Abraham Nathaniel Taylor, how can you leave for business at a time like this? Your wife has just died and the rest of your family needs you! Where's your heart?" Sari Jaymes, the favorite aunt to Sarah, and the matriarch of the Jaymes-clan voice trembled as she chided him.

He rubbed his hand over his chest, then fisted it and clinched his jaw. His heart was where it always was, with Sarah. Deciding it was better to swallow the nasty retort he was itching to tell Sari, he just kept walking.

"You can't run from this Abraham. Do you hear me?"

His gait only faltered for a second, then just as quickly, he picked up the pace and walked through the exit.

"Abraham…Abraham!" Sari called, but he kept moving. He had a plane to catch, a business to run and a wounded spirit to hide.

"Don't let this change you Abraham, let people see the other side of you."

This would be the only request he ever denied his precious wife, Sarah.

CHAPTER ONE

Six Months Later

"Lift every voice and sing, 'til earth and heaven ring'…
Lord please help me hit these notes," Keturah Birch thought, while
taking her ear-bud out, trying to make sure she was singing on key.
Although the ladies' room of the country club was not the ideal
place to rehearse the *Black National Anthem*, she had little options.

Her Uncle Emory Jenkins' words came to her mind. "What
African American doesn't know the *Black National Anthem*,
Tourie?"

She wanted to shout at her Uncle, "*Me! That's who.* Well, there's no
turning back now", she sighed and sang the next verse. "Ring
with the harmonies of liberty. Let our rejoicing rise, high as the
list'ning skies, let it resound loud as the rolling sea. Sing…"

Suddenly, raised voices coming from the lounge area caused her to
stop singing.

"You harlot! How dare you show your face at this event in
honor of my baby God rest her poor soul. Have you no shame
Hagan?"

Keturah pulled the other bud from her ear and listened as the first
woman continued her ranting, about the woman Hagan being
nothing more than an opportunist for trying to steal a dead
woman's husband. Keturah thought, "How can you steal from
the dead?" Keturah thought as the second woman, chimed in.

"Shame?!...Ha! Your precious *Sarah*, took everything from me and my son...so no Sari, I have no shame in coming here tonight. As a matter of fact, all I have is contempt for you both. Furthermore, before all is said and done, everything that you and that witch stole from me, I promise you, I'm going to get back with interest."

"Whoa!" Keturah gave a low whistle, "God, please don't let these ladies come to blows in here," she muttered, looking at her formal navy-blue gown. She was definitely not in a position to break-up two brawling debutantes. "Humph, this Abe dude must be some type of man!" Keturah thought as she continued to listen.

"If I were you, I wouldn't get too comfortable just yet, because this is far from over, Hagan!" Sari, replied.

Hagan countered, "I'll keep that in mind Sari. Now you'll have to excuse me, I really do need to get back to my date. Do enjoy the rest of your evening, because I plan to."

Keturah could hear the contempt in her voice as she heard the *swoosh* of the outer door open and close, then silence. She thought, "Wow that was quite entertaining. Thank God, I'm not mixed up in any drama like that. Just goes to show, even the rich have their share of problems that money can't solve."

Edging out of the lavatory, she looked in the mirror and checked her make-up. As an after-thought, she washed her hands, dried them, and then walked out, into the women's lounge.

To her surprise, a silver-haired woman wearing an elegant, pale lavender gown sat in one of the two chairs provided in the women's lounge. With an embroidered hankie firmly pressed against her eyes, she sat with bowed head, silently weeping.

Immediately, Keturah's heart-strings were tugged. Realizing this had to be one of the two women arguing her heart filled with compassion for her. No one should speak so harshly to the elderly. The woman looked to be the same age as her dear grandmother Gretchen Campbell, and the thought of someone speaking *to her* like that would have caused her temper to hit the ceiling. Taking a quick breath, she cleared her throat and proceeded cautiously not wanting to startle the woman who was still sobbing.

"Um-m excuse me ma'am... are you alright?" It took several minutes for the woman to collect herself, but, even then, she didn't look up, didn't speak, just shook her head, "no," and continued to cry uncontrollably. Keturah couldn't...no, she wouldn't leave anyone in this state.

"Ma'am, I realize you don't know me, but I'm a Christian who believes in the power of prayer. You seem very troubled and if you wouldn't mind, I'd like to pray for you." Keturah ventured, hoping the woman would be receptive. It was something she always welcomed anytime she felt overwhelmed; Gretta, her grandmother had taught her that God was always present and ready to help at our darkest times.

"Y-yes...I -I'd like that." The older woman's voice creaked.

Placing her hand on the woman's shoulder, Keturah began, "Father, you are the God of all comfort. You love us and are with us in good and in bad times, and you never leave us when life gets challenging. So, I pray today, that you would help this precious woman deal with whatever is troubling her. Turn her fears to faith, her doubts to belief, and her troubles into complete trust in you. Send help and let victory prevail...In Jesus' name...Amen!" As Keturah finished the prayer and was about to step back, on impulse she bent down and hugged the woman lightly.

"Thank you for the prayer. Dear heart, I..." The woman's voice came to an abrupt halt, as she lifted her head and was able to get a full view of Keturah's face. Within seconds, the woman's expression turned from gratitude, to shock, and then outrage.

As the woman's smile slowly faded away, Keturah thought, "Lord, why is this woman looking at me so strangely?" The woman's face continued contorting into a scowl. Completely baffled by the sudden shift in her attitude, Keturah took several steps back before speaking. "Ma'am, are you sure you're alright?"

The woman said in an accusing tone, "Why are you here?"

"Excuse me?" Keturah said, confused at the woman's rapid shift in attitude towards her.

The older woman lashed out at God, holding her hands on each side of her head. "Oh, God in Heaven! Why of all nights are you allowing my enemies to come and attack me?" She cried rocking back and forth. "I told Sarah this is the stuff that happens when you let trashy women hang around your man. Like buzzards, trying to get their pound of flesh." Then she directly gazed at Keturah and pointed her boney finger at her. "You're all alike nothing but a bunch of filthy vultures, but I won't let you take what's mine. Do you hear me? I won't let you!"

Whoa...whoa wait a minute...what is this woman talking about? Lord, this lady is crazy for real. Keturah thought knowing this was the first time she ever laid eyes on her and prayed it would be the last.

"What's going on in here?"

At the sound of feminine voices coming into the lounge, both Keturah and the woman turned towards the door.

"Mother Jaymes? Are you alright?"

The old woman cried hysterically, "Shannon...Tippany...oh please...please...please... make her go away."

"OMG!" Keturah exclaimed, throwing up both hands in surrender while, scolding herself, *"You have got to be kidding me! I knew I should have minded my own business."* She stepped back, so the other women entering the room could sit down by the older woman who continued sobbing. Turning her back on the three women, Keturah checked her appearance in the mirror, while keeping an eye on all of them in the mirror's reflection of the room. As one coddled the older woman like a child, the other one stood over both of them staring Keturah up and down.

"Humph, I did my good deed for the day by praying for her, so Lord, do the rest, cause I'm out." Keturah thought to herself, while fixing her smudged lipstick.

The Holy Spirit immediately spoke inside her: *As much as lies within you, live at peace with all men.*

Her heart felt a tug of conviction. Knowing that her attitude was anything but Christ like she took a deep breath and decided she would try to explain her intentions to the newcomers. She turned toward them and said, "Look, I'm not sure what's going on with her, she was in here crying. So, I asked if she would mind if I prayed for her, she said yes, so I did and that's all I did. The next thing I know, she's yelling at me."

The older woman quickly accused, "You're not innocent...Don't you dare try and act innocent, you have a part in all this too...you...you!"

The one coddling said in a protective tone, "Mom, please calm down...remember your blood pressure." Then she looked at Keturah and, in a commanding tone said, "Miss, maybe it would be better if you just go...now."

The one standing over them calmly said, "I'll walk you outside."

"NO!" the elderly woman said emphatically. "Tippany, under no circumstance are you to leave this room."

The young woman named Tippany looked at Keturah then bowed her head in submission to her mother. Keturah thought, *wow this woman is crazy and controlling.* Looking at all three women for a moment Keturah finally said, "You know what…you're right, it's time for me to go…before I say something, I'll have to repent for later…Goodbye…good riddance, too!" She said pushing the door open and exiting the room.

Resting the back of her head against the outer door of the ladies' room she said to herself, "How crazy was that?" While trying to regain her composure, still disturbed at how her good deed was rewarded with such contempt. She thought, *all I was trying to do was comfort the old biddy and how am I rewarded? By getting chewed out, that's how.*

She knew her correct response to the situation was to do the Christian thing; to turn the other cheek, and ignore the woman who was obviously suffering from dementia or something. Still frustrated she exhaled, "Argh! Who said doing the right thing was easy? Besides who did that woman think she was calling me trashy? She doesn't know me!"

Remember your purpose tonight. The spirit whispered.

Taking a breath, Keturah began to focus on her mission. She was here tonight to raise money for the finance department at the university and the girls' center. "I couldn't afford to get caught up in other people's drama." Keturah stated firmly as she pushed off the door and nearly collided with her Uncle Emory.

"Keturah, there you are. We are ready to get started, I've been looking all over for you." Emory swatted at the beads of sweat forming on his forehead and took his other hand and pulled Keturah alongside him.

Without a word Keturah obediently followed Emory who was talking about something but she couldn't focus. His words were in competition with what the woman had said. The woman's words triggered something, a memory perhaps. Whatever it was it was just out of her grasp.

"God help me!" She whispered in desperation needing her Savior to calm her nerves.

They arrived at the stage entrance Emory turned to her gave a quick kiss on the cheek and said "Don't worry honey…God's always has your back. Now go on out there and woo them with your incredible voice."

With a wobbly smile and nerves that matched Keturah followed her uncle out on stage, praying that the night would only get better.

***

"Can I freshen that up for you sir?"

"Thanks." Abraham said, sitting at the bar lost in the thought about Sarah and how they intended to celebrate this day. "Here's to you Babe." He lifted up the glass in silent salute, then downed the golden liquid in one gulp.

"Mr. Taylor is there anything else I can do or get for you?"

Abraham looked at the bartender surprised that he knew who he was. "I'm sorry but do I know you?"

"Me…no, you don't know me, it's just that I recognized you from a 'Man-Up' Seminar you did some time ago."

"Wow, I haven't done one of those in decades. Where exactly was it?"
"Right here in the city." He confessed, "It was one of the most life changing events I have ever been to. That day my life was changed for the better."

"Glad to hear it man." Abraham smiled at the bartender, then downed his drink hoping the man would drop the conversation.

"Do you want another one?"

"I'm probably already at my limit. I haven't eaten much so this will likely go straight to my head." He chuckled, hoping the bartender wouldn't talk about his past endeavors no matter how honorable they might have been, but he didn't want to be rude. "Anyway, you know my name, what's yours?"

He extended his hand and as they shook, he said, "Nicodemus Prince at your service."

"Good to meet you Nicodemus."

"Please call me Nick. My mother and wife are the only two who call me Nicodemus and when they do..." His eyes widened as he let out a low whistle.

Throwing up a hand Abraham laughed, and in a friendly tone he said, "Say no more...I completely understand. So how long have you been tending bar?"

"Oh, I don't tend bar anymore. I'm just covering for a friend who works for me. I'm the owner of St. Nick's Bar and Grill as well as Princes' Palace."

Looking surprised, Abraham smiled. "Wow I've been to Princes' Palace on several occasions. You have excellent service and cuisine; your staff is always friendly and professional."

"Coming from you Mr. Taylor that means more than you will ever know."

"Call me Abe, Nick. Why do you say that?" He said taking another sip.

"Well, like I said that Man-Up Seminar was life changing for me. At the time, all I was doing was partying and working part-time as a waiter. I had a couple kids, but I wasn't taking care of them. I was a mess. You came in that seminar and the first thing you said was, stop making excuses for the mess you've become. Man-Up about it. Everyone in here has twenty-four hours what are you doing with your time? You're a direct product of what you've done with your time. If you don't like where you are don't blame your parents stop blaming God and right here and now make a decision to change. God made men first because he expects us to stand up and be accountable. You want to tell everyone you're the man then be the man when it counts." Nick bent his head down chuckling while cleaning off the countertop. "Yeah, I went home after that seminar hating you and the guy who suckered me into going. But I just couldn't shake off your words. They kept playing in my head. It took some time but I took a hard look at myself and finally got my act together."

"Well here's to your success," Abraham raised his glass to him and finished the contents of his drink. He confessed, "I always enjoy hearing success stories."

Nick waved off the compliment and continued wiping down the bar. "My success is nothing compared to what you have accomplished, I'm just glad I wised up when I did. Now if I could only get my know-it-all- sons to listen." He breathed out a sigh.

Abraham stared at his empty glass contemplating having another drink. He didn't want to talk about his family, this city, or his successes. It all brought back memories of who he was when Sarah was alive.

"You're lucky your son is following in your footsteps," Nick said pouring Abe another without asking.

"What, what was that?" Abraham asked distracted by his own thoughts.

"Your son Isaac seems to be a chip off the old block, you must be extremely proud."

Abraham gave a smile and raised his glass to his lips. "This really needs to be my last one," he thought as the man's words registered in his ears.

Yes, he was extremely proud of how Isaac was handling himself in the business. He was still wet behind the ears in some areas, but he was learning. It seemed he had inherited a little of his business savvy and a whole lot of Sarah's attitude. No one was going to tell him 'no' or stand in his way when he wanted something, which was why he was going to be married in a few more months. No amount of coaxing him to reconsider would dissuade him. Much like his mother when he got fixated on something there was no changing his mind. He could still hear his words in his head.

Rebecca's the one, Dad. We're going to get married this summer.

Feeling his mood darken, he down more of his drink. Sarah so badly wanted to witness their union.

"Miss me Babe?" Hagan Zarah seductive voice purred in his ear.

Turning towards her he smiled, and placed his half empty glass down on the counter. "How could I not miss the most beautiful woman in the room?" He said, his voice slurring.

Playfully she nipped at his earlobe lingering for a moment then moved forward and kissed his cheek lightly. "Careful Abe you keep talking like that and you'll find yourself with your hands full tonight." She brazenly stated.

"Forgive me Sarah." Abraham said within himself but to Hagan said, "Looking forward to it darling". He gave her his killer smile all the while chiding himself in his mind. A late-night rendezvous with Hagan was definitely not wise, but he was intent on doing it anyway.

She's not your wife! A soft voice whispered.

"No… she's not…my wife is dead, but I'm still alive dealing with this painful need!" He argued within his heart. Taking Hagan to his bed was wrong. It was wrong the first time he did it and it would be wrong now, but he never knew this type of need, this hunger. When Sarah had been alive, she satisfied him completely, she was amazingly generous; always looking to please him in this aspect of their marriage. Outside of Sarah, Hagan was the only other woman who knew him intimately and from the signals he was getting from her tonight, she seemed more than willing to rekindle what they shared long ago. That was exactly what he was looking for…craved, something familiar to bring a sense of normality back to his life, even if it was temporary. He wanted to fill his arms with the soft flesh of his beloved, let his fingers play up and down the curve of her spine; feel the tremors of anticipation his hands would evoke with his caresses.

He shut his eyes to the images that played on the screen of his imagination. Shaking his head, Abraham took another gulp of his drink. He knew drinking wouldn't eliminate the memory of intimate moments he and Sarah shared, just like sex with Hagan wouldn't extinguish the loneliness in his heart. But, if God didn't do some type of divine intervention, that's exactly what was going to be on the menu that evening, meaningless sex. His grief was maddening and he needed a way out, even if it was only temporary and, if that meant losing himself in the arms of his former lover…so be it. Bottom line, he wouldn't spend this night alone. Resolved within his heart to do the deed, he put his arm around her waist and pulled her closer and tried not to see Sarah.

"You want the barkeeper to freshen your drink, Honey?" He said, as he was running his hand below her waist.

"No, and I don't want you to freshen yours up either. I want you completely alert when we're alone this evening," she said, rubbed her hip against his side suggestively.

He knew this cat-and-mouse game they were playing, all too well. Back in the day, it was always him being the cat, chasing her down, because she was too shy to initiate anything between them.

It appeared that time had changed Hagan. She was no longer the shy twenty-year-old who looked at him timidly, but a bold lioness on the prowl for prey, and she had her sights on him. Time had run out; his desires would be restrained no longer. For nine months, he had been without his wife, no hugs, or kisses, nothing…zilch…cold turkey. That was vexing. He and Hagan had arrived at the event two hours ago. Songs had been sung, dedications and speeches had been made; all that was happening now was networking; the rich trying to outdo and impress each other…Well, they could have it…it was time for a private party for two.

He stood up, downed the remainder of his drink and turned to tip the bartender. That being done, he turned to gather the woman still hanging on his arm, only to turn around to see a wall of unhappy faces. The breath left his lungs as he sighed in defeat and loosened his grip on Hagan. His family and friends had found the corner he'd been hiding in, and by the glares he was receiving from his son and his friend Emory, there was no way on God's green earth that he was going to escape the confrontation that was brewing.

Emory was the first one to break the tension-filled moment. "Abe, it's good to have you back in the country…Man!" He stepped up to give him a bear hug and whispered, "Are you okay man?"

Chuckling at the sound of the best friend's concern, Abraham stepped back and smiled. "Good ole Emory, always checking up on me," He said trying to sound more casual than he really felt.

Patting Emory on the back, he was about to say more until his eyes looked beyond his friend's head and gazed on the beautiful young woman standing behind him. Shocked, he thought, Sarah!

He shook his head slightly, knowing the woman before him couldn't be Sarah. This woman's caramel skin seemed to glow in the dimmed lighting, making her look fresh and young; her shoulder length raven- black hair cascading over her left shoulder, seemed to sparkle with those heather-grey-cat shaped eyes...Wow, they looked so much like his Sarah's. She stood there like a perfectly set jewel, just smiling beautifully at him in her stunning navy-blue gown...she reminded him so much of...*Don't take yourself there, Abe,* he said to himself, barely aware that someone was calling his name until a hand gently took hold of his.

"Are you alright, Honey?" Hagan stepped forward to put her possessive hand in his.

"Yeah. Are you okay partner?" Emory asked, his voice tensing with concern.

The room did seem to take on a slight tilt; maybe he did have a little bit more to drink than he should have. "I'm fine." Abraham gave Emory a big smile, wobbling a little as he turned. "Whoa, definitely shouldn't have had that last one." Abraham laughed it off as he sat down with assistance from Emory and Isaac who had finally stepped forward.

"Dad, I think you should go back to the hotel...don't you think so, Uncle Emory? Isaac asked his voice laced with concern.

"Zac, I'm fine...stop worrying about me." Abraham said firmly, as he turned his head and again locked gaze with the unknown woman. What was it about her? She had such a quiet strength resonating from her, it was almost tangible, as if he could reach out and claim some of it for himself.

"Clearly, you're not fine" Isaac challenged through gritted teeth; his hand fisted at his side.

"I'm sure your father is quite capable of determining if he's fine or not, Isaac." Hagan said in a matter-of-fact tone, that statement got daggers shot at her. "It's getting stuffy in here. You want to dance, Baby?" To which she received no response.

Isaac reminded Abraham so much of his mother, his complexion, the shape of his eyes...that fiery temper...all at once, uniquely Sarah's, was now his own. Abraham could see in his son's stance that he was clearly angry with his choice of dates for the evening, but he also knew that Isaac still had enough respect for him that he wouldn't outright challenge him; at least, not in public.

Isaac's fiancé, Rebecca Reynolds, who was never far behind him, stepped up and pulled on his arm and whispered something in his ear. Whatever she said, it seemed to do the trick, because Isaac was able to take a breath and swallow whatever he was about to say to Hagan. Instead he turned his attention to his father.

"Dad, please...you can't..."

"Isaac, your dad's a grown man." Hagan snidely said.

"Look, Hagan, I'm not talking to..."

Rebecca quickly chimed in while tugging on Isaac's hand, "Uncle Emory, where's Aunt Adele?"

"Oh, well, ah...she sprained her ankle playing tennis yesterday, so she's home, doctoring her foot." A soft chuckle off to his right caught his attention. "Oh Lord, where are my manners?" Emory tapped himself on the forehead with the palm of his hand, and then with tender affection, drew the unknown woman to his side and placed a protective arm around her shoulder. "Everyone, I'd like you to meet my niece, Keturah Birch, who is just about to graduate with her MBA," Emory stated smugly, his chest puffing out as if he were a proud peacock. "Keturah, this is the legend himself: Abraham Taylor and his son Isaac, of Canaan Enterprises."

She nodded her head and smiled, as everyone turned all eyes on her. "It's a pleasure to meet you both," she extended her hand to Isaac and then to Abraham. "Mr. Taylor, my uncle always brags on you and tells me all these amazing stories of the things the two of you have done over the years. So, I'm glad to finally meet *the legend* in person!" She gave a genuine smile that warmed him.

"I think, legend, might be carrying it a bit far um...Ms. umm?"

"It's Birch." She softly replied.

"Ms. Birch...your uncle has a nose for trouble and, like the politician he is, knows just the right angle to get you hooked."

"Well then, I guess I'm in good company, seeing that he uses the same sneaky tactics on me as well," she smiled affectionately up at Emory.

"Darling, aren't you going to introduce me?" Hagan nudged Abraham in the shoulder.

Realizing he was still holding Keturah's delicate hand, it surprised him at how reluctant he was to release it. Dropping his hand to his side he quickly made the introductions. "Keturah Birch...this is um...ah...is Ms. Hagan Zarah," he smiled at Keturah and then turned to look at Hagan, who immediately gave him a chilly glare he was sure they'd discuss later that evening.

"Yes, I'm the mother of Abraham's oldest son', as well as his date for the evening...Ms. Birch." She said in a miffed tone.

"Oh, well...ah...it's very nice meeting you, ...Ms. Zarah."

A loud accusatory female voice rose from behind them, "So you're the one responsible for her being here, Mr. Jenkins."

Abraham's stomach churned as they all turned. "Oh no! " he said under his breath, along with a few other choice words that he would need to repent for. He hoped not to engage in a public altercation with his family, but by the fire in his Aunt Sari Jaymes' eyes, he knew she was itching for a fight.

"And I guess you are responsible for, 'that' being here, today of all days? Abraham, how could you...how could you disrespect your wife's memory like this?" Sari demanded, while pointing an accusatory finger towards Abraham.

"Oh Lord, I should've stayed in Spain," he muttered, sitting back down at the bar- ready to order another drink and settle in for the brow beating he was sure Aunt Sari was going to dish out.

"Umm, Babe...this seems like a family matter, so I think I'll go and do a little mingling. Call me when you're ready to go back to our suite," Hagan said, in a soft voice, but loudly enough that everyone was sure to hear. With a quick caress of his cheek, she moved out of everyone's line of sight. He couldn't blame her, he wanted to do the same thing, but this was totally his fault. Never being the type of man who hid from adversity, especially when he created it, Abraham settled in for the battle before him.

CHAPTER TWO

When Keturah's uncle said he wanted to introduce her to his best friend Abraham Taylor, she felt that the evening was finally turning around. Abraham Taylor was likely one of the most influential, as well as wealthiest, men in the building... and that was no exaggeration.

An endorsement or a check from him could do wonders for her community center; even keep the land contractors, who felt it should be torn down, at bay. Butterflies fluttered in her stomach as she held the gaze of her uncle's very attractive friend. "I hope he can't detect how nervous he's making me right now. Judging how out-of-it he looks, I don't even know if he knows I'm in the room." Keturah thought.

As her uncle introduced her around, she nodded her head to each of them. Then, she slowly returned her gaze to Abraham, who was still looking intently at her. His gazed caused her to temporarily lose her voice. She felt as if his eyes were not just looking at her but somehow, he could see through her; even to her very soul. In that very moment, something shifted. His guard was down and she could see into his heart. It was as if his soul was crying out in need, as well as in pain. Like a drowning man grasping for anything to keep him afloat, she could see him going under again. His eyes still held her, as if he was searching for something.

"Hold on, Abraham!"

"Where did that come from?" She deliberated as a very shapely woman practically draped herself on him, so as to make her presence known. He gently released her hand and made the introduction. Keturah smiled, extending her hand towards the woman named Hagan Zarah, but noted the woman glared at her and barely touched her hand, as if she were contaminated or something. Pulling her hand behind her back, Keturah noticed the absence of Abraham's touch and how she would like to experience it again.

"Get a grip, girl," she softly said under her breath. "I'd have my claws out too if I had a catch like Abraham Taylor. Shoot the man has to be in his fifties but Lord he's gorgeous and even that's an understatement."

His tailored tux seemed to mold to his slightly muscular physique, this man took care of himself...Whew! Attractive, that was a word used to describe ordinary men, but a whole new word needed to be invented to classify this man with his honey-colored complexion and warm azure-colored eyes. He had a full head of brown, wavy hair, with a touch of gray at his temples, which only made him look more distinguished. Top it all off with him sporting a five-o'clock shadow...bravo!

She would have happily stood there gawking at him and loving every minute of it, but suddenly, her happy world was intruded upon by an old woman's viperous tongue.

Sari pointed her bony finger at Keturah, demanding Emory to explain himself. "Emory, why have you brought that girl here?"

Recoiling as if she's been slapped, Keturah ducked behind her uncle's arm and whispered in his ear. "That's the woman I was telling you about, you know the one from the ladies' room."

"Don't worry about her, Honey, I'll handle this," Emory assured her. "Why don't you go and mingle a little, I'll be along in a moment."

Keturah could see his tight smile and knew that, even though he was maintaining his composure, he was clearly agitated.

"Are you going to answer me or not Emory? You had no right to bring her here, as if she could ever pass for one of us."

"Ms. Jaymes, this is neither the time nor the place to discuss such matters. Besides, from what I see, your plate is already full." Quickly turning from her before she could give a retort, he turned to Abraham, while patting him on the shoulder and said, "I'm glad you're back in town, man. Look, we need to talk before you fly out again...call me." Then he tucked Keturah's hand firmly in his and whisked her away, as several pair of eyes stared at their retreating forms. Keturah remained by her uncle's side for most of the night. She was cordial to the people he'd introduced her to, but for the most part, she remained quiet.

Emory joked as he twirled her on the dance floor. "Hey, you've been awfully quiet. How are you going to raise funds for the project if you don't talk?"

"Was that her, Uncle Em...was that her?" She couldn't look in his eyes for fear of what she sensed he would say.

"Keturah, does it really matter? You're a grown woman who has done well for herself. That's what you should focus on. You have a good head on your shoulders and a bright future ahead of you. Let the past stay in the past."

"The problem is, Uncle Em...it's not staying there. It seems to follow me wherever I go. It feels terrible to have people whisper about you and look at you accusingly, and not even know why. It hasn't bothered me in a long time, but the minute I got back here, it started all over again." Keturah swallowed to keep her emotions at bay before continuing. "So, please just tell me. Is that her?" This time she spoke looking up at him, determination shining in her eyes.

With a deep sigh, Emory nodded his head in the affirmative.

With all the dignity she could muster, she said, "Thank you, I need to use the powder-room. Please, excuse me." She rushed off before he could say anything. She would hold it together for a few moments and then she'd release the tears of frustration she had towards her uncle and the shame and humiliation of being publicly denounced by her own step-mother, Sari Jaymes.

Three hours later, after dancing and mingling with as many would-be sponsors as she could stomach, she was totally exhausted, and more than ready to leave the party.

Gingerly walking on her tiptoes, she wished she could carry her shoes in her hand, which she would have done, if she wasn't so afraid that she would be photographed. She looked to retrieve her wrap, make her way to a cab and go straight to the hotel.

Seeing her uncle in the hallway conferring with Isaac and another man she didn't recognize, she gave a quick wave; not wanting to even attempt walking with her aching feet, over to where he stood.

On her way, out of the country club lobby, her only immediate thought was, *Lord, just let me make it down these steps and into a cab and I'll never wear these heels again! Okay, maybe that was an exaggeration, but not any time soon will they be back on my feet.*

God must have heard her aching feet cry for mercy. Seeing a cabbie still on duty, she quickly gave him the address of her hotel and, they were off. Her cabbie, a not-so-nice-smelling man, who had a thick Middle Eastern accent, was saying something to her in broken English. It was difficult to decipher, but she figured as long as he was going in the direction of her hotel, all the other stuff he was muttering was inconsequential.

After what seemed like forever the van finally pulled to a stop in front of her hotel. It was a little past midnight. With feet throbbing and exhaustion calling her to bed, she pulled out the price of the fare and exited the cab. Just as she started towards the hotel door, the cabbie called out to her.

"Take husband wit choo…" He said in broken English.

Too tired to comprehend what the cabbie was trying to say to her, she yelled back. "What?"

"Take him!" He commanded.

Keturah snapped with irritation, *this cabby was keeping her from her bed*, "Take who?"

The driver was nearly shouting at her as he pointed to the back seat, "Him!!"

Confused, she looked back toward the cab doors and to her surprise, a very groggy Abraham Taylor was emerging from the back seat of the van. How they managed to be in the same vehicle the entire time and she didn't notice was a testament to how tired she was.

"No…no…no…, he's not with me." She stated firmly.

The cab driver closed the door of the van and made his way back to the driver's side, and in his heavy accent said, "You say he with you when you get into the cab. He yours now…" He quickly shut his door and drove away, leaving Keturah and Abraham to fend for themselves.

Standing there looking at the tail-lights disappearing in the night, she sarcastically said, "So much for being hospitable." Turning to Abraham, she was surprised to see he was gone. Shrugging her shoulders, she went into the hotel, thinking it was rather rude of him not to pay for his share of the cab ride, but maybe that's how the rich stayed rich - by sharing cabs and staying in cheap hotels. Although, it did strike her funny that he would be staying here.

"I would have expected him to be in some five-star hotel like the Crown Plaza or Hilton; but, hey, where he stays is none of my business," she acquiesced, as she walked quickly towards the entrance, wanting to get out of the cool night's air.

Upon entering the hotel lobby, she immediately took off her shoes. "Relief!!!" she heard her feet cry, as she carried the instruments of their torture for the last five hours, in her hands. The cool, marble tile felt like Heaven, as she made her way towards a crowded elevator.

Abraham was nowhere to be seen. She thought, *"He likely has a private elevator taking him to his own suite,"* although she doubted this hotel had that type of accommodation. She muttered to herself, "Why do you even care? He probably realized he was at the wrong hotel and called his limo driver to pick him up."

As the elevator's occupants thinned out, she breathed a sigh of relief. All she wanted to do was get her weary body in a hot bath and then sink down into her queen-sized bed. She thought she'd go mad as the elevator inched its way up to her floor, letting out its occupants' one-at-a-time.

She felt relieved when the last person stepped off the elevator. She spoke out loud, while pressing the close door button, "Alone at last." Apparently, she spoke too soon, as a low groan from behind her drifted to her ears. Startled, she gasped in fright and turned towards the sound, only again to be surprised to see Abraham slouched in the corner opposite her, with a death-grip on the rails. He didn't look good. Not at all! His face was pasty white and his forehead was perspiring profusely.

"Uh...M-Mr. Taylor, I-I didn't know you were in here with me." He said nothing; he didn't even make eye contact with her. Compassion swelled in her heart as she slowly approached him. Reaching out her hand to help steady him, she spoke, "Are you all..." She couldn't get out her sentence. His head jerked up, with his blue eyes bulging. She tried leaping back from him, but it was too late. He fell face-forward, right into her cleavage, and before she could even react, he unceremoniously emptied the contents of his stomach all over the front of her dress.

"Oh crap!" she hollered right as the elevator doors opened on her floor. Thank goodness, her room was the first one to the right of the elevator. With all the strength, her tired body could muster, she half walked and half dragged a nearly passed-out Abraham to her hotel room door. Her dress was soiled and wreaked, but she couldn't worry about that right now. Her only thought was to get him in her room, call down to the front desk, and have hotel security escort him to his suite. Only after she was alone, would she try and salvage her ruined dress. "Lord will this night ever end!" she sighed.

CHAPTER THREE

"Honey, please relax. You're gonna wear a hole in the carpet if you keep pacing like that," Rebecca pleaded.

"Calm down! Are you kidding?" Isaac stopped abruptly in front of her, his fury etched into the contours of his face. "I have a right to be this upset and more. Dad was wrong!" Isaac retorted, then resumed his pacing.

"Okay!" she raised her hands in surrender. "I'm just saying maybe tonight was too much for him to deal with. After all, today is your father and mother's anni..."

"TOO MUCH FOR HIM TO DEAL WITH!?!" he yelled, suddenly grabbing her shoulders. "Becca, please stop making excuses for him! He was wrong. Plain and simple. It was bad enough that he brought a date to the event that was in honor of my mother, but of all the people to invite, he brings Hagan." Isaac said her name as if he had just tasted something repulsive. "Furthermore, to top off the evening, he gets wasted in front of everybody, including our friends, family and business associates." He ran one of his shaky hands through his hair. "Do you have any idea how his actions impacted the company's image?"

Seeing his fiancée's eyes widened with fear, he quickly released her other arm. Compassionately, he continued, "Oh, babe, I'm sorry. I'm so very sorry." He gently pulled her, trembling form, into his arms and rocked her gently back and forth. "I didn't mean to frighten you. It's just Dad's behavior tonight really did a number on me. It's like I don't even know who he is anymore." He felt her body relax as her trembling ceased. Giving an inward sigh of relief, he tilted her head back. "Babe, I promise, when we get married, I won't allow this craziness to interfere with our lives. Okay?" After she nodded her, yes, he gave her a gentle kiss then touched his forehead to hers. Closing his eyes, he longed for the day she would be his wife. She was a woman he was proud to have at his side for the entire world to see. Suddenly his eyes went wide.

"Oh, my God, the press!" He abruptly pushed away from her and said, "I've got to call Aunt Sari. If the press gets wind of what happened tonight, we'll have to do damage control." He hurried to his cell phone and began dialing a number.

Watching him make his call, Rebecca sat down on the bed and rubbed her arms. Already missing their close contact and wishing there could be more between them than a chaste kiss tonight, she rubbed her shoulders and wondered within herself, "Lord, will I always play second-fiddle to his family, and the company?" He had promised not to allow the craziness to affect their lives, but in essence, it already had. Looking down at the engagement ring that rested on her fourth finger, then back at the man who had placed it there, her eyes misted; the sting of disappointment was still fresh.

Tonight, was not just about honoring his mother, but they were also supposed to announce their engagement. Funny how Isaac showed little concern about that not happening, making her wonder just how much of a priority she would ever be in his life.

***

Tonight, was pretty much a bust, but Tippany refused to allow the events of the evening to keep her from finding out what she wanted…no…what she needed to know, about Keturah Birch. Emory had the answers and she was going to strong-arm him into telling her everything.

"Emory, tell me. I have a right to know!" Tippany argued, "Was that her? Was that my…"

"Tippany, I can't get into that right now. Abraham is missing and we need to find him, quick."

"Well, did you look in that little tramp's room?" A very cross looking Sari emerged from her room with hands on hips. She gave Emory a heated stare …. "Well, did you?"

"No. Not yet, we're just on our way…"

"On your way? That should've been your first stop!" She fired back curtly, "If you were a real friend to Abraham and not so worried about your own political career, this probably would not have happened."

Emory shot back, "We thought it prudent to first check the cab company before going on an all-out manhunt for him."

Looking for a way to bring Keturah back into the conversation, Tippany remembered the way Keturah and Abraham had looked at each other. She smirked and softly said to herself, "Nah….no way…not in a million years would those two ever hook-up."

Her mother rebuked her, "Tippy, this is no laughing matter. I just got off the phone with Isaac and he voiced the same concerns. If this debacle becomes public, it could mean disaster for the company's image and reflect badly on all of us."

Tippany rolled her eyes, while inwardly preparing for her mom's rebuttal, as she nonchalantly said, "Really, Mother. I do believe you're exaggerating. So, he had a little too much to drink. What's the harm in that? I actually think it did him a little good. I always did think he was too tightly wound. Maybe this will help people see him as a little more human."

"You make me sick, Tippany, you and that gutter trash, Conrad, you brought with you as a date tonight. Now I'll never be able to convince Lois Parnell that you and her son, Buford, could be an item." She gave a murderous glare at her daughter. "Sometimes, I don't even know why I bother."

"Me neither, Mom," Tippany smiled within herself as her mother huffed, jerked around and stormed back into her room. *Mission accomplished!* "Now Emory, back to Ket..." she stopped... seeing that she was in the hallway alone.

She gave a disappointed sigh, "You got away from me this time, Emory, but you can't dodge me forever." She smiled, then turned towards her suite,
ready for round-two with dear, ole Mom.

***

"What do you mean, he's not a guest of this hotel?" Keturah raised her voice in alarm, as she left a nauseated Abraham in her bathroom. "I don't understand. Are you sure? Okay...fine! Then can you please have someone come up and escort him out of my room?"

Keturah tapped her foot in irritation as she glared at the wall-clock as it struck one in the morning. Funny how the friendly service she received that afternoon, miraculously diminished after dark.

"Whoa...wait a second. How did he become my responsibility? I barely know this man!" She remained silent for a moment as the manager replied, while trying to ignore the stench coming from her dress. "Well, yeah. He and I shared a cab coming here, but I thought...now hold on! Call the police!?...No, no that won't be necessary. Thanks for your help," Keturah said snidely, before slamming the telephone receiver down.

Apparently, the hotel manager wasn't sympathetic about the situation. She wouldn't dream of contacting the police and having Mr. Taylor escorted out of her hotel room. It would be an embarrassment to them both and possibly put a strain on his relationship with her uncle. Running her fingers through her hair, a thought struck her. "Uncle Emory!" She straightened with the thought, quickly grabbing her purse to retrieve her cell and dial his number. "I'll call him, he'll know what to do." She only wished she had paid attention to what hotel he was staying in...it was something that ended in suites.

When his voicemail picked up, she was disappointed, but left a message for him to call her ASAP, anyway. After checking the phone book, she found there were at least ten different hotels with 'suites' at the end of the title. "Lord, this is a nightmare." She inhaled and was rewarded by the pungent odor of her gown. "Eeeww, I've got to get this off and soaked or something."

Looking at the bathroom door where Abraham had retreated; she found herself afraid to approach. Aside from her uncle's endorsement, all she knew about him was from newspaper clippings. Who was he after dark? That wasn't a question she was sure she wanted to find out.

She looked down at the beaded bracelet that one of the girls at the center had made for her and remembered the lesson Gretta taught that coincided with the arts and craft project. W.W.J.D.! As she looked at the letters, she could hear Gretta 's voice.

Listen ladies, no matter what situation you face, always ask yourself the question, What Would Jesus Do? It's important, as a young Christian, that we always try our best to be like Jesus. He's our example, the one we should strive to be like, not Beyonce, Kim Kardashian or any of those other celebrities. We most look like Jesus when we reflect his character. When He would see someone sick, He would heal them. He'd see someone hungry; He would feed them. He would provide shelter for those who didn't have any. Most of all, He would give to someone in need. Likewise, we should do the same.

Keturah thought, *Now, why did that particular lesson come screaming at her? Didn't God normally speak in a still, small voice?* She timidly advanced towards the door, giving it a light tap...nothing. Knocking a little harder, she placed her ear to the door to see if she could detect any sounds of movement...still nothing.

Quietly, she asked, "Now what?" She didn't necessarily want to go in there and find the man in his undies. That would definitely ruin the image she had of him.

What if he's passed out with his head hung over the toilet seat or was drowning in his own vomit as I'm contemplating if I'm going to help him or not? Okay, I've been watching too many episodes of NCIS. She grumbled, rubbing her face with her hands. Giving a humorless chuckle, she put her hand on the knob and boldly threw the door open, hoping the man was still conscious.

She was struck to find the only thing in the bathroom were his shoes, and his crumpled, smelly, clothes discarded on the floor. Her tiny bathroom looked as if a tornado had hit it. "Where...What.... How can one man be so messy?"

She complained praying that her uncle would call her any minute, so she could unload this burden. A low groan coming from her bedroom stopped her tidying efforts and had her staring at the room she knew he had to be in. The groaning sound came again, followed by a snore! SNORE! OMG! *This man is* not *sleeping in my bed!!!*

All timidity aside, Keturah kicked through the clothes on the floor and stomped to the bedroom door. She was gracious enough to help anyone in a jam, but it was now going on two o'clock in the morning; she was tired and smelled like puke. There was no way she was about to sleep on that lumpy sofa in her own hotel room.

Her uncle's friend, rich or not, would sleep off whatever hangover or sickness he had, on the couch. Better yet, the hall. Breathing in deeply caused her to gag. "Uck, I can't take it, I've got to get out of this dress." Spying the hotel robe on the back of the door, she quickly took it and locked the bedroom door. Peeling off the dress, she realized she was soiled through and through. "Ugh, this is so disgusting."

After discarding her soiled garments into a pile on the floor, she was about to put her robe on when she looked at herself in the full-length mirror; only then did she realize her dress wasn't the only thing that got hit. Her hair and the side of her neck were both covered in vomit.

She rushed to the shower and turned the water on as hot as she thought she could stand it. Checking the other door to make sure it was securely locked; she jumped in the hot spray and scrubbed her skin and hair until all traces of Abraham's upset stomach vanished from her skin.

She thought quietly, *you owe me Abe Taylor, big time! I've prayed for you, paid your cab fare, and not to mention, I've kept you out of jail and at least half a dozen newspapers. And, how am I rewarded? By your throwing up all over me! And if that's not bad enough, you hijack my bed! Shoot, paying for my enrichment program at the community center is the least...the very least you could do.*

"For I was hungry and you gave me food, I was thirsty and you gave me drink, I was a stranger and you took me in. I was naked and you clothed me, I was sick and you visited me, I was in prison and you came to me. I say to you, in as much as you did it one of the least of these my brothers, you did it to me."

The scripture verse immediately deflated her feelings of anger. Now, feeling thoroughly chastised by the Lord, she turned off the shower and dried herself. Stepping out of the tub, she tied the robe around her, secured it, and then went to the door again to listen.

She heard nothing but deep breathing. It was now two o'clock and somehow, she knew her uncle wasn't coming to the rescue. She had little choice, "I sure hope it's true what they say, that no good deed ever goes unnoticed," she resolutely sighed as she tiptoed into her room to grab her night gown and the extra blanket from the closet. After retrieving the items, she was about to tip back out when his voice froze her in her tracks.

"Sarah, sweetheart, come back to bed...I'm cold without you," he mumbled.

Keturah slowly peered over her shoulder, praying that the man was still sleep. She would deal with him being sick, maybe even a little hung over, but aroused? Now, that was completely out of her element! She gave a sigh of relief when she saw him lying in the same position he was in when she entered the room.

She took that as a good sign and quickly made her way out the room. She'd definitely make sure the door to the bathroom and the lounging room would remain locked. If he had to pee in the middle of the night, he would do it in his shorts, because she wouldn't be unlocking that door a minute before seven that morning. For good measure, she pushed the heavy couch against the second entrance of the bedroom. Just in case.

CHAPTER FOUR

Screaming and shouting was all around her. Why was everyone so mad at them? What had they done to make everyone shout? They were only having a picnic. What was so wrong with that? Maybe it was because she spilled ketchup on her dress. Mommy had told her to be careful and try and stay clean. Maybe that's the reason everyone was yelling; because she didn't keep her dress clean like mommy had told her to. Mommy was crying now and holding on so tightly she could hardly breathe.

"Mommy, I'm sorry about the dress."

"Hush, baby...hush!" was all her mother said as she held Keturah tightly, on her hip, as her tears mingled with her child's. The man who was standing beside them suddenly moved in front of them to keep someone away.

"Sari...you need to calm down. I told you I would handle this...now, please."

"You brought your whore and the bastard into my home and you want me to calm down? Never...never! I want this tramp gone, now. Do you hear me Kedron Jaymes...Now!" Sari shouted.

"Emory, please take them home for me!" Kedron pleaded.

"But Kedron, you promised that you would tell her...you promised that after today you, me and Keturah would finally be a family," Keturah's mom cried. Suddenly Keturah's view was blocked and she and her mom were being pulled from the room. As the person shifted, Keturah saw strangers staring back at her. The only ones she recognized were the sad grey eyes of her daddy's and the mean, light-brown eyes belonging to the one he called... "Sari!"

Startled Keturah bolted straight up out of her sleep her hand covering her racing heart. She struggled to gain her bearings while her mind slowly awoke from the dream and her heartbeat slowed to its normal rhythm. "What in the world!" she stated, looking around the darkened room, trying to make sense of what was happening and why she had fallen to sleep on the couch.

"Sarah…where are you going?" A male voice came from the bedroom.

She tensed at first, then relaxed as the dots began connecting in her brain. She was in her hotel room, sleeping on the sofa because Abraham Taylor was occupying her room, and from the sounds of it, apparently having a nightmare. "Lord, will this night ever end?" she said agitatedly, as she wiped sleep out of her eyes. She picked up her cell-phone off the coffee table to see what time it was: 4:30 a.m. "You have got to be kidding!"

She had only been asleep for two hours. Abraham was getting louder and if she didn't do something, she was sure she would be getting a call from the front desk.

Normally, she would be able to show more compassion in a situation like this, but truth be told, this entire situation was way past the point of getting on her nerves.

After all, she had already spent half the night trying to locate someone to take him off her hands, and when that didn't work, she'd spent another forty-five minutes trying to get his tux and her dress cleaned. Now she has to deal with a fifty-plus-year-old man who suffered from night terrors…Really? "Lord, I know about the story of the Good Samaritan and the importance of going the extra mile, but this is pushing it." She grumbled snatching the covers off her legs.

She walked over to the door and drew her right hand up, ready to bang on the bedroom door, when a thought struck her. Did she really want him to wake up and find himself in her bed? What would he think of her...that she tried to seduce him, or would he try and take advantage of the situation? She inwardly cringed. She knew her uncle always spoke highly of the man, but still, everyone claiming to be saved...ain't always saved, as her grandma would say.

She moved her hand closer to the door and still heard him mumbling something and thrashing around. *Is it even safe to wake a person up from a nightmare?* She asked herself, as she made her way to the bathroom door. She wasn't about to shove the couch back into its place. It was her only barricade between herself and him escaping from her bedroom. She liked the fact that anyone trying to get out of the room would find themselves blocked in.

She slowly proceeded through the bathroom and stopped at the door that joined the two rooms. She thought; *thank heavens the bathroom door leading into the bedroom locks from the side.* For one fleeting moment, she had hoped he would have quieted himself, but from the loud mumbling, he hadn't. *Shoot!*

Keturah took a steadying breath, put her hand on the doorknob and was about to open it, when fear, momentarily, overwhelmed her. She thought, *what if he's really awake and you're about to go right in there and get yourself raped... or even killed?! You don't know what kind of man he is. If he was so saved, how come he got drunk in the first place?*

What was she thinking? What if he really was up and waiting to overpower her? "Lord, what should I do?" Keturah softly asked as she continued backing away.

Then a scripture rose up in her heart: *As I walk through the valley of the shadow of death, I will fear no evil for you are with me!*

Grabbing hold of God's promise, Keturah's fears began to recede as a calming presence flooded her senses. God was with her; she didn't need to be afraid. Swallowing hard, she moved forward, feeling a boldness, she couldn't really explain.

Her hand bumped her heavy, wooden-handled brush lying on the sink. She paused and looked down at it, shrugging her shoulders as she picked it up, deciding that carrying it in there couldn't hurt, while determining in her mind that she'd beat him senseless with it if he tried anything funny.

The light from the undrawn curtains bathed the room in shadows, but it was enough to keep her from stumbling over everything. From what she could see, Abraham had knocked all the bed linens on the floor as he had tossed back and forth. She approached him slowly, still unsure of the best way to help him calm down. As she stood beside the bed, the compassion that she felt had been depleted from sleep deprivation was slowly coming back, as she saw the man, drenched in his own sweat and quite possibly feverish, as he continued to toss and turn and call for his Sarah.

She had always been told that love was a powerful drug and one of the hardest addictions to tame. Was that true for the love Abraham carried for Sarah? An addiction so strong, that the loss of her caused him to crave her, even in his sleep? "Poor man," she whispered, feeling pity for him. Was this the reason for the haunted look she had seen in his eyes earlier that evening?

"Lord, what do I do...how can I help him?" she mumbled to herself as she stood there, while fear and concern about the man played tug-of-war with her heart. Then a thought popped in her mind. She quickly turned from the bed and went into the bathroom. Placing her hairbrush down, she reached for a washcloth, turned on the faucet and dampened it in warm water. "Lord, I hope this works!" she silently prayed as she walked back into the bedroom and moved closer to where he lay. Seeing there was room to sit on the bed, she sat on the furthest edge and gently patted the sweat clinging to his brow.

"Sarah?" his raspy voice whispered. His body seemed to relax and the tortured expression on his face seemed to lessen. She didn't understand why she had a need to comfort him, but found herself speaking to him softly, "You're going to be ok, Abraham. God hasn't forgotten about you. He loves you and will comfort you…It's going to get better…just trust him."

As she continued to stroke his forehead and the sides of his face, his thrashing stopped and his talking slowly died down. "Thank God!" She breathed a sigh of relief. Tilting her head to the side, she looked at him intently and for a brief moment, allowed herself to imagine what it would be like to love someone like Abraham Taylor, one of the most eligible and wealthy bachelors in the country. Not that she was interested. After all, he was way, too old for her and she was not even close to being in his league. Although, after tonight, she didn't know exactly who was in whose league. Yet, she couldn't help but wonder what type of woman Sarah had to be to maintain such a strong hold on a man, even from the grave.

"Bet she was beautiful and smart."

Keturah looked down on Abraham's face and smiled to herself as she wiped the few remaining beads of perspiration from his forehead. "You're such a handsome man, so distinguished looking. I wonder if I'll ever be loved by a man as much as you loved your Sarah?" He gave an incoherent mumble and turned over.

He seemed to be resting now, for which she was glad. "I bet Sarah had to keep tight reins on you when you were my age. You seem like you would have been quite the ladies' man," she said softly, wondering what their marriage had been like when he was still trying to get Canaan started. She would love to know their history. "I bet you didn't leave Sarah behind with no support and a baby to raise alone," Keturah mumbled, as she felt resentment rising in her heart towards her father Kedron, who had abandoned her and her mother.

"I guess marriage works for some people and not for others. It definitely was a no-go for my parents," she mused, as fragments of the dream came back into focus.

As quickly as they came, she forced them out of her mind. None of the pictures made sense. She was always told that her mom died when she was very young and that she didn't spend a lot of time with either parent, but those memories painted an entirely different story.

"Were my parents in love like you were with Sarah?" she wondered. She didn't even realize love like this man possessed for his wife was even possible. "Must be nice!" she said, as she took one last look at a resting Abraham before getting up from the bed and heading towards the door.

Abraham Taylor was a rare breed of man. After tomorrow, when she explained to him how he ended up in her hotel room, she'd likely not see him again. Like most men, he would disappear, which was why it was her mission to open up the youth center and enrichment program for underprivileged girls. Abraham was a living relic, a mere shadow of what men used to be. She wouldn't look to anyone to rescue her and she planned to teach the girls at the center the same thing. She wanted her girls to take care of themselves and not to depend on a guy for anything.

Shutting the door with a pronounced, click, and then leaning back on it, releasing the knob; she ran her hand through her unruly curls. She thought, "You want to be disappointed? Trust a man! You want to be self-sufficient? Trust God."

She hated feeling the anger building in her soul when she thought about the untimely death of her mom, but felt powerless to contain it in her present state of mind. Feeling her throat constrict as memories of her past, like a powerful tidal wave, began dragging her under its tow, she moved from the door to the bathroom sink.

She turned the faucet on full-blast and cupped her hands under it, splashed water on her face, then grabbed a glass and filled it up under the cold stream. Taking a sip and allowing the cool sensation to combat the burning in her chest; she tried to quell the sob that rose from it.

It was tough growing up without her mom, someone who was assigned to love her no matter what. Keturah studied her face in the mirror; both tears and water drops were making a steady track down her cheeks. Her mom had gambled on love and lost, big time. Keturah felt there would never be a man who would likely make her take that gamble…Ever!

Wiping off her face, she reflected on her dear Gretta's words:

Your mom and I got a hold of some bad apple seeds when it came to men Honey, but I don't believe that it has to be the same ole story for you. Don't let our bad experiences with men set your teeth on edge. There are still some good ones out there and if you follow God's plan, he knows how to match you up with one of the good ones.

She looked back at the shut door that stood between her and Abraham and wondered if God sent her a man of his caliber, would she risk opening her heart for love?

"Humph…maybe," she chuckled to herself, "but, where's God going to find another one like him?" She flicked off the bathroom light and headed for the sofa, hoping to get in a couple hours of sleep.

Chapter Five

"Where the blazes is he?!?" Hagan fumed as she crossed the threshold to the adjoining door of their suite, for what felt like the one-hundredth time. It was bad enough he'd left the country club without her, but now it was after four in the morning and he still hadn't managed to come back. It was troubling and maddening at the same time. Troubling, because the last she saw of him he looked a little sick. He had been drinking heavily, which was something she wasn't accustomed to seeing him do. She only hoped and prayed he was all right; that no one was taking advantage of him.

A flash of the young woman Emory introduced as Keturah came to mind. Her face looked so familiar but she just couldn't place her. It was maddening because you can't very well seduce a man if he's not physically present for the seduction.

"This is all her fault!!!" Hagan hissed as images of Sari's weathered face and sour disposition erupted in her mind. "She always was an interfering witch. Abraham would be in my arms right now, if it weren't for her."

She rapidly paced back to her room and snatched her I-phone off the bed, punched in his number and wanted to scream when it immediately went to voicemail. Clicking it off, she forcefully threw it back on the bed, then plopped down on her mattress.

"Arghh! Tonight, would have been so perfect! Abraham and Sarah's special day would have been forever linked with thoughts of me and what we shared tonight. Well, that is, if the man would just come back to our suite! His memory would be of me and not of her." Hagan had been working on Abraham for the entire month to get him to this point of weakness and tonight she would have had him, and nothing would take him from her. Not this time.

The day she was forced from the house began to replay in her mind…and what an awful day that was. *Abraham had invited her and Ishmael to the lake it was going to be the three of them. Well, so she thought, until they arrived at the beach front to find Emory there with Kedron, his mistress and their little girl.*

The day had started out uneventfully enough. Abraham had asked for alone-time with just him and Ishmael. She would have loved to be a part of that; but, hey…as long as Ishmael had his dad's undivided attention, she would make do with that.

Ishmael was thirteen and really needed his dad's guidance. Abraham promised that they would all go out for a nice dinner around four o'clock, so she decided to do some shopping and then head back to the hotel for a nap.

It had not been an hour before she received a stressing voicemail from Ishmael sobbing into the phone asking for her to come and get him. Not knowing what to expect, she arrived at the beachfront to find more cars out front than were there before, and yelling that could be heard from the street.

Parking in the first available spot, she raced to the front door, not caring about anything but the safety of her son.

Walking in on Sari ranting and raving about Kedron's whore and bastard. Sari then turned her sights on her and went all in. "Oh, so you brought your whore up here, too, Abraham." Quickly shifting her eyes from Abraham to Sarah saying, "Didn't I tell you if you let gold-diggers close to your husband, they'd try to replace you one day? Well, the day is here." *In the next instant, Sarah was glaring at her with such hatred you'd never guess, at one time, they had been close friends.*

Sarah addressed her words to Abraham, but never took her eyes off Hagan.

"I will not be made a fool of, Abraham, not in my own house. I have walked in dry places with you, poured my life into making Canaan a success, but this," *she pointed an accusatory hand at Hagan,* "I cannot and will not play second fiddle to anyone, least of all...her. So, you decide, Abraham, and you decide right now; do you want what God has promised to give you with me and Isaac, or do you want this-this.... mess!"

The memory of that day cut into Hagan's gut like a sharp blade, and even though twenty-years had passed, the insult still felt as fresh as the day she spewed it.

"Sarah's dead. When will you move past this hatred? What can revenge change? The past has already been written. Release it before it destroys you." The spirit whispered.

It was so tempting to let bygones be bygones, but she couldn't. Back then to keep her head above water and food on the table, she had to work odd jobs, live in slummy neighborhoods and, although Abraham sent monthly support checks, she and Ishmael lived nothing like they had before. The only way Ishmael could have a halfway decent life was if he left her and lived with his dad. Otherwise, the measly support checks that came monthly was all they would get. It had Sarah's handwriting all over it.

Ishmael had adamantly refused to leave his mom and suffered for it when he had to go to public school. So, left with no choice, she married the first man that came along. Jamal Zarah was no Abraham Taylor, that was for sure, but he had a business and was doing well enough to take them out of the slums and back into a nice home. Ishmael was able to go back to private school and not worry about getting beat up every day. Ishmael's step-dad was less than affectionate to her but was a good father to her son, and that was enough...she would do without love...she always had.

What they had to endure was a lot to overlook and she just didn't have the stomach for that much forgiveness. Not when her son's rightful inheritance was stolen from him. Canaan Enterprise was a multibillion-dollar company and that wimp, Isaac, was about to take over as CEO. Hell would freeze over before she allowed that to happen.

With the thought of seeing her son named as the next CEO of Canaan Enterprises, a surge of renewed determination pumped in her veins. She turned and looked into her vanity and spoke boldly. "I will be the next Mrs. Abraham Taylor and Ishmael will be the next CEO of Canaan Enterprise and anyone standing in my way will get steam-rolled."

She coyly smiled at her reflection as she thought of Sari, Isaac, Emory, and for a brief moment, his niece Keturah's face flashed in her mind. Her youthful beauty and Abraham's response to her immediately wiped the smile off her face. Running into the room in search for her phone she was going to attempt reach Abraham one more time, but before she could she heard the doorknob to the suite begin to turn.

"Thank God!" she said, hurrying to the door and swinging it open. "Abe where in the…"

"What are you doing here?" Emory and Avery barged past her into the room. "Where is Abraham? I've been trying to get a hold of him all night!" Emory's demanding tone inquired.

Angered at the intrusion, she folded her arms and gave him a brazen smile. Sarcastically she said, "Yes, please do come in. Abraham and I just love when uninvited guest barge in on us this early in the morning."

Ignoring her completely, Emory began his search of the suite's bedroom, only stopping momentarily, as Hagan stood in front of the door to her adjoining suite with her arms down at her side.

"Let me stop you right now, this is my private room and only invited guest have my permission to enter." She folded her arms over her plunging neckline, daring Emory to try and move forward.

Without reserve, Avery said, "Might I remind you, Ms. Zarah that these quarters are being paid for by Canaan Enterprise and that gives me the authority to search any room I please."

She gave a hostile glare at Avery and said, "Well if you're looking for Abraham, he's not in there."

"Forgive me, if I don't take your word on that." Avery said.

Enraged, Hagan flung open the door to her suite and allowed the men to look around.

"Satisfied?" she fumed, as the men nodded at each other and walked back out. "One thing I can promise you is that Abraham will hear about this intrusion of his privacy and your lack of hospitality to me."

Ignoring her ranting, Emory questioned, "When will Abe be back? Did he say?"

"Abraham is a grown man and the last time I checked, he doesn't answer to you," she hissed, firmly standing her ground.

Avery responded curtly, "Look, Hagan. We don't have time for your foolishness. Do you know when he'll be back or not?"

In a calm, but chilly tone she said, "If I were you, Avery Jenkins, I would get an acquired taste for my brand of foolishness. You two might not know it yet, but there are going to be a lot of changes taking place very soon and my folly as you call it is going to be the least of your worries."

"Some things time doesn't change. You're just as delusional as ever." Avery gave a mirthless chuckle as he shook his head.

"You're right. Time doesn't always change things. I have as much contempt for you now as I did twenty years ago. Oh, I won't forget the role you played in your cousin's twisted scheme, and when things are in my favor, I promise to pay you back with interest."

"Keep her name out of your mouth," Avery said in a deadly calm whisper, as he moved towards Hagan.

"Whoa! Ave…don't let her bait you to do something you'll later regret. It's obvious Abraham's not been here. And from the looks of it, he never was. Making sure he's ok is our primary concern, so let's get out of here." Emory stated holding the door open.

"I'll make sure Abe's informed of your visit when he comes back," she shot back very cockily at their retreating forms. Once the door clicked shut, she went and placed the deadbolt on it.

Now alone, anxiety filled her heart. She had been sure that it was Abe coming in from the wee hours of the night. But instead, Avery and Emory came barging in as if they didn't know his whereabouts. So, where in the world was he? "Oh God, please don't let him be hurt." Panic was consuming her. She still cared for the man, even though she felt he betrayed her and Ishmael.

"Ishmael!" She shrieked grabbing her phone and punched in his number. He picked up on the fifth ring. "Yes Mother, what is it? I'm right in the middle of a business meeting."

She fussed, "Don't give me that tone of voice, and why did it take you so long to answer?"

"I'm halfway around the world and you're still nagging at me. Isn't it two-something there? What are you doing up?"

"It's three in the morning, to be exact, and your father is not here. I think he might be missing and I'm getting concerned!"

Ishmael snidely replied, "Or maybe ol' Abe is getting lucky with another woman."

Hagan gave a menacing look at the phone and wished she was able to reach out and smack Ishmael in the back of his head. "Mael, for both of our sakes you better pray that he hasn't, or our plans could be over before they ever get started."

***

"Well, Emory. Where to next? I thought he was here with her. The very thought of Abraham with Hagan leaves a nasty taste in my mouth. If Sarah were alive, it would absolutely crush her to know that Abraham would turn to Hagan after all she had put them through. Maybe we should camp out to see if he turns up" Avery stated.

Emory stayed quiet for a moment before answering. "Nah…Hagan doesn't know where Abe is, no matter how much of a front she tried to put on to convince us otherwise. Judging by the way she was dressed, she definitely had plans for him and if he's not careful, he will find himself caught up in a mess" Emory mused.

"I don't get it. Abe looked really out of it when we put him in that cab." Avery stated puzzled.

"Yeah, I know," replied Emory, as he began remembering that he had seen Keturah leaving the event around the same time. A thought popped in his mind that maybe he should give Keturah a call. He thought better of it knowing that it was a little pass four in the morning.

Leading the way outside as they were approaching the car, Emory said, "I know a couple of other spots he frequents, so let's go check them out."

Chapter Six

"Sarah, no! Don't leave! Come back, I can't go on without you," Abraham pleaded, but she kept smiling as she gently floated away.

Suddenly, there was another voice by his side. She was beautiful, angelic, her soft voice said, *"It's okay, Abraham. God hasn't forgotten you...Sarah is with him now, but God is still with you."* Her fingers gently caressed his face, wiping away tears of hurt and frustration he had bottled up for far too long. The tightness in his chest began to ease and the pain in his heart began to subside. Her touch was like a balm to his bruised ego, her words were like a salve on a blister. She softly spoke again, *"Trust and lean on him and he will see you through this time of grief. God is your friend, Abraham. He won't leave you comfortless."*

He believed her words and grabbed a hold of them like a drowning man would a life preserver. He needed to believe that life for him wasn't over. Not yet. As he continued to listen to her voice, he again turned his head towards the wall where he last saw Sarah, but she was gone. All that was left was this woman's lingering words... *"I will not leave you comfortless."* Her voice softly said them over and over again; her comforting timbre sounding like a melody that floated above his head, just out of reach.

The sense of peace he felt radiating from her was all too real. He thought to himself, as he attempted to reach for her, "If I could just touch her...maybe the hurting would stop." His hand grazed her soft, brown curls. She smiled but said nothing as she lowered her face to him. Touching her, filled him with warmth that he, at one time, only associated with Sarah. He then began noticing her amazing smile, how it captivated him; as did her sparkling grey eyes mesmerizing him, so much that he could feel his heart hammering in his chest.

Her fragrance was enchanting, causing the longing and loneliness to surge within his body. His desire to feel the lusciousness of her lips had him reaching for her, but not for comfort.

A loud humming sound startled Abraham awake. He immediately jerked himself in an upright position and looked around the darkened room. His heart was still beating rapidly, as the dream began to fade. "What was that about?" Abraham questioned, as the strange woman's face lingered in his mind. He couldn't believe how real the dream had been. He felt conflicted; never had he had such a vivid dream that aroused him in the way that only Sarah had. "It felt so real," he muttered, as he rubbed his hands over his head and face.

It was only then, that he realized he was in an unfamiliar setting. "Where am I?" He paused, looking around the small bedroom as a frown creased his brow. "This doesn't look like my suite." His head throbbed as if someone had been using it for a gong. His mouth felt like he'd been sucking on his gym socks for the last twenty-four hours, which, at the moment, he couldn't recall. "Lord, please let me have not done something stupid." He vaguely remembered a plan to seduce Hagan…but everything was foggy.

The last thing he remembered was being at the party and he was pretty sure he had one too many glasses of champagne, as well as a couple other cocktails whose names he couldn't remember. Shocked at his own over indulgence, knowing he rarely drank; how in the world had he downed so many? And it had to be quite a few for him, being he couldn't remember how he got in this room.

   "I'm probably in Emory's room," he said to himself, having a vague memory of Emory's face being the last that he had seen.

He struggled to pull himself out of the bed covers. For some reason, his whole body was wrapped in the sheets as if he had a wrestling match the entire night.

Tugging his hands and legs free, he noted he was in the buff, which was concerning, because he didn't remember undressing himself. Slowly, an unsettling feeling began to creep up his back and settle in his neck. Had he, in fact, done something foolish with Hagan? Yet, Hagan was staying in the extra bedroom of his suite and this was definitely not his hotel. He questioned himself as he pulled his feet from the covers, along with an article of clothing that fell to the floor. Immediately, a sickening feeling began churning in his stomach as he looked down at the pink lace bra. "Lord Jesus, what have I done?" he groaned loudly. At the same time, the loud humming noise coming from the connecting room ceased.

Running water was being turned off and what sounded like a shower curtain was pulled back. He caught wind of a rather lovely feminine voice humming a tune, as feet shuffled across the floor.

All traces of his hangover vanished as the reality of what he must have done settled over him. "I can't believe I did this!" he blustered, as he quickly jumped from the bed and began putting on his clothes. He had just pulled his t-shirt down over his chest when he heard a soft knock on the door.

"Hello, Mr. Taylor. You awake?"

He frantically searched for his wallet and cell phone. He had no idea where his shirt and jacket were and, at the moment, didn't really care. All he wanted was to put as much distance between himself and this mistake, as soon as possible and forget this night ever happened.

He kept searching for his belongings, when he heard a slight click of the door. He shut his eyes and gave a low groan. If only he could somehow disappear, or the floor swallow him whole, he would take any out just to keep him ignorant of the fact that he had behaved badly on the day of his wedding anniversary.

"Mr. Taylor, are you okay?"

Startled by her voice, his head snapped up and his eyes bucked as he stood, looking into the same lovely grey eyes that he had just seen in his dream.

"Would you like some coffee or something? I ran downstairs to grab a couple items off the continental breakfast bar. I figured you might be hungry after...um...well, I just thought you might want something to eat." She gave a nervous smile.

There she stood in the hotel's bathrobe looking all freshly scrubbed and deeply appealing.

"Taylor, are you insane? You're already compromised your name and the company by spending the night with this woman and all you can think of is how attracted you are to her?" He wanted to slap himself out of his own stupidity as he stood there not knowing what to do.

Opening his mouth, he tried to think of something to say, but seeing this was the first time he had found himself in this awkward situation, he stood there dumbfounded. So, he clamped his mouth shut. He didn't know what shocked him the most; the woman wasn't a figment of his imagination or the fact that she looked to be the same age as his son's fiancée.

"You don't look so good. Maybe you should lie back down."

"No!" he snapped, causing her to jump back away from him. Frustrated beyond words, he wiped a rough hand across his hair while placing his other hand on his hip and glaring at the ground, he tried to figure out his next move.

He didn't mean to snap at her, but he couldn't believe that he had slept with a perfect stranger...a perfectly young...very young stranger. *"Lord, I will never drink again. Just please, let her be over the age of eighteen."* He looked up at her and tried to formulate the words to the question he needed to know. He just blurted out what he wanted to know, "Please tell me you're over the age of twenty-one."

That brought a frown to her face. She cocked her head to the side and looked quizzically at him before answering.

"Yes, Mr. Taylor. I am."

"That's good...that's really good..." He breathed a sigh of relief. At least he wouldn't be going to jail for statutory.

"Um look, I've got to get going." His eyes didn't quite meet her gaze as he quickly side-stepped her and walked towards the opposite door; trying, without success, to open it. It wasn't locked, from what he could tell, but it wouldn't budge either. "What in the world?" he muttered to himself, pressing against it until he felt a light tap on his shoulder.

"Mr. Taylor...um, you can get out through the bathroom," said Keturah, pointing to the door she had just come out.

While she was doing her best to hide the smirk on her face, he could still see it and hear it in her voice. That did it!

"Miss, I don't really see what is so dog-gone funny about this situation at all. Maybe this is just part of your profession or because you're just immature, so it means nothing for you to jump in and out of bed with a man you don't even know!" He was shouting at her and apparently his words hit their mark, as the humor drained from her face and her eyes filled with moisture.

Good. He was glad his words shook her up. She's young and beautiful like his Sarah once was. She needed to think twice about the strange men she obviously entertained. "Lord, what are the youth of this world coming to?"

"Mr. Taylor, I..."

"Look, Miss. This is not how I operate, and if it wasn't for the fact that I had way too much to drink last night, I would not have done...what we did," he said harshly, before storming past her towards the bathroom door, making a bee-line out of her suite.

His cell was already to his mouth before he hit the door, "Call Avery!" he barked at the phone, as he fumbled with the lock, tossing it open, he walked across the threshold, never looking back.

He had made a huge mistake and needed to do damage control before the little minx could go to the reporters. Whatever the consequences for his rash actions last night, he would humble himself and pray that God would extend him some grace.

***

The days following the mishap in Charlotte went by like a blur. Abraham hated having to do it, but he needed to be honest about what happened between him and the young woman, and what he had planned to do with Hagan. Calling his longtime friend and pastor, Darius Cumming, he disclosed his indiscretion.

Of course, his pastor listened, said he understood, and prayed for him; just as Abraham knew he would. He also promised to keep his ear to the ground and make him aware of anything that might result in a scandal. Morally, Abraham felt defeated, but he didn't have time to dwell on his personal failures; he had a company to run, people to lead who depended on his leadership, and he needed to be able to deliver.

For the last week, business for Canaan consumed all of his time, and there was not much time left for anything else; just as he liked it. He spent little time doing anything other than working until late at night- that's when sparkling grey eyes would visit his dreams, arousing his senses to the point where he felt he would lose his mind.

Even when he thought of Sarah, he saw the young woman's smile, her bronze skin, her face with those haunting grey eyes; it was maddening. He thanked God that he didn't know or remember what her name was, because if he knew it, he might do something foolish -like call her.

This evening was no different, as he sat in his hotel suite attempting to catch up on paperwork, but to no avail. Visions of the little temptress in that hotel robe came crashing back to his mind. Her skin looked fresh and youthful, with a trace of innocence in the depth of her eyes. She was captivating, and in that moment, he wished he could remember parts of the night they had shared. *I must have really been drunk not to remember anything.* If he was not so wound up, he would have thanked God for protecting his mind. The last thing he needed was images of him in the arms of another woman. It was bad enough when he remembered intimate times spent with Sarah. He missed his wife and all the benefits their marriage offered, but Sarah was not coming back, and, for sanity's sake, he needed to figure out how he was going to live the rest of his life, because one-night stands were not going to cut it.

"Two are better than one," whispered the Holy Spirit. He pondered on that for a moment. He knew the word of the Lord to be true. Sarah helped him to see what he couldn't see and helped him remain balanced when business became too intense. *Abraham Taylor... you're taking a time-out right now.* He chuckled to himself as he paced his hotel suite, remembering how she would place her hands on her curvy hips, while pointing that, *don't-mess-with-me* finger at him. She would never let him work back-to-back meetings like he was doing now. As elegant and as proper as Sarah could be, when she got riled up, watch out! A fact that he and everyone else knew very well. Since her death, he felt like he was trying to put pieces of his life together. Only, he didn't have a clue as to how the pieces were to fit without her.

"Lord, she was my helpmeet. What happened the night of the benefit dinner would never have happened if ..." He blew out a strained sigh. Getting upset with God would not bring Sarah back and would only bring a rift between him and his closest Friend. He didn't need to talk about the, "if-onlies" ... with his Creator, but about what the plan would be from here on in.

"What's next, Lord?" he said, not really expecting an answer anytime soon, but immediately, a Bible verse came to his mind,

"He who finds a wife, finds a good thing and finds favor with the Lord."

He halted in mid-stride. He wasn't a stranger to the prompting of the Lord; he had been led by it the majority of his life. So, he knew the feeling in his gut wasn't from the cold pizza he'd consumed earlier that evening.

"Remarry?" He let the word roll around on his tongue, as if it was a new taste he didn't know if he quite liked yet. If he did get remarried, it would certainly solve some of his more immediate problems, as well as open the door to a few others. For instance, he hadn't been on a date in over thirty years, and to say he was rusty was an understatement. As forceful as the women were today, he would rather stay clear of the dating scene all together.

His Sarah hadn't been in the ground a good day or two before women began talking about him "getting back out there" and dating. It angered him so, that he kept his distance from as many social functions as he could, and would only go when family members insisted. Getting remarried wasn't a problem, it was *who* to marry he was worried about.

While he pondered this thought, a pair of grey eyes danced across his mind. He shook his head, trying to dislodge the image, but try as he might, her twinkling eyes would not leave.

"You're just inviting trouble!" he mumbled to himself. "She's definitely not wife material." As always, his thoughts soon drifted to Sarah. She was one-of-a-kind: beauty and brains, all in the same package. She wasn't perfect by any means. Everyone had their short-comings and he wasn't oblivious to his wife's. On more than one occasion, he had been disappointed in her lack of faith in him and God, for which they often paid dearly.

Case in point was his estranged relationship with his son, Ishmael. Abraham reached for the magazine article he had read earlier.

Ishmael was making a name for himself, but the moral integrity of his business was suffering for it. *Integrity.* The word hit him in the gut. He had no right to question anyone's integrity when he had done such a great job botching his own. Maybe the reason the young woman's eyes haunted him so was out of his own guilt, not lust.

From what he did remember before the party, he had taken his allergy medication on his flight home and then had a small glass of wine to wash it down. Once at the party, thoughts of Sarah overwhelmed him so, that he just started downing champagne. When that didn't silence the thoughts, he went to the bar for something a little stronger. All in all, he consumed quite a bit of alcohol. Apparently, the numbing effect he desired the alcohol to give him did the trick, because he didn't even remember leaving the party, or the events that led him to being in the woman's hotel room.

The blame for what transpired that night landed squarely on his shoulders. He shook his head in disgust, "Shoot, I can't even recall her name," he muttered, dropping the magazine he was holding and grabbing one of the bottled waters from the mini fridge. He twisted the cap off and took a long sip. It would be a long time before he drank alcohol again.

He couldn't believe how quickly his life seemed to be unraveling, now that Sarah was gone. How many times had he told his mentees to stay accountable- no matter what, and to have that safe friend who could talk you out of a mess? Why didn't he let Emory or Avery know he had had too much to drink? They were part of his accountability group; why he didn't use them, Heaven only knew. A safety plan only works when you follow through. When you don't...disaster usually followed.

He would be back home in the morning. That would be plenty of time to assess the damage his latest disaster had caused. A buzzing sound from the coffee table drew his attention. Truthfully, he just didn't feel like being bothered and was going to let the intruding phone-call go to voice-mail, but he paused for a moment and checked his caller ID.

"Emory! Lord, what now?" Abraham said; ready to toss his cell aside. The man had called him at least once a day since he'd been out of town; sometimes twice a day. What in the world was so important? Emory was always over-thinking everything and needed reassurance that he was making the right moves. Abraham appreciated his thoroughness, but tonight, not so much. He knew this call was likely regarding business-as-usual and could be dealt with in the morning, but his curiosity got the better of him.

Drawing in a breath, he hit the answer button and spoke.

"What can I do for you Em?" he said curtly, hoping that his tone would clue Emory that he didn't want to be disturbed.

"We need to talk."

Abraham pulled the phone away and stared at it for a brief minute. He had never known Emory to be that abrasive with him. He actually sounded angry. Well, whatever the case, Abraham didn't feel like hearing some long, drawn-out story. "Look, I have about five minutes to spare. So, can you make this quick?"

"Well, what I have to say is gonna take a little longer than five minutes. So, I guess you'll need to find some more time," he growled.

"Excuse me?" Abraham could feel his temper beginning to rise. He and Emory had been friends for years. Rarely, did they have a disagreement. Maybe it was the lateness of the evening or the fact that he had put in a long day. Whatever the case, he was in no mood for attitude. "I think you need to calm down, Emory, and tell me what the problem is."

"My problem is with how you handled my niece, Keturah, last Saturday," Emory practically yelled in the phone.

Like a missile set to explode, Abraham could feel his anger reaching its boiling point and Emory had just set himself up to be the primary target of the blast.

Last Saturday was already a sore spot with him, and he didn't feel like being reprimanded about the details of a night he could barely remember. *Shoot, I don't even remember half of what I did or said, let alone who I met.*

"Look Em, I'm in no mood to try and rehash the details of that night. So, if I promised something to your niece Keturah...," as soon as her name was off his lips, haunting grey eyes drifted through his memory, as a surge of electricity raced up his spine. There was a catch in his voice, as pieces of his memories from that night drifted in and out of his mind, but they were too fragmented to connect all the dots.

Shaking his head, he did his best to order the jumbled thoughts in his foggy mind. As more pieces came to him, a sick feeling settled in the pit of his stomach, for he had a good inkling of to whom those beautiful grey eyes belonged to now.

Dropping his head into his hands, the image of a beautiful young woman, excited about making his acquaintance and standing beside Emory, charged forth in his mind. *Oh, God! What have I done?*

He slowly exhaled a shaky breath, as all anger drained from his body, replaced with guilt and shame. With a raspy voice, he said the only thing he could, and hoped Em would forgive him and not clobber him like he deserved.

"Aw, Emory I'm so sorry."

"You're sorry for what, exactly, Abe? For acting like the Lone Ranger for the last couple of months? For pushing everyone who loves you away? For getting plastered at your company's benefit party in front of your friends, family, and even some important business associates? Or, for my personal favorite: following my niece to her hotel room and then passing out in her bed?" Emory ended his tirade in disgust.

Abraham had already sunk to the couch, clutching the phone in his hand. He couldn't believe that the man Emory was describing was him. As bits and pieces of that elusive night began to weave together into one, long, rope - strong enough to hang himself; he felt lower than a snake.

He remembered Isaac's troubled expression and the uneasy looks his friends and business associates gave him that night. Pity was something he hated, and the fact they pitied him made his stomach turn. He remembered Aunt Sari's words of admonishment, and his not-so-kind words for her, to mind her own business. Several times, his friends tried to get him to stop drinking, but he had joked, "It's a party!" Finally, Emory and Avery had taken hold of him and ushered him through the hotel lobby and called a cab. He was nearly passed out, when he heard a female get in the cab with him. He just assumed it was Hagan. He was so tired and his eyelids were so heavy, all he wanted to do was put his head back and get rid of the buzz.

"Abe...are you still there?" Emory's bark jolted him out of his thoughts.

Lord, I've made a mess of things, I need you to help me fix this and make things right, he quickly prayed before answering Emory.

"Yeah, I'm here Em, and you have every reason to be angry with me. I messed up, but I swear I'm going to make things right, if I can."

He hated having to ask Em this next part, but it had to be done. In order to fix things, he needed to know the extent of the damage he had caused; and since the details were still fuzzy, he would need to rely on Emory to fill him in. He whispered another silent prayer and braced himself, as he asked for the full details of his night spent with Keturah.

CHAPTER SEVEN

"Hey, Gretta!" Keturah shouted as she came in the front door throwing her purse down on the recliner in the living room. "How's my favorite person in the whole wide world doing today?" Keturah hugged her grandmother from behind and gave her a quick kiss on the cheek.

"Oh, are you referring to me?" Gretta stopped dusting long enough to place her hand on her chest and look wide-eyed at Keturah, which elicited a sarcastic smirk from her granddaughter. "Don't look **at** me that way, Honey. You're the one who went to the country club in Charlotte as the belle of the ball." Gretta did a mock bow to Keturah.

"Oh, Grandma," Keturah waved her hand, "I wasn't the belle of the ball. Although, I did look pretty amazing," she laughed at her own vanity. "Anyway, there were people in the room more stunning than me."

"Please! People more stunning than you? I doubt it. Like who?" Gretta challenged, as she continued dusting her living room.

Keturah looked casually at the family pictures that she had seen over a million times on the mantle, pausing at one picture in particular, she felt a chill race up her spine. Not turning away from it, she just stared at the picture of her mom as she responded. Like my half- sister, Tippany Jaymes," she said, remaining silent waiting for Gretta's response.

"Humph!" was all Gretta said.

"Gretta, why do you think my father never brought any of my siblings to see me?" She wondered out loud.

"Did you see your sister's mother, Sari?" Gretta asked pointedly.

Keturah dropped her head, and mumbled, "Yeah, I saw her.... *the old bat.*"

"Then, question answered," Gretta responded, as she continued to shuffle around the small room.

Keturah knew there was no real reason to continue the conversation about her dad. Gretta couldn't answer for the dead. She couldn't see into the dark abyss of her father's soul. Besides, he was long dead and gone; he did not bring her around his other children because he didn't want to. She had to accept that. Literally, she was the black spot on his golden-light-skinned family. She wasn't even listed in his obituary as one of his offspring. Why that still hurt, she couldn't answer.

"Girl, don't go stirring up trouble for yourself. That man's been dead over seven years now. Don't let your feet get stuck in the cesspool of his bad choices," Gretta admonished.

"I know… I know, but when you're in a room full of family who won't even acknowledge your existence, it hurts. I know mama should not have had an affair with my father, but it happened. I cannot change it, so why do I have to suffer the consequences of their mistake?" Keturah said, quickly swiping at a wayward tear that had fallen.

"Keturah, I know this is hard for you to understand because you're hurting. But, Honey, we all make mistakes: you, me, your mama… we all have difficult choices to make on this journey called life. Sometimes we do good, sometimes we don't. That's why it's so important to hold on to God, because he knows how to make every crooked path straight."

Gretta was right. She always was. Sighing, Keturah started helping her grandmother straighten up before going to the community center. "We're still on for tonight right, Gretta?"

"Roast is already thawing in the fridge. Make sure you bring your game-face with you, little girl cuz I'm gonna beat the pants off you in checkers tonight," she winked, as Keturah rolled her eyes.

***

"You did what?!!" Emory chided, "Girl, have you lost your mind!"

"He's your friend and he seemed sick and what else was I supposed to do? Let him sleep it off in the hall?" Keturah argued.

"Yes, that's exactly what you should have done."

"As Christians, it's our duty to be good Samaritans."

"Augh! That's the type of thing that can get you hurt, raped and even killed, Keturah," he scolded.

"But Uncle Emory, it was Abraham Taylor, your friend," she tried reasoning with him once more.

"I don't care if it was Apostle Paul. Don't you ever allow any man, especially a drunk one in your room! Are we clear on this?"

"Yes, Sir."

"Good. Now, I've got to go, there is somebody I need to speak with." he said firmly.

"You're not going to call him, are you?" She held the receiver tightly to her ear, mortified at the thought of her uncle having this conversation with him.

"I'll handle things from here on in."

"Okay?" she said dejectedly, knowing the "somebody" he referred to was Abraham.

"Bye, Babygirl."

"Bye, Uncle Em."

It had been a week ago that Keturah had that conversation with her uncle and disclosed what had happened between her and Abraham the night after the party. The memory of his scolding still caused her to cringe. Gretta had responded much in the same manner, minus the yelling. Blowing out a sigh of frustration, she continued her tedious chore of painting the rec room, repurposed from the old gym. "What good is it to believe God is able to keep you, when deep down, most Christians believe in keeping themselves? She wondered out loud. Besides, she wasn't an idiot. She understood the ramifications of her actions and would be cautious in the future. But, two things factored in when she decided to help Abraham. One, she felt safe and, more importantly, she felt God's presence. Anyway, she was just glad she hadn't told Gretta the humiliating remarks that Abraham had made before his departure from her hotel suite. The thought of them still stung. Why she felt a need to keep those details to herself, God only knew. It was bad enough she had to tell her uncle that his longtime friend, the one he had bragged to her about for years, ended up stoned and passed out in his undies.

"Humph, and he had the gall to say he wouldn't be bothered with a woman like me. If it wasn't for a woman like me, his rep would be totally trashed by now." She murmured, while jabbing her paintbrush into the can of paint more forcefully than necessary and was rewarded with a hand covered in blue liquid.

Giving a frustrated sigh, she reached for a rag to wipe it off. "The nerve of him thinking I'd be the type of woman to allow a total stranger in my bed, just like that," she snapped her fingers for added affect, "all because he's rich?"

Well, technically, you did allow him in your bed, just like that.

"Yeah, but it was completely innocent." she warred with her own conscious. *I was being a Good Samaritan, nothing more. Shoot, for putting up with all his craziness, I should've gotten a doggone medal!* She continued to fuss.

Emory told her not to worry, that he'd handle it. Well, that had been more than a week ago and she still hadn't heard anything. Not that she expected to, although an apology from her accuser would've been nice. "But I guess the great and mighty, Abraham Taylor, doesn't feel the need to apologize to lowly, common-folk like me," Keturah griped, while putting her paint brush down. She stood up with her hands gripping her hips and stretched her back out. *Whew!* She was tired. Spying the wall clock, it was three-thirty already and her stomach was grumbling louder than the music she had pulsing in her ears.

Time to finish up. She blew out a sigh and mopped her brow with her arm, as she stepped back and looked at her handiwork; slow but steady progress was being made, and, finally, she was beginning to see things come together for the youth center and she couldn't be more pleased. It was her and Gretta's dream to secure a building, so an achievement center for girls could be established. And, now, the dream was becoming reality.

She had worked tirelessly to procure the funding and donations needed to get this building, and with a little more money, she hoped they would be able to open by November. Being able to go to the Taylor's benefit party had helped her personally, as well as it had helped her department. She had found additional funding and support from the university's finance department, but, in addition, she was able to discuss her project at the center with a few people who seemed genuinely interested in her efforts to work with inner-city girls. All in all, she would've deemed the night a complete success, until she met up with the Taylors.

"No need to rehash that fiasco," she thought. Besides, she needed to get moving if she wanted to run home before going to Gretta's.

"Hmmm, if I leave now, I can make the last bus and get to Gretta's place and help her fix dinner. That way, she can keep off that hip like Dr. Morgan told her," she mused, looking at the time and knowing full well that, in order to do that, she'd need to pack up now. However, she hesitated, then cocked her head to the side.

"Um, that line looks crooked and the paint in that corner is a little smudged. I'll fix it really quick and then go," she reasoned, while looking around for something to stand on, so she could reach the offending smear. Spotting an old wooden chair that looked as though it had seen many a summer, she purposefully turned and walked in its direction. The chair seemed to cringe at her approach, as Keturah snatched it up and set her face towards the task at hand. "Give me one minute, three at the most," she begged the creaking chair. She stood on the seat, doing her best to balance herself; a paintbrush in one hand and a half-empty bucket of paint in the other.

Somewhere in the back of her mind, reason was telling her this wasn't a sound idea, but she ignored the warning. She had just dunked her brush, coating its bristles with the thick, colored liquid, when she felt the chair make a sharp sway to the left. Before she could correct herself, the chair jerked to the right and she went flying in the opposite direction. She was going down fast and hard, her back likely about to pay the painful price for her stupidity. Squeezing her eyes shut, she tightened her body, bracing herself for the jarring impact of the floor, but instead of the hard cement, she felt strong arms catching her mid-air in a tight embrace. *What just happened?*

Opening one eye to see who her savior was, her mouth hung open in utter shock, as she looked up at her unexpected rescuer's twinkling bluish-grey eyes. Before she could utter a word, she gave another gasp, as thick globs of blue liquid showered them both.

***

What is he doing here? was all her mind kept wondering, as she walked from the bathroom, back to the gymnasium where she had left Abraham covered in paint. *How did he know where to find me?* That question piqued her interest more than anything. Emory maybe? *No, not even Uncle Em knows my whereabouts on Saturday, I don't think. So how did he know?* She continued her inner dialogue until she reached the gym. Seeing him standing there in his jeans and tee-shirt caused her heart to beat a little faster, as a sense of awareness rushed over her.

He might be older, but the man sure did take extra-special care of his body, she thought, looking appreciatively at his firm biceps that fit snuggly in his black tee-shirt. Not an ounce of fat could be caught on his midsection, and what a mid-section he had, Keturah thought, as an image of him lying in her bed under the covers came to mind. "Forgive me Lord!" She shook her head to dislodge the thought, as she found herself doing often when she thought back to that night. He suddenly looked up and caught her staring. Quickly, she averted her eyes, but not before she noticed a hint of a smile reaching the corners of his mouth. *Oh great...he saw me gawking at him!*

Flustered at being caught and struggling to tamp down strange unruly feelings, she advanced in the room. Hesitating as she came closer, she chanced taking another glance at him, while he checked his arms for more paint. *Wow this man is handsome....*she inwardly sighed as she allowed her eyes to travel over him wantonly. *Um...sexy as all get out, well respected, rich...a big plus, and loves God...everything on my, 'What I want in a husband list.' Wow, God! He'd be perfect if he wasn't so much older than me and for the fact that he thinks I'm a loose woman.* "Too bad!" she sighed deeply.

"You're watching me again, Ms. Birch," he said with a low chuckle, revealing deep dimples that only accentuated his good looks, "And exactly what's, *too bad?*"

Keturah's eyes went wide. She wasn't aware she had spoken out loud, and now that he turned his piercing eyes in her direction, she feared he might have picked up on more than her slip of the tongue. *Lord, please don't let him be a mind reader.*

Struggling to come up with an explanation that wouldn't leave her completely humiliated, she stuck out her hand towards him offering the moist hand-towel she had brought. He lowered his gaze momentarily to the towel, giving her a brief moment to collect herself.

No wonder this man is so successful in business. One look with those intensive eyes and he probably sends his competition running home with their tails tucked between their legs.

Looking him in the eyes was like looking directly into the sun's fiery blaze. There was no way you'd ever win, no way you could tell him no. There would only be one of two outcomes: go blind or concede to his dominance. Abraham Taylor was definitely not a man to be messed with, although why he was at her center was still a mystery. She'd decided it was best that she tread softly with him. But, as quickly as fear and intimidation of the man tried to sweep over her, her mind reflected back to the night she held him in her arms and rubbed his forehead, to chase his nightmare away. He wasn't nearly as intimidating then, but quite vulnerable and in need of comfort...her comfort. She gave it and he took it. It would likely never happen again, but still, she would always remember that moment and the lesson God taught her from it.

Money can buy you comfortable things in life, but true comfort only comes from God. But that was then, the man standing before her now wasn't hung-over and was in complete control of his emotions. This man didn't need anything...well, except for maybe a shirt. With this thought in mind, she kept her gaze slightly lower. *No more sun gazing for me,* she said to herself before clearing her tightening throat.

"Um...your shirt. It's too bad about your shirt, Mr. T-Taylor. It's completely ruined. Oh, I can pay to have it dry cleaned," she offered, shrugging her shoulders. Once again, she felt trapped by his intense stare.

"I can assure you, Ms. Birch, my shirt can easily be replaced. However, the damage you were about to inflict on your body by being careless could've been permanent. What in the world would possess you to stand on that old rickety chair in the first place?" he said reproachfully.

"Well, I-I needed to reach that spot over there in the corner," she pointed towards the area that still went untouched, "and I'm not tall enough to reach it on my own. So, I thought the chair would hold me..." She let her sentence end in a whisper as she looked into his eyes again and was met with a critical glare.

Defensively, she folded her arms across her chest, trying to shield herself from his scrutiny. She shuddered at the powerful gaze he was giving her right now and remembering, all too well, this look and the stinging words that accompanied it. *I wouldn't be bothered with a woman like you.* That thought sobered her.

"Next time, you should consider hiring professionals, so the work can be done properly. It will save you a lot of pain and paint," he said tersely, still using the moist towel to clean a spot of blue paint off his hands.

Her admiration was rapidly fading and quickly turning into something more like annoyance. She was hoping that his brutish behavior the day after the party was nothing more than a fluke. That his being a jerk was alcohol induced, and not his true self. But, from what she was seeing, maybe this was just who he was.

Millionaire or not, she was tired of his attitude and wasn't going to put up with it a moment longer. As far as she was concerned, he could take his chivalry and unsolicited opinions and get out. She clenched her fists then released them, allowing the blood-flow to circulate again, in her hands. Swallowing several choice words back, she turned towards him and spoke with such calmness, it shocked even her.

"Unlike you, Mr. Taylor, I don't have the luxury of throwing money at problems that are an inconvenience to me. As I said, I'm sorry about your clothes and you can send me the bill for the dry- cleaning or I'll replace them," Keturah said tersely.

"If you can't afford to get a professional painter, I highly doubt you could afford to replace my shirt," he snapped.

Gasping at his words, her head snapped up and fury showed in her stormy gray eyes. *You arrogant self-important....ooohh! God, if you don't get this man out of my face, I swear I'm going to jail!* It was bad enough that he had ruined last Saturday for her, but she refused to allow him to ruin another day or take up any more of her time. He was leaving now...but this time she'd have the last words.

"You know, Mr. Taylor, you would think that with all your money, you could afford to have a better personality!" she challenged, doing her best to give him an intense glare of her own. "I mean, really! Who do you think you are? So what, you have money. Does that give you some special privilege to be a jerk from sun-up, to sun-down? No, you're right. I can't afford to replace your expensive *silk* shirts, nor could I afford to replace the dress I borrowed last Saturday night. You know, the one you ruined when you got sick all over me...but no, you probably don't remember, seeing how you were too drunk to remember much of anything, but that's neither here nor there. I'm a Christian woman and that means something to me, so when I give my word, I keep it."

She couldn't tell what he was thinking. His facial expression remained as hard as granite, the same as it was when she began her tirade. The only thing she could see was the pulsing of a vein in the side of his neck, or maybe it was more like ticking like a time-bomb ready to go off. No matter, she would have her say.

"Are you quite finished, Ms. Birch?"

His voice was low and a little unnerving, but she wouldn't be stopped. Not this time.

"As a matter of fact, Mr. Taylor, I am not. How dare you look down your nose at me as if I'm beneath you? I take offense to it. Since I was a teenager, I've looked up to you. Not because of your title of being a self-made millionaire, as some people called you, but because you always confessed the very opposite.

'I'm not self- made, I'm God made,' you used to say. *All that I am is a direct result of my relationship with the Great I AM. If you learn nothing else from me, learn this: The richest person in the world is one who's learned to become God's friend.* The man who spoke at my school that day would have never treated me the way you have, Mr. Taylor."

Somehow, telling him off didn't feel as good as she thought it would. She hadn't looked away from him the entire time she was talking. Well, yelling, but now his pained expression was something she could hardly bear. She had definitely hit her mark, hard. Well, she had said her peace; there was nothing left to say. "Like I said earlier, I'll pay for your shirt and anything else the paint happened to damage. Now, if you'll excuse me, I've work to complete."

She turned around to stalk off, wondering what her Uncle Emory would think if Mr. Taylor decided to share their confrontation; but, before she could set her mind to worry about that, a warm hand wrapped around her forearm, restraining her from going any further. At first, she thought to panic, but then her body calmed as his hold on her arm relaxed. Keturah heard him inhale and slowly let his breath out before speaking.

"I'll help you finish," he said in a gruff voice, squeezing her arm before releasing it. Then, he turned to pick up a paint brush.

"What? . . . I-I," she stammered as she turned. She watched him walk towards the overturned paint can, pick up a brush and proceed to paint where she had left off.

***

They had worked for at least an hour in relative silence, him speaking only when needing to know what else needed painted. He hadn't said much and neither had she; mainly because she didn't know exactly what to say. One minute he was criticizing her, the next minute, he was painting her walls like a madman.

Several times, she had told him that he need not bother, but he kept working as if she'd said nothing. If it wasn't for the fact that he was such a close friend of her uncle's, his irrational behavior might be cause for concern.

Right now, he was giving her a helping hand, and she wasn't about to refuse it. Taking a quick look at her watch, she cringed. She had worked longer than she had intended and had missed her bus. "I'll never get to Gretta's on time now," she sighed heavily.

"What did you say?" Abraham inquired, as he swiped at the sweat on his brow. His shirt was soaked with sweat, but it didn't seem to bother him.

"Umm...nothing," she said over her shoulder, still a little taken aback that he had stayed and helped her. She preferred he tell her where she could shove her opinion and walk out in a huff. That's what she expected him to do. So, why hadn't he taken the bait?

The entire time they were painting, she was getting an earful from God. *Love covers a multitude of sins... Judge not, lest you be judged...They will know we are Christians by the love we show one to another. . . When you see a brother overtaken in a sin, you that are spiritual restore him.*

Okay Lord, I get it. She sighed inwardly, realizing she had become Abraham's judge, jury and executioner. The only recourse she had was to make things right. *Put on your big girl pants and turn to face the music.* "Uhh, listen, Mr. Taylor. I um...well, about what I said before...I was..."

"You were right and you have every right to be angry with me," he said softly, all traces of arrogance and criticism in his tone gone, as he took a long drink from the water-bottle she'd given him earlier.

"I am a Christian, Ms. Birch, but my recent actions..." he bowed his head and closed his eyes momentarily before continuing, "well, let's just say, I haven't been the best witness for our Lord, not for a long time... but I plan on changing things. Starting now."

With hands outstretched, he spoke with sincerity, "Ms. Birch, I'm truly sorry for my behavior towards you last Saturday. I make and give no excuses. Please, forgive me."

Keturah stood, momentarily stunned at his admission.

"As for today, I didn't mean to offend you. It's just that you could have really gotten hurt and with you being here all alone," sighing while rubbing a hand over his head he finished, "well, I guess I over-reacted, again." He gave a small smile that caused a shiver to skip down Keturah's spine.

His severe look was replaced by a humble one, causing the indignation she had felt earlier, to drain out of her like water out of the sink. By the way things had started; she hadn't expected an apology from him. But now that she had it, she felt remorseful that she had talked about him so negatively. And besides that, he did save her from what would likely have been a nasty fall.

With that final acknowledgement, she gave him a genuine smile, "Mr. Taylor, I do forgive you and I want to thank you as well. I had my doubts about getting in that old chair, but sometimes I can be impulsive. I really could've been hurt if you had not been here."

"Do you normally come here and work alone? I mean, this doesn't seem like the safest of neighborhoods," he said, giving the place a visual appraisal before looking back at her.

Throwing up her hand dismissively, she bent over and started picking up empty paint cans. "This is my Saturday stomping ground. I've been coming here as long as I can remember," she smiled, then went back to cleaning up.

"Do you mind if I ask why?" he looked a little confused at

her admission, "I mean, most women your age are doing a lot of things besides hanging out in an old building, painting over graffiti-littered walls."

"True, but then most of them aren't trying to open a youth center, either."

"A youth center?" he questioned.

"Yes!" She smiled at him then, turned to pick up more of the soiled newspapers that covered the floor to catch paint drippings.

For a moment, she battled within herself as to whether or not to tell him her reasons for working on the center. She didn't want to broach the subject and come off as if she was making a play for a donation or something, but another part of her still wanted vindication from his comment about the type of woman he thought her to be.

She was a strong, Christian woman with upstanding morals. She didn't go around letting strange men in her hotel room. Why? Because of the things Gretta taught her, right in this very room. Every Saturday morning, Gretta would stand up in front of twenty or more elementary girls talking about what it meant to be a woman of standards, and one day soon, she hoped she'd be able to teach some young girl the very same thing.

"Oh no, Gretta!" Keturah bopped herself upside her forehead, realizing the lateness of the hour. "Lord, I'm going to be so late!" Moving quickly, she pushed the remaining unopened cans to the side and tossed the paint brushes in an open container of turpentine.

"Is there a problem?" Abraham inquired; his brows knitted together in a frown.

"Well, no. I mean, yes. Actually, there is." She gave in to a groan while shaking her head. Her need to get to Gretta's was more important than her need to exonerate herself in the eyes of Abraham Taylor.

She knew what type of woman she was and, more importantly, God knew. That would have to be enough. "I stayed longer today than I intended to, and now I'm going to be late for dinner at my grandmother's."

"No problem, I'd be happy to drive you to your grandmother's home," he offered without hesitation.

"Oh no, I couldn't ask you to do that. I . . ."

"Whoa, hold on! First off, you didn't ask me, I volunteered. Secondly, you wouldn't be running late, if it wasn't for me interrupting you in the first place."

"True, but I hate to think of what would have happened if you had not come. I'd likely be sprawled out on the floor covered in blue paint, hurt, and possibly stranded here all night. So, your presence, along with your help today, was truly a Godsend. Besides, it's getting late and I'm not about to take up any more of your time."

"Keturah, this is an argument you're not going to win. There's no way I'm going to leave you at a bus stop in this neighborhood, this late in the evening. I'm taking you. Period!"

The finality in his tone squashed any other protest she had. To tell him that she was actually *in* her neighborhood would probably do little to deter him. So, why bother? Besides, by accepting the ride, she could spend more time at Gretta's house, which was something they'd both relish. Shrugging her shoulders, she decided to enjoy his company for what was, most likely, the last time. After all, it wasn't every day she got a chance to hang out with the man she had idolized and secretly crushed on, when she was in junior high.

CHAPTER EIGHT

She felt downright giddy, speeding down the beltway, sitting in the passenger's seat of Abraham's silver, Mercedes-Coup, heading towards Gretta's neighborhood.

It had been a rather warm, September night, so Abraham decided it would be nice to drive with the top down and she was glad he did. It felt exhilarating: the wind blowing in her hair, the taste of summer still lingering in the air. This was a far cry from traveling by the transit bus system. Her bus-stop was the last pick-up before getting on the expressway. This meant that on most nights, it was standing- room only.

Rarely, did she get an opportunity to look out the window and see the city lights shining in the semi-darken sky, let alone experience the night-life of her fair city. Most of her Saturday nights were filled with mundane work. Not that she was complaining; her work was important and hopefully some girl would have the chance to get out of Centennial City like she had. So, she'd gladly sacrifice her social life for now. It wasn't forever.

Right now, she planned on enjoying this experience and maybe even the man sitting beside her. Tonight, whizzing by downtown in Abraham's silver bullet, watching the world go by in a blur was priceless and a memory she would revisit many times over. Turning towards her chauffeur for the evening, she noticed how young and carefree he appeared. Although she knew he was about thirty-years her senior, and could never see herself with a man that much older than she; he still was very attractive and appealing. *He'd be perfect, God, if he wasn't so much older than me.*

Age is only a number…it's what's in a man's heart that truly counts! She heard a soft voice within herself say.

Yeah, but his numbers are really high! Keturah argued. *What happens if I eventually want children? I would, at least, want him around to help raise his kids...and then what about our twilight years? Shoot, we're not even married and he's already in his.* She frowned.

"You're staring again, Ms. Birch."

"Oh, was I? Sorry." Embarrassed, she quickly looked the other way, but not before noticing a smile grace his lips. *Great, he caught me! Again!* She tried to calm herself but couldn't. *I'm in the car with Abraham Taylor!* She wanted to take a selfie, but refrained. However, she definitely would blog about it later.

"What's going on in that little head of yours?" he questioned.

"Oh, nothing."

"Right. So, I guess you're not going to tell me why you keep staring?"

She wasn't trying to stare. It was just that today he looked so different than he did at the party. He looked relaxed, carefree; definitely a change for the better. Not knowing how to say it she just blurted out the first thing that came to mind. "You look different with clothes on."

"What?"

"Oh...oh...my goodness! I didn't mean that the way it sounded, Mr. Taylor. I meant you look different without your tux on." She shook her head, horrified at what she implied. "Oh, I didn't mean to suggest that I saw you undressed or anything...well, I guess I did, but you were already in my bed under the sheets, so you weren't exposed or anything."

"STOP TALKING!!!" her insides screamed. By this time, he was laughing so hard, tears were streaming down his cheeks. She was sure her cheeks would have turned five shades of red, if her skin wasn't so dark. "I just meant you look nice in regular clothes." She blew out a breath, her left hand rubbing her temple as she felt her head pulsing.

"Keturah, you're a treasure," he said, wiping the side of his face.

"Normally, I don't babble. I guess I'm nervous is all."

"Well, I promise the big, bad wolf won't bite Little Red," he teased.

She smirked, but remained quiet. She wasn't sure if he would bite or not. Looking up at the city skyline, she smiled. "I love seeing the city on a clear night like this. It's really beautiful when it's all lit up, don't you think?"

"It's alright as far as cities go, I guess," he said nonchalantly.

"I take it you don't like our city?"

"What makes you say that?"

She shrugged her shoulders, "I don't know. It seems like you stay away from here quite a bit."

"You do know I run a multi-billion-dollar company all over the country, right? I can't always be here."

Keturah detected the tightness in his voice and decided to tread lightly. They were having such a nice ride; she didn't want her curiosity to ruin things. "So, since you're well-travelled, what cities in the world do you like the best?"

"Venice!"

"Really? What's so special about Venice?"

"Are you always this inquisitive?" He gave her a sideways

"Yep! So, what's so special about Venice?"

"The young people aren't so nosy," he said sarcastically.

"Ha-ha-ha, very funny," she scrunched her nose at him, noticing his smile, "I'm not being nosy. I just like being well-informed. By the way, how come you don't mentor women?"

"How did we go from Venice to mentoring?" he asked, perplexed.

"Well, you've already told me that its young people are dull; therefore, the city must be just as dull and boring. So, on to the next topic; which is why your company doesn't sponsor mentoring for women? That's pretty chauvinistic, if you ask me," she folded her arms.

"First off, no one asked you!" he said to her in a loud huff. "And second, I have my reasons for not having girls in the program," he said matter-of-factly.

"I understand why you wouldn't have girls in your program," she said, just as sarcastically, "but as you can clearly see, I'm not a girl. I'm a woman and you do us a disservice when you bar us from programs that could really help us in the business world. After all, we are not living in an age where women need men to clothe and shelter them. We can fend for ourselves."

"This is exactly why I don't have *women* in the program. They're more focused on proving why they should be there than focusing on the job."

She felt that anything she would say in defense of women would only strengthen his viewpoint; so, she decided not to take the bait and looked out the window to enjoy the nightlife. They rode in silence for a few moments.

Abraham asked, "Penny for your thoughts?"

"A penny? My thoughts are worth way more than that, Mr. Taylor," she said, playfully.

"Aye...how about we stop with the, Mr. Taylor, business; call me Abe." He turned quickly and gave her his one-hundred-watt smile.

Feeling a charge of electricity race up her left arm caused her body to shiver slightly with the sensation. She nodded her head and gave him a small smile, hoping he didn't notice her reaction. The knitting of his brows alerted her that he had.

"Are you getting too chilly with the top down? I can put it up," he said, reaching towards his dashboard to hit the button that would cause the roof to automatically glide into place.

"Oh, please don't, Mr.....um, Abe," she stressed. Reaching out, she grasped his fingers to stop him. His fingers were so warm and firm, soft, yet strong. Her nimble fingers looked like twigs in comparison. For a brief moment, she wondered what that firm hand would feel like holding hers, or caressing her shoulders as he held her close. *Oh, my God, what is the matter with me? This guy is old enough to be my dad!* Snapping herself out of her own delusional thoughts, she quickly returned her hand to her lap.

"I-I enjoy the top being down. The air really feels good tonight."

"Then, down it will stay. Now, what's on your mind Keturah?" he inquired in his deep tenor.

You're pretty attractive...downright sexy, for a man in his fifties. I wish you were younger and we had more in common. I really would love to get to know you better...how about it, are you interested? She didn't dare tell him that, although she wished she had the boldness to say it.

"You're not at all what I expected," she confessed, choosing her words carefully. It seemed like a burden had been lifted off his shoulders this evening, they were genuinely having a nice time. She didn't want to spoil it.

"Well, what exactly did you expect?" he probed, light-heartedly, with a trace of curiosity laced in his voice.

What had she expected? The night of the party, when her uncle said he'd introduce her to Abraham, she was so nervous, yet bursting with excitement that she'd had the good fortune of meeting someone who had greatly impacted her life. She thought remembering back to her high school days.

One day, a guest-speaker came to her school. There stood a slightly younger Abraham Taylor sharing his story about his life, where he came from, and what God had done for this kid from the wrong side of town; how he had turned tragedy into triumph. His testimony had mesmerized her. This man hadn't come from anyone special and he wasn't a super genius; "just an ordinary man serving an extraordinary God," was how he described himself. Keturah remembered leaving the assembly that night feeling something she had never felt in seventeen years. Hope! There was hope for Keturah Birch to land on her feet. His last words that day had been, "If you've been helped today, help someone else. If you've been encouraged, then remember to encourage someone else. A kind word can go a long way."

For years, she had wanted, in some way, to thank him for what he said. Let him know how inspired she'd been by it. She had followed his advice and cherished it, as if it was a lesson coming from her father. She learned, early in life, that she had to grab hold of wisdom whenever she could. She wasn't blessed like her friends who had parents; she only had Gretta.

So, yes, maybe she was a little star-struck and had carried that view of him in the back of her mind, all those years. So, to see her mentor, her idol - *drunk* was rather shocking, to say the least. For him to end up spending the night in her hotel room... she had no words.

"Oh, come on! It can't be that bad! Haven't I redeemed myself in your eyes just a little?" he jested, tugging on her short-sleeved shirt; hoping to prod a response after her lengthy silence.

Smiling at him, she gave a light laugh, "Yes, you have redeemed yourself. A little." Moving a stray curl from her face, she looked straight ahead; still unsure of what to reveal. She decided it was best to keep things light. "I don't know. I knew you were a good-hearted person, who has a keen business-sense, but I didn't expect you to get a kick out of doing normal things."

At that admission, he threw back his head and laughed, "Yes, Keturah. Although I have money, I still like to do *normal* things that other people do like, eat, sleep, go to the bathroom, and spend time on a Saturday evening in the company of a charming young lady, such as you. I know. Shocking, isn't it?" He laughed again.

He thinks I'm charming? Wow! Oh, wait. Should I respond? Is he actually flirting with me? I hate the fact that I haven't dated much. I'm not sure what to do! Keep things light; don't read too much into it. Besides, this man could be with any woman he wanted. So, why would he be interested in you? Not to mention, that you are younger than his youngest son! That thought sobered her giddy mind.

"I realize you do normal things, but I'm surprised that, okay, for instance, I can tell you're enjoying yourself right now, pushing this silver beauty to its limits." She extended her hands to indicate his car, and when she looked at him; she was rewarded with a devastatingly handsome smile. Apparently, she had guessed right.

"I don't get a chance to drive as much as I used to, but when I do…I believe in enjoying the journey."

She simply smiled, trying to take it all in. For her, this was a heaven-sent moment; one that she hoped to share one day with her girls. *I wonder if taking a selfie right now would be totally inappropriate.* Getting pointers from one of the best-in-the-business was a dream; but, speeding down the highway with Abraham Taylor was *priceless*!

"When I first started this journey with God, I had no idea that he would lead me to all that I have now. All I wanted was to live an obedient life and follow the voice of my friend. I think if God would have shown me his full plan, I would've bolted," he relayed in earnest.

"Really? You seem so at-ease with your life, with everything; so in control."

"I think last Saturday night proved that that's not the case," he chuckled, "I've learned to be at ease with who God is creating me to be. When I listen to and follow Him, the Lord keeps me grounded. When I don't, he has his own methods of sending me wake-up calls, to smack me back in line." He turned towards her and smiled and was compensated with a shy blush.

"Do you feel success has changed you a lot, compared to how you used to be and who you are now?"

"What, are you doing an interview, Ms. Birch?" His smile warmed her through and through.

"No, I just… well," she stammered, feeling the heat of his gaze resting on her. "I wanted my girls to know and understand that success is defined by them, not someone else. Success shouldn't determine how you act or treat others and it comes in all different forms," she finished softly.

His prolonged silence made her finally look up from her hands, folded in her lap, and take a sideways glance at him. For some reason, there seemed to be a shift in his countenance as his face went blank and his fingers tightened around the steering wheel.

"I wasn't aware that you had children, Ms. Birch. Are you married, as well?"

"Oh, I don't and I'm not," she laughed and raised her hands, turning them, front and back, so he could see she wore no ring. "I'm completely unattached," she stated, pausing a few moments to emphasize that point. He appeared to get the message as she saw the white-knuckled grip he had on the steering-wheel relax, as did the muscles in his face.
Interesting! She thought.

"The only kids I have are the girls at the youth center. I inherit them every day, from three to six, Monday through Friday and Saturday, from nine to noon," she finished, still puzzled as to why her marital status mattered to him.

"So, here you are; a young woman in her prime marrying and childbearing years, filling your weekdays teaching other people's children and then you fill your weekends alone, in an empty building, standing on old unreliable chairs painting, I assume." He looked at her for confirmation. No sarcasm was in his voice.

"Well, when you put it like, that it makes me sound...*boring, dull, completely void of a social life, uninteresting!*" She settled for that word, hoping it didn't sound as bad as the words she had rambled off in her head.

"No. I definitely wouldn't say you are uninteresting." He smiled at her, and then with a smirk on his face he was barely able to hide, he turned his attention back to the road.

Keturah squinted her eyes and studied him closely for a moment, causing him to chuckle even more. "Okay, then what?" She said with an exasperated huff.

"What...what?" he said, continuing to smile.

Rolling her eyes, she twisted in the seat to look at him head-on. He was being a typical, evasive male; dodging her questions with a question, although, his method seemed more flirtatious and fun. *Flirtatious? Wow! Where did that thought come from?* She definitely been out of the dating arena for too long to think this conversation had even a hint of flirting in it. *Why do you even care?* She yelled at herself inwardly. *Why does his opinion matter so doggone much?*

"You said you didn't think I was uninteresting. So, what do you think?" She bit down on her inner lip, nervous about what he was going to say, as well as annoyed that she wanted to know.

"I think you care too much about what other people think about you." he said in a matter-of-fact tone, "I also think that this is your grandmother's turn off."

"You're right. Make a left at the light," she said, and then went back to their conversation. "So, it doesn't bother you what people think?"

"Not so much," he said casually, as he turned when she directed him to.

"So, if what people think about you doesn't bother you, how come you came down to the center to apologize to me?"

"There's a clear difference in worrying about someone's opinion of you and knowing when you've wronged someone and striving to make it right. If I worried about how someone's going to take something I say, or how my employees and business rivals perceive me, I'd never get anything accomplished," he said seriously. "Don't get me wrong. It's important to have good morals and to walk in integrity, and when you do the opposite of what you stand for, I believe in making amends. But aside from that, I can't live out my days worrying about what a person thinks of me. I just don't have the time, and even if I did, I wouldn't waste it on that."

Keturah was quiet; allowing his words to sink in deep. She wished she was at a place in life where other people's opinions didn't matter. But truthfully, other people's opinions were a big deal to her. Her job required her to make a good impression, especially when trying to get people to part with large sums of cash. Maybe when she was further in her career, had the center running strong, and banked her first million, she could decide not to care what others thought. But right now, that would be a "someday" goal she prayed one day to attain.

"Well, I have an opinion of you, too, Mr. Abraham Taylor," she said softly.

"Oh really? Do tell, Ms. Birch."

"Oh, no...I wouldn't dare waste your time with something as insignificant as my opinion," she said with a hint of mystery in her voice, as she watched familiar streets go by in blissful blur.

"I welcome your opinion of me."

"Fine, since you asked so nicely," she said with a cheeky smile. "I can tell you're a high stakes player who enjoys the challenge of something new and exciting. A thrill-seeker, who definitely does not like staying in one place for too long, you are an extrovert and where other people would play it safe, you enjoy taking leaps of faith and risking it all, just to see how God is going to catch you," Keturah stated, looking towards him and was again, rewarded with his charming grin, confirming that she was correct.

"Have you been reading up on me, Ms. Birch?"

Yes, ever since I was seventeen! She thought inwardly but said, "I'm just a good judge of character, that's all. I know a risk- taker when I see one."

"Well, aren't you the pot calling the kettle black?" He stated. Then, when he saw the mystified look on her face he clarified, "Oh, I forgot. That expression's probably before your time. I simply meant it takes one, to know one," he said plainly.

"Why would you think that I was a risk-taker?" she questioned. As far as she was concerned, she was as dull as they came. "No, I don't think so. I'm as boring a person as you'll ever meet and I have the empty, daily-planner to prove it."

"So, you're denying that you're a risk taker?" he looked at her incredulously, as she nodded her head.

"Okay, so you've already forgotten how we came to meet today; with you about to land on your back on the hard cement floor?"

"I would've bounced back," she rebutted.

"Yeah, right," he said sarcastically, "and what about our initial meeting? Things could have gotten out of hand, very quickly." He pinned her with a pointed gaze before turning his eyes back to the road.

"But that was completely innocent, a misunderstanding. It could've happened to anyone," Keturah said dismissively.

"Keturah, I'm a total stranger to you and yet you let me in your hotel room to sleep off a hangover. Who does that?"

Sighing heavily, Keturah tried to keep her irritation at bay. First Gretta, then Uncle Emory, now it was him getting on her case. Didn't anyone give her even the slightest bit of credit that she had survived this long, practically on her own, and was able to take care of herself?

"Look, for the one hundredth time, I'm a big girl and I know how to handle myself. I could've taken care of any situation if it arose, but it didn't. So, case closed." Seeing him about to protest, she talked right over him. "Besides, I knew of you even before Uncle Emory introduced us, and Uncle Em has the highest regard for you. So, I just couldn't leave you out in the hall sick, where anyone could've recognized you or even taken advantage of you."

"Keturah, that's not the point. The fact that you were looking out for me was good of you, and I am grateful to you for that but..." he held up his hand to stop her from interrupting, "if things would've gotten out of hand..." he sighed remorsefully, "I just don't think you should have put yourself at risk like that for me, or anyone else."

"I know this is likely a blow to most men's egos, but all women are not the helpless little Red Riding Hood-types, needing rescue from the big bad wolf," she shrugged off his concern as they pulled up to the front of her grandmother's house.

"Is that so?" he questioned, as he cut off the engine.

"Yes, that's so! This is one girl who knows how to handle herself in intense situations," she said smugly, while climbing out of his two-seat coup. When she turned around to shut the door, she was surprised to see that he had already exited the car.

Turning back around, she shrieked, startled to find him directly in front of her and extremely close. Too close. She tried backing away, but found herself pinned up against his car.

"Here I am, the big bad wolf...so now what, Little Red?" he said in a deep tenor, while arching an eyebrow at her.

Suddenly, she couldn't get enough air in her lungs. Her mouth went dry and, though she tried swallowing, her throat refused the command. In that moment, there was only him. Being that close to him felt so wonderful, the heat radiating off his chest made her want to wrap herself around him, as if he were an electric blanket on a cold winter day.

Instead of pressing as far away as possible, her traitorous body leaned forward, drawn to the steady rhythm of his heartbeat.

"Keturah?" Abraham said.

His timbre seemed to vibrate to her very core. His azure gaze held her fast. His spicy scented cologne was intoxicating and drawing her in like a bee to nectar. *His lips looked so soft and inviting, I wonder what they'd taste like.* She thought feeling herself rise on her tippy toes as they came closer.

"Keturah!" he said even more firmly.

"Yes, Abraham?" she felt her voice softly whisper his name as the tips of their noses brushed each other's.

Placing his fingers under her chin, he smirked, "Score one, for the big bad wolf," he said, mirth evident in his voice as he tapped her under the chin. With a sigh, he placed both hands on her shoulders and pushed them apart, putting some much-needed distance between their bodies.

"You better be very glad I passed out last Saturday night; for both our sakes. Now, off with you, before I forget I'm a reformed wolf," he said, pointing to her grandmother's porch.

Turning towards the porch, Keturah saw Gretta standing there with a little smirk on her face. With her hands on her ample hips, she looked at Abraham, then back at Keturah, and gave a chuckle. "Well, well, well! If you two are finished making a spectacle of yourselves, why don't you come on in. Supper is ready," she said, waving them forward, as she turned around and walked back into the house.

Keturah wasn't quite sure what to say, so she turned to Abraham, who still looked quite amused.
"I guess you're invited to dinner," she gave a shrug and turned and walked towards the house. Half-hoping, he would refuse, but so glad when she heard his car doors lock, as he fell in step behind her.

CHAPTER NINE

"Ms. Campbell, you sure do fix a mean pot roast." Abraham grinned as he wiped his mouth after his second helping. He was going to have to do two workouts, just to burn off the calories from the pot roast. The homemade apple pie was a whole other matter. He'd gladly work it off though. He couldn't remember the last time he had such a mouth-watering, home-cooked meal and the enjoyable company. He hadn't intended to stay when he dropped Keturah off, but Gretta didn't appear to be a woman who'd take, no, for an answer. Not being one to disrespect his elders, he graciously complied and was so happy that he did.

"I'm gonna swat you, if you call me Ms. Campbell one more time, young man." Gretta took her cloth napkin and shook it at him for emphasis.

"Yes, Mama…I mean Gretta." He held up his hands in surrender.

"How long has it been since you've eaten a home-cooked meal, Son?"

"Funny, I was just wondering that myself. It has definitely been quite some time," he mused.

"Well, you're more than welcome to stop on by here anytime your taste buds get to hankerin' for some down-home southern comforts," she winked as she got up to move about, clearing the table.

"Oh, no you don't, Gretta. You sit yourself down. I'm cleaning up. You know good-and-well, you shouldn't be doing half the stuff you've been doing around here, anyway. I told you I was going to help rearrange your living room and here you've gone and done it yourself," Keturah accused.

"Oh, girl, hush up. Them doctors don't know everything, and they definitely can't tell me about my own body. Hmmph, give a man a piece of paper and let him hang it on his wall in an office, and all of a sudden, he's an expert about me. Shoot, I can smell the breast milk on some of these so-called experts' breath. Please!" Gretta fussed as she limped around, gathering things off the table.

Keturah gave a helpless shrug at Abraham; he empathized with her. Gretta was seventy-five years old, the same age his father was when he passed away and he was as stubborn as a mule right up until the end. Couldn't get the man to listen for anything, and was as cantankerous as all get out. He only prayed that he didn't get that way as he aged.

"Ms. Cam...I mean Gretta," he quickly corrected, remembering her threat, "it would be my pleasure, if you'd allow me to clean up. Honestly, it's the least I could do for you feeding me so well. Besides, my mom would have a conniption if she knew I came to someone's home, unannounced and empty- handed."

Gretta gave him a hard stare for a moment, and then broke out in a laugh that caused her belly to shake.

"Umm hmph, boy you're one silver-tongued devil, if I ever did see one." She gave a laugh again, and then turned towards Keturah.

"You gonna have to watch out for this one, Keturah. He's good looking and smooth talking. Umm, girl, man like this will have you wrapped around his finger before you can give a second blink."

"Gretta!" Keturah said, wide-eyed and exasperated. "What? I didn't tell the man something he didn't already know. The man is fine! He knows it, I know it, and you've known it since the eleventh grade," she rolled her eyes and shook her head.

"Oh, Lord. You should've seen this girl, Abraham. Eleven years ago. Every time a magazine article came out about you, she collected it and put it in her scrapbook. She was such a nerdy girl. When most girls were looking at the latest boy group, she was clipping articles form *Forbes* and *Money Magazine*. Shoot, she used to quote you more than she did the Bible. Lord, you'd a thought you were the "great black hope of finance," the way she carried on and on and on. I didn't know what she was talking about half the time, all I knew was that it kept her head in the books and out of the boys' faces and away from the clubs."

Gretta continued to straighten the table as she talked, "You were the first black man she had seen make it to the top in finances, and she was determined to be the first from this area to be successful, too." Gretta then stopped and stared at Keturah, pride and love filling the woman's facial features.

"Mighty proud of you, Tourie, you've done good. And it is so sweet of you to get that youth center open, so you can continue to encourage those coming behind you."

"I'd like to hear more about the center and what you're trying to do with it. My company also has a charitable foundation and it is always on the lookout to support community-based projects," he said, looking in Keturah's direction.

"That's a great idea. Tourie, take Abraham on the porch and tell him all about it while I clean up in here."

"But, Gretta!" They both stated at the same time.

"But, my butt!" She put her hands on her hips again and stared them both down. "Ya'll should know by now, that you ain't running this show. Now, git!" She waved them off and disappeared into the kitchen.

"I've dealt with a lot of imposing figures in my day, but I don't think any of them could hold a candle to Ms. Gretta Campbell."

"In her heyday, she'd have some of my toughest professors trembling," Keturah chimed in.

He hated to leave Gretta in the kitchen just as much as Keturah did; he had seen the way she was favoring her right leg. He thought she needed to sit down and rest up a bit as well, but he knew that type of stubbornness. He had witnessed it a hundred times in his dad. If they insisted, she rest, she'd just dig her heels in and refuse to do anything they suggested. So, with a sigh, he cuffed Keturah under the elbow and slowly walked her towards the front door.

It was a picture-perfect night. The air skirting across the back of his neck was not too hot, or too cool, but perfect for just sitting and talking. Surprisingly, it was something he was looking forward to. Keturah was a puzzle he just couldn't figure out. She wasn't the decadent woman he first thought her to be last Saturday. On the contrary, she had a big heart for others, especially the girls in her community. Most women her age would be out partying or somewhere out on a date. So, the fact that his personal assistant tracked her down to the center in a rundown part of the city amazed him. But for her to be there alone and unprotected, enraged him. Why she seemed to constantly place herself in risky situations was unsettling.

When he held her close earlier that evening, it was only to show her that she needed to be careful; that a casual situation could turn, in a heartbeat. He had no idea he'd like holding her so much! He hadn't had a woman in his arms, since Sarah that day in the hospital before she died. Shaking his head slightly, he tried to dislodge the memories of that day that were reemerging in his mind.

Twice, he had his arms around this vibrant young woman, and admittedly, it felt good. He led her to the only seat available on the small porch, a wrought-iron swing.

He let Keturah settle in, and then sat down beside her. The swaying movement was comforting, reminding him of the times spent with Sarah after dinner, when they would sit on the porch of their starter-home and gaze into the sky; talking about endless dreams and the family they'd one day have. It was the best time of the day for him back then, and was proving to be enjoyable now, he thought, as they swayed back and forth, in companionable silence.

"Do you really think we should be out here? I mean she seemed to be limping pretty bad tonight," Keturah said, worry etched on her face.

Her words snapped him out of his wayward thoughts. "How about you give me the short version of your project, then we will go back in. And, on the drive to your place, you can fill in what you left out," he suggested and she smiled her approval.

Engrossed in their conversation, Abraham sat transfixed at Keturah's animated presentation. He had definitely misjudged her the night after the party. Her passion for her work reminded him of himself at her age. He remembered having the zeal and, like her, would have stood on three or four rickety old chairs, if he thought it would get his goal accomplished.

"There's a lot of unused land in the back and I wanted to cultivate it and eventually plant a garden full of organic vegetables and have the girls develop a farmer's market. We could sell the vegetables directly and partner with local stores," Keturah explained.

It was a solid plan and doable. It was definitely a project his foundation would support. Keturah had a good head on her shoulders and a good heart. An idea was beginning to congeal in his mind. He needed time to think all the particulars through but, before he could focus his thoughts, a loud crash and scream came from the inside of the house.

Keturah was already up and making a mad dash for the kitchen and Abraham was right on her heels. Entering the kitchen, Abraham saw water soaking the floor and a crumpled Gretta sprawled on it in an awkward position. Keturah was about to go to her, but he restrained her by grabbing both of her arms.

"Call an ambulance," he commanded as he pushed her out of the way and towards the phone hanging on the wall. He could tell she was on the verge of panic, but he needed her to be level-headed right now. She knew their whereabouts better than he, and they would likely want to know things regarding Gretta that he didn't have a clue about.

Being careful to step around the soapy water so he would not slip and land on her, he made his way to her side. "Gretta, can you hear me?"

She moaned, giving the only indication that she was still conscious. She attempted to move but her efforts caused her to gasp in pain.

"Try not to move to much Gretta, help is on the way, okay?" He said in a gentle whisper, while watching her struggle to focus on him. He could hear Keturah in the background, frantically rambling off information to the 911 operator. Looking towards her, he could see the frustration and worry etched in her brows. He only wished he could somehow ease those worries. Only God could heal the body lying out on the floor. With that thought in mind, he laid hands on Gretta's shoulder and moved closer to her.

He prayed with confidence,

Father, your word says the prayer of the righteous avails much and that those prayers could heal the sick. So, I'm coming to you on Gretta 's behalf. Heal her body and bring into alignment anything this fall has caused to be out of place. Restore her health completely and fully. Let this test become a testimony in Jesus' name."

He could feel her hand tightening on his and a smile creasing her face. "Bless you, child. Bless you. I've been waiting a long time for you to come and take care of my baby," she gave a heavy sigh, "She's young, but God's got something special in store for the two of you. Just trust him, man of God…trust him."

Abraham could feel the hairs standing up on the back of his neck as her words resonated deep within his heart. He had felt an unexplainable pull towards Keturah the very first time they met, but after the morning in her hotel room, he immediately dismissed it. Incredibly, that same feeling came over him today when he was with her at the center. Again, he was going to brush it off as just being lonely and seeking out female companionship; but now, he wasn't so sure.

There was only one other time he could recall, when he sensed purpose calling to him, urging him to act - back when the Lord spoke to him about leaving his family and pursuing Canaan. He felt that same press and sense of urgency now. However, Gretta needed him. He would figure all this other stuff out later. A trembling hand touching his shoulder caused him to refocus on the situation at hand. Looking up, he could see Keturah's tear-stained face come into his line of vision.

"How is she?" her voice and fingers trembled as she looked down at him for some kind status on her grandmother's condition.

"Don't worry; everything is going to be alright." He answered her with such assurance in his voice that it momentarily startled even him.

Needing to stretch and clear his head, he slowly rose from his crouched position over Gretta, and turned towards Keturah.

"Hey, why don't we trade places," he directed Keturah, as they switched positions; Abraham being careful not to bump into Gretta's contorted form.

"I'll go outside and move my car, so the ambulance can take my place," he said, already hearing sirens in the distance. *Thank God, they're almost here*, he thought as he quickly moved from the small kitchen into the dining room.

Picking up his keys off the coffee table, he was out the door and in his car within minutes. He quickly moved from the parking space just as the ambulance turned the corner and was coming down the street. Signaling for them to move right where he just exited, he waited for them to park and gave them a brief status of Gretta's condition as they were all walking into the house, stretcher in tow.

***

Five hours later Abraham and Keturah rode back to Gretta's house, both deep in thought about the doctor's prognosis of Gretta's condition.

She's sustained a broken hip and a mild concussion when her head hit the counter. Her right leg has a lot of bruising and is very badly swollen; this also could be due to her elevated sugar levels. With her age, along with her blood-pressure being so high right now, we can't operate on her hip until we get that under control. She's medicated for now, and will need to stay here until we can get her blood pressure regulated, and then we'll proceed from there.

It took the remainder of Abraham's mental strength to convince Keturah to leave the hospital and go home that night. Finally realizing there was absolutely nothing she could do for Gretta, she acquiesced and left with him some time after midnight.

They were in such a rush to get Gretta to the hospital that they needed to return to her home to make sure the lights were off and everything was secure.

They were both exhausted and a little on edge, so hardly any words passed between them on the ride back.

Pulling up to the curb to park, he was in the process of turning off the car engine when Keturah touched his arm, causing him to turn towards her. Her face was hidden within the shadows of his car. He didn't know what to expect, until her hand gently travelled up his arm and trembling fingers lightly touched his jawline. Timidly she drew his face downward and whispered,

"Gretta told me to give you a kiss on the cheek for being there for her. Hope you don't mind," she said quietly, as she closed the distance between them, brushing his face ever so softly with her lips, lingering there for a moment, before she withdrew to gaze into his eyes again.

"You've been so wonderful today Abe; I can't imagine what I'd have done without you. Thank you for everything," she whispered as she drew his face towards hers again, only this time, she surprised him when she kissed his lips slowly. It took him only a second to decide what his response would be. Slowly, his hand rose to the back of her neck to cradle her head in his palm, while he responded in kind.

CHAPTER TEN

"I finally met her, Conrad. At the benefit, I met my sister, Keturah," Tippany Jaymes whispered the words, as if talking to herself.

"That's nice babe," Conrad Jessup mumbled as he turned away from her to snuggle down into the comforter.

"She wasn't at all what I expected. She seemed nice, even showed concern for Mother, if you can believe that," Tippany snickered, as silence emanated from the other side of the bed.

"You should have seen Mom's reaction when I was about to leave the room with her. She nearly bit my head off!" Tippany rubbed her chin, wondering why her mom responded that way.

"Mother always told me to stay away from her. Heck, we weren't even allowed to mention her name. But I always wanted to know her. Wondered what her life was like. Wanted to be able to talk to her, to see what she's really like for myself. Now that I'm older, I still want that. I know it probably sounds crazy, but after all this time, I would still like for us to become friends." Heaving out a long sigh, she turned to her boyfriend.

"Conrad, do you think I'm being silly? Should I just leave things alone?" No response came from the other side, "Conrad, are you listening?"

"Mmm...hmm," he muttered from under the comforter. "Okay then. What did I say?" she challenged.

"Love you too, babe," he slurred, before snoring loudly. She glared at his covered head for a long time, hating the fact that her mother was right about him.

I bred you to be a debutante, not a garbage collector. You need to learn how to pick a man who has pedigree, the right breeding and class. I didn't spend all that money putting you in finishing schools and an Ivy League college, just so you can date trailer trash. You keep dating men of Conrad's class and, mark my words, you'll soon find yourself in the gutter. Her mother's hateful words still rang in her ears.

"I hate it when she's right," she mumbled. Maybe he was just using her name to build a reputation for himself. She knew she should likely dump him, but still he did serve two important purposes. One, he irritated the mess out of her mother, which was priceless. Second, he kept all her mother's would-be suitors at bay.

Do you love him?

She already knew she didn't. There was no denying it. At times, she couldn't stand the sight of him. He was notorious for his flirting and being self-absorbed.

All true but he is cute and good in bed and that's more than some women ever get in their marriages, would be the response of her sorority sisters. But, even if that thought wasn't ringing in her ears, she knew first-hand that most marriages were not made in Heaven. In fact, she would guess that her dad would say his marriage to her mom was birthed right out of hell.

Hate is a strong word, but it was the only one fitting, when describing how her parents felt about each other. It was torture growing up in her home. If her parents weren't fighting, they were giving each other the silent treatment. She was certain her mom was responsible for sending her father to an early grave. Many a night, she'd prayed they'd just end everyone's misery and get a divorce, after which she would've happily lived with her dad. But they didn't.

Shivering with the thought, Tippany looked over at Conrad, once again. She would never in a million years subject herself to that type of torture. Hearing a loud snoring sound from under the covers, she nudged her partner in the back, hard.

"If you're going to be snoring all night, you can get your stuff and go," she snapped.

"Ouch! Babe, what's wrong with you? Why you got to be so mean!" Conrad flipped the covers down groggily staring at her.

"I didn't call you over here so you can sleep all night. If that's all you want to do, then get dressed and go home," she flared at him, angrily throwing the bed-covers back and jumping out of bed; snatching up the discarded robe on the bedroom floor and covering herself with it. She was angry, but not really with him. He was the closest one around, so he was going to get the brunt of her fury.

"Aw, Babe, don't be like that. You know, I know how to satisfy my woman." He gave her his killer smile as he exited the bed in all his glory, walking over to her side and embracing her fully, giving her neck long, exaggerated kisses.

Pushing him away, she faced him with her hands on her hips. "I want more than sex, Conrad. If you're really going to be in a relationship with me, I want more than photo-ops and quick rolls in the hay. I want your attention as well as your time," she demanded, wondering where all this was coming from.

"Whoa!" he said, wide-eyed, while holding both hands up as if surrendering. "Where's all this coming from Tippy? I thought we were just kicking it. You know, having a good time. When did things become so serious?"

Turning from him, she belted her robe and wrapped her arms around her middle. When did things become so serious? She wasn't looking for any complications in their relationship. But something happened when she saw Keturah the other night. She wanted something permanent, something lasting in her relationship. She was tired of the superficial. "I don't know, Conrad," she said while turning her back to him, "I'm tired of just *kicking it*. I want more."

She allowed her words to trail off. It was time, and she knew it. Breathing out a sigh, she gathered her wits, so she could say what she knew was long overdue. Facing him she simply said, "Listen, I'm sorry I snapped at you. I think we need to call it a night."

"Sure Babe, if that's what you want. I'll call you." he said, already sitting on the bed getting dressed.

"Yeah right," she said knowing that call would never come. Smiling as she watched the man quickly put his clothes on, already knowing she was going to make her mother a happy soul when she learned that their causal relationship was over; but probably as mad as all-get-out, when she learned the new friendship she thoroughly intended to embark on with her half-sister.

Imagining the steamy vapors emanating from her mother's head only made her smile harder. With a plan in mind, she began thinking of ways she could connect with Keturah.

"Emory!" she thought out loud, instead of in her head.

"What?" Conrad looked up.

"Oh nothing...nothing at all." She smiled as her plan began to formulate. First thing in the morning, she was in Emory's office waiting for him. He might have dodged her all last week, but she'd see to it that he didn't do it tomorrow.

***

"Hi Emory, how's Adelle's ankle?"

Startled Emory turned around quickly, nearly spilling his coffee. "Tippany! You startled me."

"Sorry about that." She apologized with a smile.

"What are you doing here so early?" He asked, putting his coffee down and sitting behind his desk.

"You're a tough man to track down," Tippany remarked. Getting up, she roamed around his office looking at various pictures, her eyes coming to rest on one in particular.

"So, what can I do for you, Tippy?" he asked cautiously. "I think you know," she said, turning her hand, which was resting on the picture of him and Keturah, at what appeared to be her graduation.

"So, we're back to that," he resolutely sighed.

"Did we ever leave it?" She moved towards him and sat down in a chair in front of his desk.

"Look, Emory, I know my father had other children besides my brothers and myself. Keturah looks just like us, except for her darker complexion. Besides that, the way my mother reacted in just seeing her at the benefit seals it. Keturah Birch is my half- sister."

"It seems you have all the answers, Tippany. Why do you need me to confirm anything?"

"Because I want the truth. You were Dad's best friend. So, it's no coincidence that she is in your care. What I want to know is, why the secrecy, and why have you kept her hidden all these years, until now?" she demanded with conviction.

"I think those questions can only be answered by one person, Tippany." he said cryptically.

"Dad's dead. He can't answer anything. I want to know Emory," she said, irritated.

"The answers you want to know can best be answered by your mother." he said flatly.

"What? What are you saying?"

"What I'm saying, dear-heart, is your mother is the reason for all of this." He restated tersely. "Now, I'm sorry. I have a meeting in a few minutes. If there's anything else you need to know, confront your mother," he said picking up the phone and effectively ending the impromptu meeting.

"Thanks for your time," Tippany muttered after being dismissed.

Slowly walking towards the door, she felt as if she were leaving with more questions than answers. *What's mom's role in all this?* She already knew that her dad hadn't been faithful to her mother. She stumbled on that fact years ago, when she overheard her oldest brother, Malcom talking to her dad about having half-siblings from his birth mom. *Why did Mom accept Malcom, but not Keturah?*

Oh, how she would have loved having an older sister to hang with. Maybe her life as the only daughter wouldn't have been so stifling. Mother's only concern was proper etiquette and her prestigious education. *"She could have cared less if I enjoyed my childhood."* Tippany thought bitterly.

Hitting the elevator button, she pondered how best to get the information she needed from dear ole Mom. They had been on the outs since their fight over Conrad on the night of the party. Maybe knowing she and Conrad weren't an item anymore might get her in her good grace. *It's worth a try?* She thought, smiling and walking into the elevator. It was time to go to work.

CHAPTER ELEVEN

"You're right, Hagan. You're absolutely right; it was wrong of me not to call you before now." *The woman was such a drama queen.* Abraham absently shook his head, knowing this was an argument he wasn't going to win. "Honey, all I'm asking is that you try and understand the position I put my family in that night." He knew trying to reason with her was pointless, but it was worth a shot. Besides, he deserved her anger. He had left her stranded at the party and then went out of town the next day, without a word. It was thoughtless.

In truth, he should have told her from the beginning that they weren't going to work out, but the idea of reuniting with Ishmael was too enticing. He would do anything to have his oldest son back in his life.

"You want me to try and understand! What, exactly, would you have me understand Abraham?" Hagan spat at him like a cat clawing at her prey. "That pleasing your dead wife's relatives is more important to you than I am? That revelation is abundantly clear to me now," she gave a mirthless laugh, "Ugh, I'm so done taking this type of abuse from you and Sarah. I did it when I was young and stupid, but that girl is dead, Abraham. Dead! You and that wife of yours killed her a long time ago. You have to deal with the woman I am now. And that woman will not take a backseat in your life ever again. Ishmael and I had to survive on our own for years without you, and will continue to do so."

"Hagan, I know I messed up, but let's not drag Ishmael into this." He felt his heart pounding hard within his chest at the thought of losing his son, even before they had a chance to reunite.

"Why not, you think I don't know why you've been milling around for all this time? I know you want Ishmael back in your life, but here's a newsflash for you Abe: we are a package deal *honey* always have been, and always will be. Now that I see how attached to Sarah's family you evidently still are, I really don't know if it's in our best interest to be involved with you at all."

"Now, you just wait one minute, Hagan..." clutching the phone to his ear he spoke through clenched teeth, already knowing he had reached his boiling point. He didn't like ultimatums or coercions for that matter regardless of who it came from.

"No, Abraham. I've waited for you far too long. Now it's your turn to see how waiting feels. I'll need some time to reevaluate this entire relationship between us. See if it's in Ishmael's and my best interest to allow you to be involved in our lives again."

"Hagan, please don't," He urged, but she kept right on talking.

"So, we won't be joining you overseas like we previously discussed. Oh, and you'll have to fend for yourself with the business venture with my brother-in-law."

"Hagan...don't you dare..."

"Don't worry, darling. I won't let the cat out of the bag and tell Hassin the status of our relationship. I'll let you do the honors," she said snidely.

The dial tone was the only indication that she'd hung up. "Well, that didn't go as planned," Abraham said sarcastically. Dropping the phone on table, he rubbed his eyes. What had happened between them only confirmed what he already knew in his heart. He and Hagan weren't right for each other, no matter how much history, good and bad, they had between them.

"Lord, what now?" He wondered out loud. Looking out at the skyline from his high-rise apartment, he allowed the golden sunset to calm his frazzled nerves. He'd wanted *Canaan* to delve into international waters for some time now. It would be the final piece that would make the company a global force to be reckoned with, and then he could finally retire and let Isaac take over. He thought to himself, *"If that's going to happen, you better get back on that phone and beg Hagan for forgiveness"*.

The idea caused the veins in his neck to restrict. He twisted his neck from side to side, to release the building tension. He wasn't in the habit of begging anyone for anything. If God couldn't do it for him, then it wouldn't be done, or he didn't need it. Of course, Hagan was instrumental in getting him an initial meeting with Hassin Zarah, CEO of Globe International; after all, Hassin was her brother-in-law. He had been trying for months to set up a meeting with the man who was as busy as he was. One call from Hagan, and they were meeting for lunch within an hour.

It was God who had orchestrated the meeting, not Hagan. She was just a tool God used; not the architect. Trusting God brought him this far, not man. He'd do well to remember that truth.

He thought to himself, *Hassin is all about family and will only do business with those with traditional family values. To him, a man with a stable family runs a strong company. Right now, Isaac and I are in the same boat. It's taken Isaac three years to finally commit to Rebekah, and I haven't been in a serious relationship since Sarah. Now with Hagan gone, I'm definitely not the poster-child for stability. I need to prove that I have a stable home life. In essence, I need a wife.*

Rubbing his forehead, he shut his eyes momentarily and immediately saw twinkling grey eyes fill his mind as her name rang in his head like a sweet melody.

Keturah.

Of all the women in the world, why did this young woman's smile and bubbly personality wreak havoc with his soul? Since the time after Sarah's death, all he could think about was her and the legacy they had built. Now, when he saw those familiar eyes, it wasn't Sarah on his mind, which was unsettling, because until now, he never imagined any other woman could captivate his thoughts. A smile softened his chiseled features, as his hand absently rubbed his chest; the memory of the kiss they shared in his car still lingering in his mind. Although he could detect her innocence around men, she certainly wasn't a shy thing. Yes, Keturah Pamela Birch was undeniably full of surprises.

The biggest was her being the daughter of his late uncle, Kedron Jaymes. Looking at the envelope the private investigator dropped off that afternoon, he was shocked at the contents. Using her mother's maiden name, Birch, Keturah proved to be far different than the spoiled, rich kids that Sari and Kedron had raised. Keturah was smart and tenacious, working her way through undergrad and graduate schools by winning scholarships and working part-time jobs. And, to top it off, she still took time to check on her grandmother.

He shook his head and smiled. She had a lot of spunk for being only twenty-five. Her age kept drumming in his mind. Twenty-five! He rubbed a hand down his unshaven face. She was younger than Isaac. Kedron would wallop him for sure, if he knew of his intentions!

His mind drifted back to the first time he remembered seeing her. It was one of the worst days of his life. She might have been, maybe three or four years old. He remembered her clutching her mother's thigh, crying at the scene of Aunt Sari, lunging at her mother calling her all types of filthy names. Kedron stood between them taking the brunt of his wife's fury. The little summer house where he and Kedron were going to spend time with their children turned into a war zone. So much yelling, screaming arguing, blaming...it was crushing. It all took place right in front of the kids. Then Sarah's ultimatum: *"It's either us or them. Choose!"* Abraham gave an involuntary shudder remembering those words. Watching Sarah walk out on him, with Isaac screaming behind her and Ishmael leaning on his mom, while sensing the gravity of the situation was heart-wrenching. Kedron had Emory usher Keturah and her mother out of the house and into his car, all while aunt Sari screamed obscenities to the top of her lungs. How could such a beautiful day end so horribly?

He got up and paced the floor. More than twenty years had passed since that event occurred, and it still hurt. The scar was still tender to the touch. If he hurt like that, he could only imagine how Keturah and Ishmael had felt. Back then, it was like he was caught between two warring countries, powerless to fix the situation; and it cost him dearly.

"ENOUGH!" He stood up shaking his head, needing to rid himself of that horrible memory.

"Forgetting those things that are behind me, reaching for those things that are before me." The Holy Spirit whispered.

Keturah was beautiful, charming, and very giving; everything his Sarah had been before she became obsessed about having his baby. Although they had similarities, he wasn't gullible enough to think they were the same. Keturah was definitely not the stay-at-home type. She was young and energetic; the type of woman who wanted to make her own way in life, and he admired that about her. He liked her need for independence; understood it. But, would it prove to be an issue if she took him up on his proposal? After all, he wasn't really looking for anything too serious: just a temporary arrangement that would satisfy Hassin, and keep unwanted suitors, like Hagan at bay.

He surmised his biggest obstacle would be getting Emory on board. He had not known his friend kept tabs on Kedron's child all these years. Back in the day, Emory and Kedron were frat brothers, and although they all eventually went their separate ways, Emory and Kedron had apparently remained close. Emory always looked out for Kedron, up until his untimely death, and was apparently was still doing so. He only prayed Emory would be agreeable to all this. He didn't want to butt heads with his good friend, remembering the last argument they had over his treatment of Keturah. He thought the man was going to wring his neck for passing out in her hotel room. Chuckling at the thought, he blew out a breath.

"I'm going to ask Kedron's twenty-five-year old daughter to be my wife!" he said out loud, to hear how it sounded. *Crazy*, he thought, cradling his head with both hands. Was God really orchestrating this or was this the irrational actions of a grieving man? He wasn't known to act on a whim. He always prided himself on making solid decisions. This would likely push his family over the edge. He could envision his aunt Sari now:

"....Boy, have you lost the good sense the Lord has given you? Why in the world would you take up with an infant? Abraham, come to your senses, you're still grieving is all, and you're being irrational."

He shook his head. If she said half those things, she'd be right. Every one of those points was valid and things that he'd already said to himself.

"There is no guarantee Keturah will even say yes!" He grunted, pacing back and forth, "I'm not even sure that I'd say yes, after our first encounter. She very well might laugh her head off." He flopped back down on the bed and again allowed his head to drop in his hands. He hated indecision on his part; it always leads to doubt.

Trust in the Lord with all your heart and lean not to your own understanding. In all your ways acknowledge Him and he will direct your path. As the familiar scripture rose in his heart, he took comfort in it; a reassuring promise from God that he had carried in his heart when he first began pursuing *Canaan Enterprise.*

Bowing his head, he prayed earnestly to the Father, "Lord, you've always been a friend to me, directing my steps as I navigate these uncharted waters. I know I can trust you now and I do. The direction I'm about to take looks kind of crazy to me, so I can only imagine how it will probably look to others; but I don't care. I've been called crazy and far worse. As long as I know you're in this, I'm going to trust you."

Chapter Twelve

"Another glamour-free Friday night for me!" Keturah huffed her resignation as she shuffled from the bedroom to her living-room, wearing her old cut-off sweatpants and favorite faded sweatshirt; comfy clothes. "Once the pizza arrives, my boring weekend can officially begin." she said sarcastically before flopping down on her sofa and putting her feet on the coffee table, frowning at a smudge on her middle toe where the nail polish had chipped.

"Whatever!" she said to the minor offense. She'd let nothing disrupt her evening of solitude. God had been good and had gotten her through another tough week. So, there was no real reason to complain. She had just left the hospital and from the doctors' report, Gretta's vitals were improving and it was possible to do the hip surgery she desperately needed.

The hospital bills were going to be astronomical, but she'd manage. She always did. Her grandma was all she had in the world; she'd take care of her, no matter what. Abraham's brilliant blue eyes drifted in her mind like always. She smiled dreamily as she thought of Abraham. Like a prince, he had called everyday just to check on her and Gretta. It was so sweet. He might be a shrewd business man, but there was a tender side hidden under that tough exterior.

"He'd be a great catch if he wasn't so old. Lord, why are all the good ones taken, or not ready to commit, or too doggone old?" she grumbled to herself.

"Should his age make a difference?" the spirit whispered.

"I couldn't possibly get with someone that much older than me." Keturah warred within herself. "What could we possibly have in common?" She said out loud shaking her head, trying to dismiss the thought.

Abraham Taylor was at least twenty-five years her senior and they lived in two separate worlds. Granted, her heart did this funny little flip-flop every time he called her, but she knew it was nothing more than infatuation. He rescued her when she needed it the most that's all. She was just being silly. Anyway, he wouldn't give her the time of day. She was mistaking his caring nature for more than what it really was. She was enamored by the man who turned out to be her knight in shining armor, and she'd likely never forget it.

With him continuing to call and then sending Gretta flowers, well, it was enough to get a woman thinking. "Shoot, if he was just closer to my own age, he'd be perfect." She had been talking this way, the entire two weeks Abraham had been gone on his business trip.

"Arrgh!" Keturah huffed out in frustration. *No wonder you're home alone on a Friday night. Men don't want to attach themselves to needy women. They can see your neediness coming a mile away. Abraham...Mr. Taylor is a Christian, as well as a gentleman. Of course, he would check on us. He was just taking care of his friend's family. That's it! See it for what it is,* she chided herself.

This was her fatal flaw when it came to men. She only saw them in the context of husbands. Not every man was going to be her husband, and Abraham Taylor sure wasn't going to be that to her. He did a good deed that was it.

Dismissing the daydream of her being in the same class as Abraham and his circle of prominent friends, she snatched up the remote and turned on the TV, wishing that her pizza would arrive soon. Not that she was starving, but if she had to be alone on a Friday night, it always went better with sauce and cheese. Flipping through the channels to see if anything caught her attention, aside from the steamy love-scene she had to quickly turn from if she wanted to keep her sensual side tame that night; she kept flicking through the channels.

"Lord, I'm going to have to fight off thoughts tonight," she mused. As she settled down to watch a promising love-story on the *Hallmark Channel*, she let her mind wonder as to what it would really be like to be married with a family of her own. It could happen, maybe with her co-worker, Carlton Parson, at her side, if he would take five minutes to see her as a woman and not just his good buddy.

What about Abraham?

It was a passing thought she wasn't willing to entertain. First of all, they came from two different worlds; his was one in which she'd never fit. Secondly, the difference in their ages was too great. For heaven's sakes, he was old enough to be her father, or at best, her older uncle. If that wasn't enough, both of his sons were older than she. She'd be deemed a gold-digger and Abraham, a dirty old man. "Why am I even thinking like this? Besides, nothing would ever happen between us in a million years anyway. If it did, that would be a divine act from God," she said to herself, as she pulled the comforter over her shoulders to get in a more comfortable position, just as the doorbell rang.

"Finally!" Keturah huffed shrugging off the comforter and snatched up her purse to retrieve the money. It was pizza and romance stories night, and she was going to enjoy it.

Shuffling towards the door, and hoping not to smug her remaining wet nails, she reached the door and flung it open. "I'm happy to see..." she stopped mid-sentence, her mouth hanging open as she stood there looking at Abraham Taylor. He was standing in her doorway dressed in a tailor-made suit that looked as if he was poured into it. He had a pizza in his hand and a thousand-watt smile on his face that lit up her porch and her heart.

"You're happy to see me, or the pizza?" he said, his deep voice rumbling through his chest.

Keturah, standing there, mouth wide-open and gawking couldn't speak.

"I realize I'm coming here unexpected. I hope I'm not interrupting your evening," he questioned, his gaze never leaving hers.

She needed to say something, anything, so he won't deem her a total idiot. "Is that pepperoni?" She pointed at the box he held in his hand. *Brilliant, Keturah, always thinking about your stomach,* she inwardly chided herself, but outwardly gave him a lopsided grin. "Is there any other kind?" he chuckled, looking devilishly handsome.

"Oh, my goodness, where are my manners? Please, come in." She hurriedly stepped aside to allow him access into her apartment. As he passed her, she inhaled and couldn't determine what smelled better; the pizza or Abraham. Without a doubt, *he* did. Unable to get over the fact that he was there; she quickly checked her reflection in the TV and frowned at how frumpy her comfy clothes made her look. Running her fingers through her hair, she smoothed out her clothes and put on her best smile. The man who had been invading her dreams nightly and bringing on bouts of nervous jitters was actually in her apartment, and she looked worse than a bag lady. "Lord, help!" she mustered up a prayer before she shut her door and quickly ushered him to the living room.

"Hey, listen. I didn't mean to disturb your Friday night. I realize that I've come unannounced, but I wanted to check on you and your grandmother. I thought coming here would kill two birds with one stone, seeing that visiting hours at the hospital were over. I hope you don't mind," he said sounding a little hesitant.

"Oh, no, I don't mind; not at all. I didn't really have much planned, just pizza and a movie." Keturah shrugged, realizing how much of a bore she must sound like. Thinking of a way to change the subject from her dull Friday night routine, she quickly added, "Have you eaten anything yet? I mean, I know it's not much, but since you're here, why don't you stay and have a slice?" she really didn't expect him to, but it was the least she could offer.

So, it was quite a surprise when he gave a nod of agreement and took a seat on her couch. "Great, let me get us some plates." Quickly, she went into the kitchen. She wished she had not been so lazy and had done some house cleaning like she knew to. *Oh well*, she thought, as she grabbed two plates and glasses. Then she thought to make a quick salad, so at least the meal would be healthier. She was bustling around in the frig, making the salad preparations, when his deep voice sounded from behind, startling her.

"Hey, I don't want you going through all this trouble for me…Keturah. I have been known to dine on pizza alone, you know," he said with warmth in his voice that seemed to caress her, even though his hands never left his side.

"You've been so kind to me and my grandma, I wish I could do more," she quickly turned her back to him before he could see tears filling her eyes. Of all the times to get emotional, *Lord, why in the world did I have to go and say all that sappy stuff like a big dope? There's nothing I have that he could ever want. Well, if he was another type of man, he might want something else; but that's not how Abraham operates. He is genuine; the real deal.*

Her reasoning screamed, *HE'S AS OLD AS SIN!!!*

No, he's not; just older than me, she rationalized, with the warring thoughts raging within her mind. *He's a good man. I wish…I,* she stopped herself. She didn't want to voice her thoughts, not even to herself. *A man like this will only want one thing from a girl like you. Trust me! Abraham can have any woman he wants…so why settle for me? He's a kind-hearted man, looking after Emory's family. That's all, end of discussion.*

A touch on her shoulder drew her attention to the man with her in the small kitchen. She hadn't even known he had gotten so close, until she turned around and realized he was only an arm-length away.

Abraham said softly, "Did it ever occur to you that God's been tallying up your acts of kindness towards your grandmother, as well as what you're doing with the girls in the youth center, and now you're receiving the overflow? God sees the good and bad stuff and chooses to place more emphasis on the good, because that's when we resemble his likeness the most."

He voice was so tender, it settled around her heart and squeezed it a little, while his finger quickly whisked away a stray tear that had fallen on to her cheek.

"Mr., I mean, Abraham, you describe God in such a way, it's like you've just sat down and had coffee with him or something, like he's your BFF. Looking at his wrinkled brow, she gathered he didn't get her meaning and interpreted it for him, "You know BFF, best friend forever?

He cocked his head to the side in thought, "Yeah, I guess that would be a good way to describe us."

"But, don't you think that's kind of bold to say, 'I'm the friend of God!' Jesus is my brotha!'" she joked as she handed him his plate.

"Well, Jesus is your brother and God wants your friendship. Why is that so hard to believe?" he questioned.

"Who am I, and what do I have to give? I mean, I gave him my heart a while back, and I do my best to live in a way that is pleasing. But, it's not like I'm going to be a preacher or something important. I'm just ordinary me." She shrugged her shoulders as she walked him back to the living room, and sat down on the couch next to him.

"You're far from ordinary Keturah; far from it." Abraham pinned her with a compassionate gaze.

Blushing at the intensity of his stare, she turned her head slightly, to break eye contact. What was it about this man that made her so jittery inside? She'd leave that question for her private time later.

"I like the way you talk about your relationship with the Lord; it's like you're actually friends." She looked at him with wide eyes, fascinated at this new concept he described.

"Well, I like to think so," he said, adjusting his position on her couch to get a better view of her. "Over the years our relationship grew, as I obeyed his word and followed the leading of his Spirit. Not that I did everything perfectly, and I have received plenty of correction; but what he's done in my life has been so amazing that I have no regrets."

"No regrets? Now that, in itself, is amazing." She relaxed a little more on the couch while biting into her pizza, crust first. "There are so many things I wish I could change in my life", she said but thought to herself, *like growing up without parents.*

"Like what?" he pressed.

"I don't know." She wasn't too keen on telling him her whole life story yet, just the parts that wouldn't make her look so bad. "I guess the biggest regret is not having the ability to take care of Gretta right now like she deserves, and fix the center for the girls." Shrugging her shoulders, she hoped she didn't sound corny to a man who was a multi-millionaire and who dealt with more serious issues than an aging grandparent and a dilapidated building.

"Wanting to take care of your loved ones is admirable, Keturah. That's all I wanted in the beginning, to take care of my wife and our future family." He snagged another slice of pizza from the box and continued, "I was scared to venture out on my own. I mean, here I was, a man with no business-sense and hardly any money, ready to launch out into the great unknown, with only an inner voice prodding me to keep going. My family thought I had lost my mind, and at times, so had I. But I know what I heard and I had a burning desire to take a chance and I followed God's voice."

"Your family abandoned you?" she said softly as she curled her feet under her thighs and hugged herself.

"Yes, my dad thought I was being reckless and irresponsible, having just gotten married. I was ready to uproot my bride and nephew from the only home they knew, to go traipsing across country to follow this voice." Abraham chuckled at the memory, "I actually thought for a moment, that he was going to have me committed. They practically disowned me, but Sarah and my nephew Lot stayed. So, the Lord became everything: my father, mother, doctor, lawyer, etc. Back then, I had no clue *Canaan* would be what it is today. I just obeyed his voice," he finished with a shrug of his own.

"Wow, it must have been hard to have the only family you ever had, act as if you didn't exist," her voice caught with emotion; she forcibly swallowed to keep the swelling of feelings at bay. She knew firsthand that type of rejection, from her absent father. The abandonment of her father was like being punched in the gut repeatedly.

"Keturah?"

Her head snapped up to look into Abraham's frowning face, a trace of concern evident in his stormy gaze. "Oh, I'm sorry. Did you say something?"

"You looked so lost for a minute. What's wrong?" Shrugging her shoulders, she gave a shy smile, "I admire how much of a courageous person you are. I mean to just up and leave your loved ones and step out into an uncertain future. I don't think I'd have done something like that; especially, if I didn't have family to support me."

Moving closer to her on the couch, Abraham spoke, "You truly underestimate yourself, Tourie. You're a lot tougher than you think," he said softly, allowing his gaze to connect with hers. "You're taking care of your grandmother, when most people your age would be off doing their own thing. You have a heart to give back to your community by mentoring at-risk youth, and you take your disadvantages and use them to your advantage. If that's not courage, then honey, I don't know what is."

His fingertips on her face were making the skin he touched pulsate with the awareness of him. His cobalt eyes had a hypnotic effect on her and before she could catch herself, she was in his embrace and kissing him deeply and wishing somehow it could last forever. She suspected he must have been feeling the same way, for they had shared several more lingering kisses before he tore himself away.

Not knowing what to say, she stared back into his eyes- the intensity of his look was still there, but something else was smoldering just beneath the surface. Why this man happened in her life was a mystery, but what she could possibly do to entice him to stay would be her secret mission.

She could lie and say she wanted him as a mentor, or even a father-figure, but seeing how badly she wanted to kiss him again, she knew that would be creepy. Endless possibilities bombarded her mind with such force that she didn't hear him when he spoke. It was a gentle tap to her shoulder that brought her mind back in focus to the attractive smile on Abraham's face.

"Did you hear what I asked?" he inquired.

Knowing she hadn't, she slowly shook her head no.

Placing both of his hands on either side of her face, he placed his forehead on hers and spoke in a low whisper,

"Keturah Pamela Birch-Jaymes, will you be my wife?"

CHAPTER THIRTEEN

"Earth to Keturah, come in, Keturah!" A male voice spoke from behind.

Startled, Keturah jumped, as the hand waving in front of her face came into view. "Carlton L. Parson, what in the world?" she laughed, then quickly stood up from behind her office desk, ready to receive his bear-hug. If there was ever a person, she couldn't be happier to see, it was him. "When did you get in?" she said, as she breathed in the musky scent of his cologne: just what she needed to counter the effect of Abraham's memory.

"Just a little over an hour ago," he said casually, as he tossed his jacket in the opposite chair and gave her one last hug. "Umm, don't make any sense that such a good-smelling, gorgeous-looking woman like you is still single. What in the world is wrong with men today? Shoot, any man coming from a long trip would be proud and eager to come home to a woman like you!" he winked, pulling one of her spiraling curls in the process, before letting her go.

"I agree one hundred percent. What's wrong with you men today?" she gave him a challenging glare that he completely ignored. He was laying it on pretty thick, *must want something*, she mused to herself.

"So, did you miss me?" he wiggled his bushy eyebrows in a suggestive way that caused Keturah to burst out laughing. "I know I missed *you* something terrible!"

"I'm sure you did," Keturah said, walking back around her desk and having a seat. "So, you couldn't get that Malibu-Barbie-grad-assistant of yours to do all your work, like you normally have me doing?"

"Now, now, now, be nice and retract your claws." He put his hands up in surrender, "I had a perfectly good reason for choosing Melody, over you," he said diplomatically.

"Yeah, size thirty-six, twenty-four, thirty-eight reasons and you know it. One of these days, your reasons are going to land you in the president's office trying to explain away a sexual harassment suit from a ticked off boyfriend or husband!"

"Naw, it'll never happen," he denied. "Shoot, I'd marry you and be working on our third child before I'd let it come to that." He winked at her as she rolled her eyes back at him. "Furthermore, one look at you and anyone in their right mind would never believe I'd stray," he gave his signature, full smile.

Keturah stared at him hard for several long minutes, then shook her head, "You'll never change, Parson. You'll always be the world's biggest flirt."

There was a time when she had first started working in that department that she believed she had heard from God that Parson was "the one". The fact he was very attractive, always flirted with her and had some serious cash didn't hurt either. Any time his name was mentioned, her heart would do somersaults. She was constantly trying to get closer to him or simply catch a glimpse of him walking by. She even, on occasion, found herself making any and every excuse to go into his office under the guise of delivering paperwork or his mail, just so she could put anointing oil in strategic places: She was claiming him for the Kingdom and herself.

Then about a year ago, the day she'd prayed for had finally come. He had rededicated his heart to the Lord and was attending her church. Surely, God was on the move, and since he answered her first request, of course, he would answer the other one. All last year, she was his "dear" and "sweetheart." They'd hold hands while at the movies, eat dinner together, and go to school events. He even fought for her to get the position in their department that she currently held.

What woman wouldn't think that the man cared for her; felt something on a more personal level? Yeah, he gave her more and more of his work to do, but hey, since they were unofficially dating, what was wrong with helping her man out? Then six months ago, her neatly stacked pre-fabricated world came crashing down, when he introduced her to his new grad-assistant, Melody Ingstrum, daughter of Elliott Ingstrum, the lucrative textile manufacturer who just happened to be looking for a new CFO, and sweet, ole Melody thought Parson would be perfect. Ever since then, they were tied to each other's hip and lips. The only problem was the girl didn't have a working brain and was lazy as all-get- out. Nevertheless, Melody was in, and she was out. It was hurtful, but a reality that she'd lived with for last six months.

Now, with Gretta's health in jeopardy, to say nothing of Abraham's unexpected proposal, a proposal she didn't intend to let anyone know about. Parson's needs didn't make the list of her concerns right now. "I think what you meant to say was that you and Melody will be working on your first child and that *her* beauty will cause you to never stray," she corrected him.

"Naw, me and Mel won't work. She's extremely needy and bossy! And if there's one thing in the world I can't stand is a bossy woman." He looked at Keturah for a reaction before continuing, "Anyway, how 'bout you and me dine at *Combine's* tonight and talk? We've not done that in some time. What do you say?"

"Why not?" shaking her head, she laughed. Parson was definitely one of a kind. "By the way, I'm very glad you're back!" She confessed, wiping moisture from her eyes.

"But of course, you are, Madame," he said with a fake French accent, while he extended his arm for her to take.

***

After a long week of meetings and travel, Abraham dragged his weary body back to his office. Dropping his briefcase on his desk, he headed straight for the little refrigerator where he stored his favorite late-night drink, Red Bull. He needed the pick-me-up to pull the all-nighter needed so he could be properly prepared for the business-meeting first thing in the morning. So, why couldn't he concentrate? Soft grey eyes appeared in his mind. They kept haunting him; breaking into his thoughts all times of the day and night, no matter how much he tried to ignore them. He still hadn't heard from Keturah, and it made him worry. *She must think I'm crazy!* He huffed. "Maybe I should call her," he thought, already reaching for his phone.

Patience, Abraham. Be patient. The Holy Spirit whispered.

Looking at the picture hanging on the mantle of Sarah, he smiled remembering how she would always tell him that very same thing.

Sarah...How I miss you! He felt the familiar numbness in his chest, while looking around the office she had personally designed. He hadn't changed a single thing since she passed. This was their office. The wall exhibited all they had achieved over the decades. The center of it showcased his most prize possession. He remembered the day she came in and caught him placing her portrait at the top of his massive array of awards. She protested, "Baby, what on earth? What are you doing? My picture doesn't belong on this wall," she said as she grabbed a chair to stand beside him, so she could promptly take it down. But, before she could, he stopped her.

"Sweetheart, having your love and support over these past years is the greatest honor I've known, and it means more to me than any plaque nailed to this wall," he said softly, as he wiped the solitary tear that had spilled onto her cheek. The love she lavished on him in his office that day was enough to make him long for what they once shared. The memory gave him a melancholy sort of feeling. "God...if only ..."

He stopped himself and let the sentence go unfinished. It was pointless to talk about it. It was her time. She was home with the Lord and he refused to allow his faith to waiver by questioning God's plan. He had learned early-on in his journey when he had nothing, to trust God completely. So, he wouldn't start questioning him now. Shaking the memories of yesterday out of his head, he took a big gulp of his drink. *Living in the past won't help me prepare for this meeting tomorrow*; he thought as he stood up and strode to his desk to grab the files he needed to prepare. *Time to get to work.*

Fifteen minutes later, his mind was wandering again, "Focus man." As much as he tried, his thoughts kept going back to proposing to Keturah and likely what a big mistake he had made. Dropping his head in his hands, he shook it in disgust. "Man…what were you thinking?" Abraham wondered, as he propped his tired feet on the mahogany desk. He should never have asked her in the first place. It wasn't like him to do something that rash. *She probably did me a favor, not taking me up on the offer. If Aunt Sari found out that I asked her step-daughter to be my wife, she'd knock me upside my head,* he thought, chuckling. He hated to think of the repercussions of bringing those two under the same roof could cause.

Keturah.

She was so enthused about life. She was young and still had that fresh idealism that hadn't been spoiled by the harsh realities of life. Keturah wanted to do so many things, make a difference; her enthusiasm and zeal for life reminded him of Sarah, as well as himself, in their younger days. Back then, they were full of life and driven to make their own way. Together, they were going to set the world on fire and make lasting changes. Would Keturah want the same?

Really Abe! You know she's way, too young for you.
Somehow, Sarah's portrait seemed to be shooting daggers at him.
He sighed wearily. She was young, that was for sure; twenty-five
years old, to be exact. No wonder she stared at him the night he
proposed, as if he had sprouted three heads. *You want me to
marry you?* He remembered her saying, confusion laced in her
voice as she tilted her head to the side, as if she was trying to
determine if he was only joking. It felt as if everything went
downhill from there, as he tried explaining the marriage in name
only between the two of them. *Mr. Taylor, I don't know what to
say.* He had just asked this woman to be his wife; yet, she still
called him *Mr. Taylor,* which only emphasized the fact that he was
so much older than she was. To date, this had to be the craziest
thing he had done by far. "Abe, you never cease to amaze
yourself," he laughed out loud. Then he picked up off his desk,
the files that needed his attention, and settled back for what was
sure to be a long night.

CHAPTER FOURTEEN

Perched on the edge of Gretta's bed, Keturah absently nibbled on her bottom lip, while listening to the heart monitor's steady blip.

I want you to consider this: be my wife for one year.

She remembered laughing. It was only when he didn't laugh; she realized he was being serious. Rubbing her hands down her face, she blew out a sigh of frustration.

"Lord, why did Gretta have to fall?" she questioned, glad that her grandmother couldn't witness her wavering faith. It was only because of Gretta's dire condition that she was even considering his crazy proposal.

Looking over at her purse, she knew the mountain of bills that were hidden inside. Several of them where due immediately, but she just didn't have the money. As if things weren't already tight, the hospital social-worker had just finished talking to her about the co-pay that was due up front. *Five-thousand dollars.* It rolled off the woman's tongue, as if she had said fifty dollars, which, at the moment, she didn't have either.

"Lord, what are we going to do?"

Marry him!

She shook her head, trying to rid herself of the unwanted thought. *This couldn't possibly be your will;* she thought adamantly, *could it?*

One side of her mind was telling her to take the offer and all the benefits marriage to a millionaire would present, while the subtle side was saying marriage was something not to be entered into lightly. *He's too old for you. You don't belong in his world. This could be an answer to prayer; God's ram-in-the-bush for you.*

Desperation was colliding with her good judgment and it seemed that all voices were clamoring to be heard. Suddenly, a jerking movement from the bed caused her head to snap up. Gretta's body was shaking like a leaf and then suddenly, all movement stopped as her heart monitor's rhythmic sound gave out one, long beep. "Oh My God...NO!!! Keturah jumped off the bed, panicking; not knowing what to do or which way to turn.

Go get help!!!! Her mind screamed at her, but her feet seemed rooted to the floor. Suddenly, the door burst open, as the nurse came flying in.

"Code Blue.... Code Blue," the nurse shouted.

Within seconds, Gretta's room began filling with blue-scrubbed individuals. Still frozen, Keturah found herself jostled out of the way, while her eyes remained transfixed on her grandmother, whose body and soul struggled to remain in the land of the living.

"Don't leave me Gretta, please don't go!" she broke down crying. "God, I'll do it! I'll do anything. Just let her live; please, let her live," Keturah bargained. "I'll marry whoever, whenever, but please don't take her; not now," she said within herself, as she felt someone wrapping their arm around her shoulder and gently leading her out of the room. She was so overwhelmed, she just clutched on to the other person and drank in their strength.

"We'll be in the chapel!" a masculine voice said.

Uncle Emory!! She thought it was strange for him to be here, smack-dab in the middle of the day, but she didn't care. "I'm so glad you came," she said in a wobbly voice, while hugging him tighter. It was a short distance to the hospital chapel and they quickly went inside and sat down. There, she allowed her tears to flow freely in the safety of his arms.

After some time, feeling more comforted, her sobs finally began to subside. In better control of her emotions, she looked up to take the handkerchief being offered. It was only then, that she noticed it wasn't her uncle's hand. Bolting straight up, Keturah was speechless, realizing it was in Abraham's embrace she had found comfort.

"It's okay, Keturah. Everything is going to be all right," he assured her.

Finally, her tongue loosened enough for her to speak. Embarrassed, she immediately began to babble, "Mr. Taylor, I'm so sorry. I thought you were…I mean, I didn't realize…" she fumbled over her words, "Oh, my God. Look what I did," she exclaimed, pointing to a wet spot her tears had made on his suit jacket. "I don't know what's the matter with me that I keep messing up your clothes!" she said tearfully, which brought on another crying spell.

"Nothing matters to me right now, but you and Gretta," he said, gently kissing her forehead, while cradling her in his arms.

His care and compassion pushed her over the edge of reason and sanity, as she found herself telling him the unthinkable, "Mr. Taylor, I accept your proposal," she said quietly, allowing the gravity of her words to sink in to her conscious.

"Shhh…. you have enough to think about. Let's get through this and we'll talk about that later," he said while still cradling her in his arms.

"No, seriously, Mr. Taylor, I really want to."

"Honey, you're not thinking clearly right now."

Doesn't he want me anymore? She thought alarmed. She couldn't bear it if he rejected her. She knew it was crazy logic, but his proposal gave her an option; even hope. She was desperate for hope, no matter what form it came in.

Panicking, she clung to his arm and pleaded with him, "You're wrong, I am thinking clearly. I truly am," she said, pressing a kiss to his lips that caught them both off guard. She knew she was being irrational and was about to pull back when she felt his resolve weaken as he gave in, kissing her back. The swing of the chapel doors broke them apart. Keturah did her best to control her breathing as Abraham stood.

"Doctor, what is it? How is Ms. Campbell?"

"Well, it seems you two are celebrating even before I came to give you the good news," he chuckled, then continued, "Ms. Birch, your grandmother is stabilized and is resting comfortably. We did have to transfer her to our ICU unit though. If she does well, we will likely transfer her back to her own room tomorrow morning."

"Can we see her?" Abraham and Keturah both inquired at the same time.

"Yes, but the visit will need to be brief," the doctor stated firmly.

Relief flooding her soul, Keturah hugged Abraham's arm, and leaned her head on his shoulder, as she allowed herself to shed a few more tears. It was only mid-afternoon, but she felt exhausted already. Abraham was saying something else to the doctor, but she didn't hear it. All she knew was that Gretta was out of danger for now, and she had just committed herself to marrying Abraham Taylor. The latter she'd freak-out about later. Right now, she allowed her soul and body to dissolve into restful peace.

She didn't know why, but somehow Abraham's presence and take-charge attitude soothed her restless soul; so much so, that after their brief visit with Gretta, she allowed him to ease her out of the hospital doors without protest for lunch.

They were seated quickly at the small bistro that was only a block from the hospital. It was a brisk walk, but Keturah used the time to help corral her raging thoughts. When they had left Gretta, she was sleeping peacefully and there wasn't much more she could do, other than watch the rise and fall of the woman's chest. That was when Abraham stepped in and took over, telling the head-nurse to call him immediately, if any changes occurred. Grateful to have someone take such a heavy burden off her shoulders, she stepped back and allowed him to issue orders.

They fell into comfortable silence as they walked to the Italian bistro. Now seated, she used her menu as barrier between them.

"Would you like me to order for you?" he asked.

With a nod, she placed her menu down, as he began placing their order with the waitress. It didn't much matter what he ordered for her; she was sure she wouldn't be able to eat anything, with her stomach tied in so many knots.

Looking anywhere but at him, she began noticing how quaint the Italian restaurant was. The aroma emanating from the kitchen had her stomach grumbling. Maybe she would be able to eat something after all. Any other day, she would've drunk in how handsome Abraham looked in his three-piece, designer suit that fit him perfectly. *He must have his own tailor*, she thought, as she gave him a quick once-over, while he was talking to their waitress. His hair was shorter than before, *Must have gotten a fresh cut,* she mused. She quickly averted her gaze once their orders were taken and the waitress walked away. Butterflies began doing somersaults in her belly, as she now, had no choice but to look at the man who was looking intently at her. Sighing, she decided there was no need to beat around the bush. Ignoring the big elephant in the room wouldn't make it disappear. Besides, she had questions of her own. Like, how had he known she was a Jaymes?

"So, I guess my "Yes," came as a surprise?" Twirling her straw in her ice water, she was still struggling to make eye-contact.

"It did," he said.

"Why did you come down here?" She quickly took a couple sips of water. All the crying she had done had left her throat tight; the man sitting across from her wasn't making matters any better.

"I wanted to see how Gretta was doing." He let a few moments of silence pass before asking, "Why did you say yes?" "I think it's the right thing to do," she shrugged

He nodded his head and took a sip of his water, and then remained silent.

Keturah thought, *maybe he's being quiet because he's thinking of how to withdraw his proposal."* Her heart sank, *I waited too late and now he doesn't want to marry me! Lord, what am I going to do?*

"Keturah, relax. I still want us to get married," he smiled. Knitting her eyebrows together, she looked at him with a frown, "How'd you know I was thinking that?"

"Well, for one, I make a very profitable living knowing how to read people. Secondly, your eyes are like windows to your soul. They speak before you even open your mouth," he said keenly. "So, what made you change your mind? You looked pretty decided last week when I left."

There was no need to lie, she was sure he'd be able to tell that she was, after what he just said. She hung her head, ashamed as to why, but feeling the need to be as honest as possible with her would-be fiancé.

"I need the money," her heart ripped at the words while a lone tear slipped down her cheek. She quickly swiped at it as anger and humiliation seeped into her soul. She hated needing anyone, hated she couldn't shoulder this responsibility on her own, but Gretta 's health was too important to allow pride to best her. Besides, she was out of options.

"Oh, I see," he said casually.

Her head snapped up as heat flushed her cheeks, "No, Mr. Taylor, you don't see. I realize how this might look to you, but I'm not one of those girls who has a price-tag attached to her body. I didn't come to this decision lightly. I prayed and believe that this is the direction God has for me to take. I swear I will pay you back every dime for Gretta's care. I don't care how long it takes me. I...I...," she couldn't finish. She was shaking so hard; she gripped her arms around her waist to steady her nerves.

"Keturah, I am well-aware of the type of woman you are. It's one of the reasons I proposed to you in the first place. And, to ease your mind further, I'm not looking for you to share my bed, either."

"I don't understand. What?"

He held both hands up to stop her, "This would only be a temporary arrangement: six to nine months; a year, max. Keturah, in this business, who you are in private, is just as big of a factor as how you run your business in public. People invest in *Canaan* because they see at its head, a stable, family-man, who would be as careful with their money, as he is with his own." He rubbed his head and looked pointedly at her, "I think we both know that my recent behaviors speak contrary to that image." He shrugged a shoulder, "Marriage is one way for me to reclaim that image."

"But why me, I'm sure there are thousands of women out there who would love to be the next Mrs. Abraham Taylor."

He chuckled at that, "You flatter me. I wouldn't say thousands, maybe a few hundred or so. But the problem with that is most women would not want what I'm offering. Nine months to a year, with no strings attached. We would be married in name only, just long enough to secure *Canaan* in the international market."

"And then, after *Canaan* is secure?"

"Then, we get the marriage annulled and you get your life back. The only difference is that you would be debt-free."

"Okay, but I still want to know one thing."

"What's that?"

"Why me?"

He didn't answer right away. Looking down at the plate of food the waitress just delivered, he appeared deep in thought. "I felt it was one way for me to help the daughter of one of my closet friends."

***

Later that evening, Keturah sat on her grandmother's bed on pins and needles waiting for her to respond to her big news.

"Oh, my Lord!" Gretta shook her head in wonder.

"I know it sounds a little odd, as well as sudden, Gretta, but you said so yourself, that Mr. Taylor was a nice man. As a matter of fact, you said he was a decent person the way he didn't take advantage of me that night after the party.

"My lord...my...my....my...my Lord," Gretta repeated herself.

"Oh Gretta, please stop saying that.

"Father in Heaven, please watch over this girl once I'm gone, Dear Jesus."

Gretta definitely wasn't making this any easier on her. She had been irrational in accepting the proposal, but when she thought of all the things marriage to a man like Mr. Taylor could mean, the good outweighed the bad. "Gretta this is a good thing. I really feel this is the right way for me to go."

"Do you love this man?" Gretta's watery orbs pierced her granddaughter's gaze.

"I-I'm," she looked down at the oatmeal-colored, frayed blanket covering the bed. She could never lie to Gretta when she was younger, and there was no need to try and do so now. With an inner strength, she didn't know she possessed, she looked her grandmother in the eyes.

"No, Grandma, I don't love him. I've always been infatuated with him, but, love?" she again shook her head no. "But what I do have is a peace about what I'm doing. Otherwise, I'd never even consider it."

Gretta closed her eyes and remained silent for so long, Keturah thought she might have fallen asleep. She was about to move off the bed and leave her to rest, when she heard the old woman sigh.

"I always knew God had a special man in store for you. My only prayer was that I would remain alive long enough to see him, even sit down and have a meal with him. I guess God does have a funny way of doing things in his own time." She opened her eyes and smiled at Keturah.

It was then that Keturah noticed the moisture that had collected in their corners. "You could have done a lot worse, like your mom and I did. I'm thankful that this man wants to do right by you, Sweetheart. Let the peace of God guide and you'll be alright."

She patted Keturah's hand and shut her eyes. Keturah stayed where she was until she saw the steady rhythm of her grandmother's breathing and knew she for sure was fast asleep.

She doesn't need to know all the particulars about my arrangement with Abraham, Keturah reasoned within herself. She would tell her grandmother those details once she was out of the hospital and back on her feet. She was sure Gretta would likely disapprove and her high opinion of Abraham may take a beating, and so might he. But for now, with Gretta's approval and the peace of God still resting on her shoulders, she headed home for some much-needed sleep.

CHAPTER FIFTEEN

Keturah looked at the clock and gave a big stretch and yawn, then buried her head under the covers. From the brightness coming from her window, she perceived it was going to be a nice day, even if the cold air would send her in search of her long, winter coat when she went to visit Gretta that afternoon.

Charlotte was unseasonably cold for this time of year, but dealing with the mid-fifties was a breeze compared to the one-degree temperatures that Chicago was getting.

It had been two weeks since Gretta had been in the hospital. They were still struggling to get her sugar under control, but at least they were able to move her to a nursing home. Today, Keturah had off and since she had no major plans, she had decided to be a little lazy and stay in bed longer than usual.

A ring of her cell phone broke into her thoughts, "It's Abraham!" she said, clutching the phone to her chest as her heart sped up with nervous anticipation. She sat up and did her best to straighten up her hair as if he could see her. It had been a week since they had dinner at the quaint little restaurant where they discussed the terms of their marriage arrangement and where Abe revealed of his close friendship with her deceased father, Kedron Jaymes.

Her father, the sperm donor, as she deemed him, was nothing more to her than a name on her birth certificate. She has some memories that were too fuzzy to have any true significance, but listening to Abraham and his stories of their friendship somehow made him more real to her. He told her he would be out of the country for a few days on business and they'd connect when he come back in town. "Guess he's back," she said before clicking over.

"Good morning, sunshine."

The endearment and deep tenor sent warm chills through her.

Maybe deep down I am attracted to him." She then shook her head, *No I'm not!* she chided herself inwardly, before speaking. "Oh, hi Mr. Taylor."

"Keturah, you have to stop calling me that. It's Abraham or Abe, which ever you prefer. I'd hate for people to think that I make my fiancé call me mister."

"Sorry, mister, um, Abraham. Good morning."

"That's a little better," he chuckled. "Listen, I hate to spring this on you right now, but there needs to be a slight change in the timetable of our wedding plans."

"Oh, really? Do you need to push things back a bit?" she almost hoped.

"No, I was actually hoping we could move the time up a bit."

"A bit?" she scrunched her face up in a frown. "Exactly how soon are you talking about Abe?" she asked timidly.

"Well, I have two out-of-town functions coming up in the next couple of weeks and I'd really like you to be there as my wife," Abraham pressed.

Panic gripped her. It was one thing to think about being married to him in the not-so-distant future but it was another thing all together to have it happen in a few weeks. Things were going way too fast and all she could think of doing was stalling. "But, what about Gretta? She hasn't had her surgery. I can't just up and leave her!"

She was grasping at straws, but she needed more time. Yes, she knew she had agreed to go through with the marriage, but now she wondered if this hare-brained idea was something she should seriously consider backing out of. Maybe he would allow her to do some type of payment plan, so she could give him the money back that he'd already shelled out for Gretta's expenses. She appreciated how caring and thoughtful Abraham had been. His getting a specialist to help treat Gretta's diabetes had really been crucial in her overall progress.

He said her health wasn't part of the deal. He wanted to make sure Gretta was okay. Keturah was thankful and felt a little overwhelmed with the obligation to pay him back, but becoming his wife. That was major. She said to herself, *Lord, I really need more time.*

Too afraid to tell him no, she circumvented her fears and doubts and used a different tactic.

"What if something happened while I was a way, I'd never be able to live with myself if something like that occurred."

"Keturah, I'll have her moved to a private facility where she'll receive the best twenty-four-hour care available, as well as a private nurse. I've already had my assistant make the necessary arrangements."

Ugh, idiot! The man is a multi-millionaire; he probably owns hospital. Not knowing what other excuse to give, she remained quiet.

"Keturah, are you having second thoughts about our arrangement?"

She could hear his voice tense as he spoke the words. *God, this is my chance to back out and run like a bat out of hell, she thought.* After all, would God really have her do this anyway?

But you said yes, the Spirit whispered.

"Yeah, I know! But I thought Gretta was dying and I was scared and I thought this was the only way to save her. Can't I just plead insanity and we forget the whole thing?" She reasoned within herself.

You gave him your word, the Holy Spirit prodded.

Keturah bowed her head. Gretta would always tell her, "There is nothing more important than your word, and if you can't keep it don't give it." There, she had her answer. She knew what she needed to say, but still cringed when she heard the words coming out of her mouth.

"Yes, I am; but no, I'm not backing out on you," she hoped he could get used to her blatant honesty. "So, when do you want to do this?"

She had to swallow several times to get the words to come out around the lump rising in her throat.

"I was hoping as soon as tomorrow."

"What?!" she said ending in a high-pitched screech.

"I know...I know, it is sudden, but the next time I'm available will be a month from now, and I really do need to get this business settled," he said firmly.

"This business, as you call it, happens to be my life, Mr. Taylor," she huffed. The way he talked; he was doing nothing more than conducting one of his many business deals. Yet, this was far from that. He was negotiating her and Gretta's lives. She didn't want to be penciled in on a calendar or some need to-do list. She had plans, and now they were being infringed upon by his need to get this "deal" settled.

"Listen, Mr. Taylor. I know you're used to doing mergers and making business deals and all, but I don't appreciate you lumping me and Gretta in that category. This is my life, and I still want it to be a good one, even after you blow through it," she finished, a little surprised at herself for speaking up. Maybe he'd decided to back out, now that he could see she wasn't going to be a push-over.

"Ms. Jaymes, I can assure you that I've never negotiated a business deal quite like this; especially, with someone as attractive and as feisty as yourself," he said, amusement evident in his voice. "I can also assure you that my intentions are to make you and Gretta very comfortable and I believe after I, "blow through your life," you'll be very happy that I did."

"That remains to be seen, Mr. Taylor," she said, now with a hint of a smile in her voice.

"It's Abraham, and I never make a promise that I don't intend to keep."

***

The next day, she found herself in the home of a judge who happened to be Abraham's good friend. It was surreal; reciting marriage vows to a man who was little more than a stranger to her. It pained her heart. This was definitely not the way she envisioned her wedding day would be. Her mind remained on auto-pilot until the judge made the proclamation that they were man and wife.

"Abraham, you may kiss your bride," the judge announced in his deep baritone.

Her mind jumped back into her body and it was all she could do to keep herself from jerking back, when she looked up at Abraham, already closing in for a kiss. It was a brief brush of his lips to hers that she barely felt. Standing back, he smiled, chucked her under the chin with his hand and then turned away to shake the judge's hand.

"That's it?" she muttered to herself. *He kissed me better in the car, the night of Gretta's accident,* she thought. Quelling her frustration, she smiled at the judge's wife who greeted her.

From that point, everything happened rapidly: from the signing of their marriage certificate, to being ushered out the front door.
In the blink of an eye, she was being seated in the passenger side of Abraham's Mercedes coupe. She plopped down with a loud sigh, not sure if it was from relief, utter frustration, or maybe a little of both.

They were legally bound in marriage. She felt a strange surge of panic grip her, just as Abraham slid into the driver's seat while talking to someone on his cell. Although she knew that this was a temporary arrangement and in six to nine months, she'd have her freedom, still somehow, she felt this whole set-up was just wrong. Looking down at her ring-finger now incased in a simple platinum band, made the fact that she was now, Mrs. Abraham Taylor, a reality. Yet, she felt hollow on the inside.

"Okay, ready the jet. I want to be in the air within the hour," he stated, and then hung up. Turning to Keturah, he sighed, "Listen; there's been another change of plans. I need to leave for Europe, now. Would you like me to drop you back at your place, or take you to see Gretta?" He gave a sideways glance as he started up the motor.

He was leaving already? With wide eyes she jerked back, as if he had splashed cold water in her face.

"But I thought we were *both* going to see Gretta?" Keturah waved the hand that supported her wedding band in his face. Was he really going to just leave her to face Gretta alone?

"Honey calm down. I know I'm springing this on you and I'm sorry about that, but it can't be helped. I must fly out of town and leave a lot sooner than I'd planned. It's just that this issue has come up with this new business venture, and I have to take care of it in person. Otherwise, I'd stay. Look, why don't we do this, let's hold off telling our families until we can do it together. I shouldn't be out of town for more than two days. I'll come back, we'll tell Gretta and then I'll introduce you to my family. How does that sound?"

She couldn't argue with his logic, but keeping secrets from Gretta was just something she didn't like doing. However, Gretta's health was a priority, so if keeping the fact that she and Abraham were officially man and wife was the way he wanted it, then fine.

CHAPTER SIXTEEN

Tippany didn't want to play nicely with her mom, but if she wanted the information, she knew her mother could provide, she'd have no choice. "You were right mom. Conrad was just using me to gain status. I should've listened to you," she thought she might gag with that last admission.

"Of course, I was right. I always am. You better be glad you got rid of him before he could ruin the rest of your reputation. God knows I've done my best to salvage what little of it I could," Sari said with a demeaning sneer.

Remember the goal, you want information about Keturah, Tippany chanted in her head over and over, hoping to quiet the anger brewing in her chest. "Well, I was thinking that maybe I could be a little more useful around here; help you with some foundation stuff," she said perkily.

Her mother looked at her hard, suspicion evident in her glare. "What are you up to now girl?" she barked.

"Up to?" she repeated innocently. "What makes you think that?" Tippany asked, vying for some time. She hoped somehow, she hadn't allowed her eagerness to show.

"Well, you've never wanted to help before. Why now?" her mother pinned her cold stare on Tippany.

Used to her mother's interrogations by now, she used her own cunning to throw her mother off the scent.

"Well, if you must know, I was trying to impress Jefferson Pickerington III. He asked me out last week and I know he'll want to know all the goings-on here, so I at least thought to have something interesting to tell him," she said casually.

"That stuffed shirt? I'm surprised you'd give him the time of day," Malcolm Jaymes said, coming in from the back of the room. "Hello, Mother. You wanted to see me?"

"He might be a stuffed shirt, but he does carry a lot of influence in this town, which we could definitely use when you run for governor," Sari tapped her chin, her mind well at work.

"Mom, for the last time, I'm not running for office. Shannon and I aren't at a good place right now. We definitely don't need the press prying into our affairs."

You mean your *affairs!* Tippany wanted to shout, but remained silent. Her poor sister-in-law had been through the wringer with his multiple affairs. She was talking of divorce and it couldn't have made Tippany happier. No one should have to put up with a man who can't keep his pants zipped. Her mind immediately went to her dad, and her heart softened a little. Her dad was definitely no saint. Maybe that was why Malcolm was like he was, a chip off the old block.

"You leave Shannon to me. She's not going anywhere but to the governor's mansion with you," Sari declared.

Needing to get some air, and quick, Tippany spoke up, "Listen, Mom. Call me when you have something for me to do," she said starting to stand, "I..."

"Hold on. Hold your horses, girl. It just so happens; I do have something I need you to attend to in my stead. Abraham is investing funds from the *Sarah Jaymes Foundation* for a mentoring project, and I want to make sure he doesn't go beyond the scope of what the foundation allows," she said briskly.

"Okay, when is it?"

"You'll meet him down in the parking garage in ten minutes," she barked.

Tippany was about to become irritated, when she took a quick look at the name of the school and those heading the project. There was no way her mother knew what she was passing up! Inwardly smiling, she took the packet of information, got up and headed towards the door.

She prayed her brother didn't notice the lilt in her step as she walked out her mother's office. This meeting was going to be with none other than Keturah Birch, herself. She smiled broadly. *This is the break I needed.*

***

"Hey, Grace. We're here for the board meeting," Parson gave her a warm, flirtatious smile that he quickly shut down as he looked at Keturah's cynical glare.

"I know. I was told to have you both go in immediately. Everyone else is already in there waiting on you two," she said warmly.

Keturah and Parson both exchanged surprised glances. Normally, they were the first at every one of these board meetings. Members of the board typically came in late. But, for all the members to be present or accounted for, meant something was up and usually, it wasn't anything good.

"Grace, I even see the president's car is here. What's going on? I mean he's not here for this meeting? Is he?"

"Yeah, he's here for the meeting, and brought a few other notable people as well. You two must have one, special presentation to put on. I was called by the president himself, yesterday and told to call the entire board and confirm their presence at the meeting today."

"Well, I guess we better get in there Keturah. Thanks Grace," Parson said calmly.

Walking towards the conference room, Parson placed a hand on the doorknob. He gave her a quick look and mouthed, "Are you ready?" Keturah nodded, yes. Opening the door, he walked with Keturah on his heels. Suddenly, he stopped abruptly, causing Keturah to slam into his broad back.

"Ouch!" Keturah said quietly, as she stepped back to massage her smarting nose. Parson was six-three with broad shoulders, so she couldn't see around him and didn't understand the reason for his sudden pause until she heard him speak.

"Oh. Mr. Taylor and Ms. Jaymes, what a pleasant surprise. I wasn't made aware that you'd be present today," Parson managed to say in an even tone.

Keturah's head snapped up. *Abraham!? What's he doing here?* She could feel her whole-body quiver from anticipation or frustration, she couldn't determine. The last time she laid eyes on him was a week ago, after they had their impromptu wedding ceremony at the judge's home. Except for a few brief texts checking on her and Gretta, she hadn't heard from him.

The fact that she missed him- missed his kisses; only frustrated her more. Now, she'd have to sit in a board meeting with him and pretend that they had no connection at all. "Boy, he has more faith in me than I have in myself." Keturah thought as she heard Abraham speak.

"Is Ms. Birch with you?" Abraham inquired.

"Yes, yes she's right behind me," Parson replied, turning his back on the crowded room to gaze at Keturah. "Your presence is being requested," Parson whispered and winked at her. "Right this way, Ms. Birch," he said in a loud voice, while ushering her into the room.

Afraid to look at him, she allowed her eyes only to look as high as his neck tie with a nervous smile, she extended her hand. "Good morning, Mr. Taylor," she said, hoping to breeze past him, without too much fanfare.

"Ms. Birch, as always, it's a pleasure," his tenor was warm and inviting.

The soft caress of his fingers warmed her from head to toe. His musky cologne made her head spin. Luckily, she refrained herself before doing something wonderfully stupid like kissing him in front of the entire board. Giving her hand a soft squeeze, he released it and let her pass. Parson directed her to a seat next to him. It was only after putting the distance of the conference table between them that she dared look up at Abraham.

His chestnut brown suit only enhanced his toned physique. He accessorized it by wearing a light blue shirt with a white collar and a coordinating tie and handkerchief. "Gorgeous," she muttered.

"What'd you say?" Parson asked.

"Nothing, nothing at all," she whispered back, looking at him unable to ignore the smirk on his face. She cut her eyes at Parson, embarrassed that she'd been caught drooling. Pretending to look at the business report her thoughts quickly turned towards how much she missed Abraham over the few weeks he'd been gone. Finally, no longer able to make her eyes obey she quickly looked up to find him staring intently at her. She felt as if she'd been caught up in some type of mystical trance, that she couldn't break away from even if she tried. What was happening to her? Was her admiration for his business savvy turning into something else...? She was afraid to admit even to herself that the feelings budding in her heart had nothing to do with his success and everything to do with the man. With a nod of his head and a slight smile meant only for her, Abraham dropped her gaze and turned his attention to others in the room. Keturah gave a slight sigh and was about to relax when suddenly a discomforting feeling as though she was being watched washed over her. Her heartbeat began to elevate, had someone been observing the exchange between her and Abraham. She did a quick sweep of the room to see who it was. Immediately her eyes locked on a distinctive pair of grey eyes very similar to hers. She inhaled sharply as she looked at the woman she encountered at the banquet. What did her mother call her? Tiffany...wasn't it? Keturah could feel the unsettling emotions from her childhood rising in her throat. How terribly unfair it was for her to have to grow up alone, when she had siblings who lived in the very same city as she did. A gentle hand covered hers pulling her out of those dreary memories.

"You alright Tourie? Parson whispered in her ear.

"Yes…I'm fine just a little nervous I guess." She said with a tight smile.

"Don't worry partner, I got you covered." He said patting her hand that unbeknown to her was balled up in a fist.

With a controlled smile, she turned towards the woman who was still looking at her. Keturah thought for a moment of what she could say to her sister but before she could form the words. The woman gave her a quick nod then turned back to focus on the others in the room. Keturah breathed a sigh of relief now that all eyes were off her. Feeling more relaxed she twisted around to talk with Parson again. "What 's that Jaymes woman 's first name?" Keturah mumbled to Parson, who was engaged in small-talk with one of the board members who sat next to him.

Looking in the direction she was staring, he replied. "Tippany Jaymes," was all he said before returning to his conversation with the board member. Apparently, whatever was being said was good news, because Parson was talking enthusiastically; excitement evident in his voice.

Tippany Jaymes…*my half-sister!* She swallowed several times to keep her emotions at bay. She already knew that Kedron had other children. Most of them resembled him, but this woman only favored him in skin-tone and eye color. But the funny thing was the way she was holding her head reminded her a little bit of her mother, but that wasn't possible? Keturah had so many questions, but knew they would have to wait as she heard the chairman of the board call the meeting to order.

After thanking everyone for coming on such a short notice, the chairman welcomed Abraham and Tippany, and then discussed the order of business.

Out of the corner of her eye, Keturah saw Abraham lean over and whisper something in the president's ear. Immediately, President Morris cleared his throat and interrupted the chairman.

"Mr. Franks, I hate to interrupt you, but Mr. Taylor is a very busy man. If we could just skip your usual business and address the part that concerns *Canaan Enterprises* that would be greatly appreciated."

"Oh...yes...yes, certainly." Franks cleared his throat, quickly rearranged several papers that were in front of him and continued, "We've called everyone together to announce that Mr. Taylor has agreed to fully fund the mentoring project." Speechless, Keturah looked at Parson, then at Abraham. *We're fully funded!* The words pulsated in her brain like a heartbeat. This was beyond anything she ever imagined! At long last, her girls' mentoring program would be fully operational.

She couldn't wait to tell Gretta the news. She wanted to jump out of her seat and scream with excitement, but most of all, she wanted to thank Abraham in a very private and personal way. Her wayward thoughts brought an immediate flush to her cheeks. Thankfully, because of her skin tone it went undetected.

"Since *Canaan Enterprises* already has its own mentoring program; they will be able to easily absorb what is currently being done in our program," the chairman continued, "We'll just need to make a few adaptations, in order to fit their model."

That brought a frown to her face. The university's mentoring program was strictly for boys. *But what about my girls?* She thought as Parson was already verbalizing the same sentiment.

"What about the girls' component? Will funding also be supplied for that as well?" Parson stated with a frown of his own.

"Unfortunately, the mentoring model *Canaan Enterprises* has developed is strictly for males. Although we do recognize the need for young ladies to be properly mentored in business and finance, right now our funding will only cover the male mentoring portion of your program," Tippany Jaymes spoke up.

Keturah could already feel her dander rising and was ready to argue the point, when she again felt Parson's hand cover hers as he spoke up.

"Mr. Taylor and Ms. Jaymes, on behalf of our university, we are extremely appreciative of the financial support you've offered, and maybe in a year or two, we might revisit the girls' portion of the program."

Keturah remained calm, but with that statement, she could visualize bopping both Parson and the Jaymes woman upside their heads. She swallowed hard, trying not to show her hurt and rising anger. The girls mentoring project deserved to be looked at *now;* not in one or two years! As a matter of fact, she had presented the girls' portion of the program to the board before the boys. This only made her more determined to make the girls' mentoring program a success.

They didn't have to do anything for you at all, she thought, realizing she should be happy the boys' program would be taken over by Taylor's mentoring course. It was a good program and any school would be thrilled to have the backing of the Taylor name, but still the victory for her was hollow. A squeeze of her hand pulled her out of her own head. She looked up at Parson who was smiling down at her. She needed to be grateful.

"Yes, thank you, Mr. Taylor and Ms. Jaymes, for your financial support. I know our youth will benefit greatly, due to your generosity." Keturah smiled at Ms. Jaymes, then towards Abraham. It was only then that she noticed his eyes not connecting with her, but with her hand. She hadn't realized that Parson still had a hold of it. She quickly retracted it and placed it on her lap under the table.

Later that evening...

"Keturah, I think we need to discuss your behavior at the board meeting today!" Abraham said sternly.

Pulling the phone away from her ear, she stared at it for several minutes, as if the man on the other end had lost his mind. It was late and she was already in bed and had no intention of discussing anything; especially, the board meeting. "Abraham, I'm tired. Can't this wait until morning?" She rubbed her eyes only wanting to go to sleep and forget this miserable day.

"Where I am, it is morning," he said harshly. "Now, exactly what is your relationship with this Parson guy?"

"Parson? What?" Abraham hadn't funded her project, something he knew she cared deeply about but all he wanted to discuss was Parson? "What are you talking about? Parson and I work together," she said plainly.

"Do you normally hold hands with your other colleagues?" he said sarcastically.

If she hadn't known better, she would've thought he was jealous. But they weren't married for real, so the nature of her relationship with Parson shouldn't matter. What's more, she should be the one with an attitude over her project not being funded. Feeling spiteful, she gave a snippy reply, "Actually, I do when a few of us have Morning Prayer." She said snidely.

"Well, you weren't having prayer in the board meeting this afternoon, Keturah," he shot back. "Look, as my wife, I expect you to demonstrate proper decorum both in and out of my presence. I don't know if you and that guy had something going on, but we're married now and you need to cut it off!" He demanded. "When we announce our marriage in a few weeks, I won't have any scandalous behavior thrown in my face. This business deal for *Canaan* is too important to allow any type of impropriety on *your* part."

"*Mr. Taylor,* I will not be chastised like a child by you or anyone else, especially since I've done nothing wrong. Parson is a colleague and friend and was simply trying to take my feelings into consideration, when my portion of the mentoring program was dismissed by my husband and half-sister." Keturah paused for added affect, "Parson knows how much the girls' mentoring portion meant to me. He was trying to be supportive. That's all."

"I hate it when you call me *Mr. Taylor,* you say it like a curse word," he grumbled.

"Oh, I'm so sorry, did I not take your feelings into account?" her words dripped with sarcasm.

"Alright, I get it Keturah," Abraham huffed in frustration. "So, your co-worker knows how you feel better than I do. I get the point," he said.

"Well, I guess he would, seeing that he takes an interest in my well-being before dashing off to another business meeting on the other side of the world," she's in a snippy tone. Well aware, that she was being spiteful but didn't care.

"Fine, maybe I should ask Parson to come with me to the Caribbean next week, so he can tell me all about you?" he muttered.

His tone had shifted from quarrelsome, to amiable, in seconds. Was this some type of peace offering, she wondered? As much as she always wanted to go to the Caribbean, she still felt the need to make him stew a few minutes more before accepting. "Why, that sounds great. Hey maybe if you're not so grouchy, Parson might even let you steal a kiss," she said mockingly.

Caught off guard by the remark, there was a long pause before his deep laughter broke into her ear. *"Lord I love the way his tenor makes my insides dance,"* Keturah thought.

"Parson might be a great kisser, but my lips fancy yours, Mrs. Taylor."

CHAPTER SEVENTEEN

The days leading up to their Caribbean get-away went by like one big blur. Gretta was still weak but appeared to be doing much better. So, she wouldn't hear of Keturah staying behind to tend to her needs. *What can you do that the doctors and nurses can't? Besides that's their job. Your job is to keep that big smile on your handsome fiancé's face.* After a few more protests, Gretta kicked her out of her room with a threat to beat her with a stick, if she didn't get going. Keturah left begrudgingly feeling guilty that she was leaving without telling Gretta the truth about already marrying Abraham. She hated lying to her but Abraham assured her they'd tell both of their families as soon as they got back.

Parson was already fully immersed in the mentoring project, so she had little time to see him, something she felt Abraham had orchestrated. So, with bags packed, Abraham's private car came to pick her up and take them to the airport by one o'clock that afternoon. Within the hour, they were in the air.

She was doing her best to relax, but her death-grip on the armrest was very evident. She had never flown in a private jet before, and the little bit of turbulence was making her nauseated.

"So, tell me what makes a beautiful young woman like yourself tick," Abraham said casually, obviously not in the least bit affected by the bumpy ride.

He wanted to talk, but all she wanted to do was keep her lunch inside her stomach. Another hard dip of the jet sent her stomach reeling. She clenched her eyes shut and committed herself to prayer. She was sure, by the way the plane was shaking that she would soon see God face to face, therefore, ending the need to answer any of Abraham's forty-million questions. Somewhere between her panic and prayer something cool touched her forehead then slid down her cheek followed by soft, warm lips.

Startled by his touch Keturah opened her eye's "Wh-what are you doing?"

"I've done everything I could think of to put your mind at ease, and nothing seems to be working...so." Shrugging a shoulder, he gave a bashful smile, "seems to me this is the one thing we do that gives me your full attention." As if to prove his point, he kissed her again, this time allowing the contact to linger for quite a while. Finally, he broke away, but not before hearing her give a contented sigh.

She hadn't realized that her hands were interlocked behind his head and that she was practically in his lap. However, what she did notice was she wasn't frightened anymore, and if the plane was shaking, she couldn't feel it. She felt nothing but Abraham pressing gentle kisses on her forehead and cheek then lower, to her neck. Yes, there were some perks to having a pretend-husband like Abraham!

***

It all started with a simple glass of vintage wine and slow dancing in the moonlight on the balcony of their hotel. She had no idea Abraham could be so totally charming and, dare she say, sexy. This man, who was twice her age, was luring her into his clutches like a lion marking his prey. She was helpless to escape, and frankly didn't want to. She wanted to blame what happened next between them, on the alcohol, as the song says, but truthfully, that had little to do with it. Gretta had told her that intimacy between husband and wife was the most beautiful experience two people could share. Because of that she had saved herself for marriage. Only, she had no idea that it would be with Abraham. All she knew was that what she was feeling for her husband was right; she would never regret their love-making and hoped it would happen again. There was no denying it; theirs was not a marriage in name only anymore, and the tiny bond she was beginning to develop for Abraham was proof. But this revelation she decided to keep to herself.

"SARAH!"

Startled awake by Abraham's voice, a half-groggy Keturah momentarily scanned the darken room, realizing that morning was still far off. Taking her hand from underneath the warm covers, she reached out to snag her cell-phone to check the time, but the phone wasn't there. *It must have fallen on the floor,* she mused. Placing her hand on her damp forehead, she rolled onto her side and bumped into Abraham's bare chest. At first, she lurched away from him, not understanding what he was doing there. But, then she remembered and smiled. Yes, she remembered everything that took place that night, and how their pretense of a honeymoon ended up being the real thing; something she was utterly thrilled about. Feeling safe and protected in her husband's arms, she placed her arms around his waist and kissed him under his neck.

"Umm, Sarah," he mumbled, while pulling her against him. Her heart plummeted. Sarah! Could her ears have deceived her? No, she heard right. Abraham was only thinking of Sarah! She covered her mouth thinking she might hurl. Wanting to pull away, but finding it impossible to leave his side, as his arms were still wrapped around her waist tightly even in sleep, she willed herself not to cry. However, the humiliation of giving herself to a man who does not love her had already begun pricking the edge of her nerves. So, when moisture began seeping down her face, her shame was complete. *Sarah... He was thinking of Sarah the whole time,* Keturah silently cried.

"Tourie, what's the matter?"

At the sound of Abraham's groggy tenor, she froze. If she could crawl under a rock, she would have. It was bad enough for him to be thinking of Sarah the first time they were intimate, but to catch her crying about it was humiliating. After all, hadn't he said this was a bogus marriage? He had made it very clear that he wasn't in love with her, but like every man, he had needs. And if she was willing to give in to that, then what man wouldn't take her up on the offer? She had to face it; she had become a victim of her own romance story. She had made a mistake, but now it was time to correct it. Blowing out a breath, she swallowed deeply and then spoke.

"I'm fine, Abraham. I'm fine."

"Then, why the tears?" he said softly, rolling her over on her back, using his finger tips to wipe the moisture, evident on her cheeks.

Abraham, please stop asking questions, she said within herself. She didn't want to lie, but was not ready to get into this discussion after they had just made love. Well, had sex, since he didn't love her. Yet she had to say something. The intense look on his face made her know he wasn't going to drop it. Keturah fumbled for something to say. "Well, I mean, it's just that..." Muffled chimes went off from under her pillow cutting off her words. *My cell-phone. Perfect timing,* she thought. Turning away from Abraham's penetrating gaze, she frantically searched the sheets for the phone. Abraham's cell also began to ring as well. *Good. Hopefully, it's business. That will distract him for sure,* she prayed.

"Hello?" they said simultaneously. Smiling at each other, they both turned their backs to the other to answer their callers.

"Hey, Uncle Em," she greeted him cheerfully. "What's going on with you and Auntie?" she said looking at the table-clock to check the time. She and Abraham were at least five hours behind her uncle, making it at least nearly one in the morning, for Emory. It wasn't like him to call this late. She prayed that nothing was wrong, yet an unsettling feeling began creeping over her.

"Tourie, honey, I-I have something to tell you." He said in a somber tone.

A cold chill filled her soul, as she felt Abraham scoot behind her and wrap his arms around her waist. *No...no...no! NO LORD!* She cried within.

"Tourie, are you still there?" Emory raised his voice, the tension evident.

"I don't...I won't..." She began to vehemently shake her head in denial of what her heart was already telling her. "She would not have sent me here, if she wasn't going to...."

"Give me the phone, Honey. Let me talk to him," Abraham whispered in her ear, as he gently took the phone from her trembling fingers.

"Em, this is Abe, I'm here with her. Let me break it to her."

"What... wait a minute? What are you doing with her?" Emory demanded.

"Now's not the time, Em. We'll talk about it later," Abraham said firmly.

"Abraham, I told you not to mess with my niece. Where are you two anyway?" he pressed.

"Emory, we'll discuss it later. Right now, Keturah is all that's important," Abraham insisted before saying a brusque goodbye, and hung up.

Keturah had already moved from the bed and was standing in front of the window, ignorant of the fact she was unclothed, until she felt something silky covering her shoulders followed by Abraham's arms wrapping her in an embrace. His breath on her scalp made her body shudder as the words he spoke brought tears to her eyes.

"Baby, I'm so sorry, but Gretta's gone home to be with our Lord tonight," he said in a strained voice.

She wasn't aware that her legs gave way at those words, or that she had begun screaming, with uncontrollable sobs. Her grief was so instantaneous, so raw, she thought nothing could ever or would ever hurt as badly as the loss of her grandmother. She clutched onto Abraham, asking him when. However, he didn't answer, only kissed her forehead and rocked her. She let all her grief out right there, cradled in her husband's lap.

How long they stayed that way, she didn't know. For that matter, she didn't care. She could hear Abraham murmur quiet prayers while he continued to comfort her. Why was everyone leaving her? First, it was her mom, then her dad- even though he was never truly in the picture. Now, Gretta was gone and, soon, Abraham would leave her, too. Why couldn't people love her enough to stay? "I'm all alone now. I have no one; no family, nothing," she said, barely above a whisper.

Placing his fingers under her chin, he made her look up at him, "No, Honey, that's not true. That's so, not true Tourie. You've got your uncle and aunt; your friends. They'll be your family now," Abraham said quietly, rubbing her arms with his hands.

For a moment, she thought she saw something, maybe a touch of care in his eyes, but then it was gone. She also noticed he didn't mention himself in the circle of people who cared for her, only further driving the point home that he too would eventually leave her.

Now that Gretta was gone, she had no one to take care of, no one to love and, what she desperately needed someone to love. Amid her grief, a plan began to slowly churn in her mind. She should've immediately dismissed the thought, but she couldn't. Common sense should have told her that what she was contemplating was wrong; especially without Abraham's consent. But, for all she knew, his consent could be a moot point, seeing they had already been intimate, without the use of protection. What could a few more times hurt? Was this plan wrong? Maybe, but she had no choice. She wouldn't be left all alone in this world, without anyone to care for. Her mind in a daze of confusion, she blurted the words out, before she had a chance to back out.

"Hold me, Abraham, make love to me please," she clutched at him in desperation.

Startled by her abrupt request, he tried pulling back from her grasp. "Honey, I don't think that's what you need right now. Give yourself time to…"

"No, no, please. I hate this empty feeling inside. I can't take it, Abraham. I can't take it!" She was holding her head with both hands, almost on the brink of hysteria as she pleaded with him. Then she reached up and kissed his arm, his chest and neck. She was determined to bend the will of this stubborn man to hers.

It was nearly three in the morning. Abraham stood at the window of their suite looking into the night sky then turned to look at his sleeping wife and sighed. He felt like the biggest hypocrite. It was bad enough that he had gone back on his word by being intimate with her the first time. He hadn't meant to blur the line of their arrangement, but she was so lovely and desirable. He only meant to keep things at the kissing stage with her, to sample her loveliness. But then one thing led to another. He weaved his fingers behind the back of his head and looked up to the ceiling and sighed. Who was he trying to fool? Everything that happened tonight had all been orchestrated by him. From the gifts, the expensive clothing he had bought her just for this night, dinner at the best restaurant followed up by an evening of dancing was all leading to sleeping with her. To deny it would make him a liar. He was her first, and the fact that he took something as precious as her virginity, only tore at his conscious, all the more.

He knew from the moment they met that she was different; there was a purity about her that was refreshing. It was her innocence that appealed to him, that reminded him of Sarah when she was young and full of life. He just wanted to remember what it was like. He missed Sarah so, and it had been such a long time since he had been this close to anyone who made him feel like the old Abe.

He wouldn't lie, he enjoyed the intimacy they had just shared. The awkwardness of her touch, the shy way she smiled when he let her know he was pleased, the way she responded with wide-eyed curiosity. She was the enchantress and he was the enchanted. So many memories swirled around in his head; he had to shut his eyes to keep from getting dizzy. Cherished memories of his time with Sarah barged in his mind.

Their first-time making love as man and wife, how she clung to him and the secrets they whispered to each other between kisses. Their honeymoon was unforgettable. The long walks on the beach, the way she stepped on his toes when they danced, and her infectious laughter. Lord knew he miss the sound of Sarah's laughter. He'd do anything to have her in his arms. All those memories came flooding back to him when he was with Keturah. It was only having heard himself mutter Sarah's name that he realized what he was doing and with whom he was doing it. By then, it was too late; the deed had been done. He had taken Keturah's virtue and had given her nothing in return. He only prayed she hadn't heard him call out Sarah's name, but when he felt her hot tears on his chest, he knew that she had. "Idiot!" he slapped his thigh hard.

Did you really think you could play with fire and not get burned? The Holy Spirit said softly.

Shaking his head in silence, he berated himself. Once was bad enough, but this time it was far worse. He couldn't blame it on trying to capture memories of Sarah, or that he had done it under duress because she pressured him. No, this had nothing to do with any of that. This had everything to do with a much darker urge pressing on him. *With Gretta gone, she'd have only me, and if I play my cards right, I could make our little arrangement permanent*, he thought. Keturah reminded him so much of Sarah, and he felt so much like his old self when they were together, that maybe somehow, he could get his old life back, he could be happy again.

Forgetting those things which are behind me I press toward the things that are before me.

He shook his head to clear it, as the Bible verse he learned as a young man began to surface in his mind. His old life with Sarah was behind him. He needed to reach for his future. That meant a future without Sarah. That wasn't a future he wanted to be part of but what choice did he have? But, when Keturah kissed him so frantically, he responded out of his own desperation.

He found himself promising her things he knew he couldn't deliver, knowing that at summer's end, he still had every intention of ending their farce of a marriage.

"But was it wrong to want to comfort someone who's hurting?" He found his heart defending his actions.

It's wrong when you don't plan on keeping your word, his conscious replied.

Ouch! Keeping his word was a major area for him. He was always big on his word. Making sure he followed through. If there was one thing he couldn't tolerate, was a man who wouldn't stand by his word. Now, it looked as if he were that man. He needed to fix this. The problem was, he didn't know how. He had opened up a can of worms but wasn't quite sure how to get the squirmy things back in the can.

Confess your faults to one another. The effective and fervent prayers of the righteous avail much.

He smiled to himself. He seemed to be a scripture-magnet today. God was clearly showing him the way out was by being honest. Something he seemed to be struggling with lately. Bowing his head, he said a quiet prayer of repentance and vowed to come clean with Keturah in the morning. His I-phone on the night stand began to vibrate. Grabbing it quickly, he looked over to see if Keturah had stirred. She was still sleeping.

Looking down at the caller ID, his stomach dropped. It was Emory. *God, you don't pull any punches when you test a man to see if he's going to keep his word*, Abraham thought, as he turned the volume down and quickly moved from their balcony into the living room and out of earshot. He knew this wasn't going to be a pleasant call, but if he was going to do the honesty thing, he might as well start with Em. Taking a steadying breath, he clicked over, "Hey, Em. Yeah, I know I've got a lot of explaining to do."

CHAPTER EIGHTEEN

"Keturah, would you like something to eat?" Abraham inquired, knowing she'd likely say no but still he needed to try.

Turning her head towards him, she shook her head "no" then went back to staring out the window again.

Inwardly, he groaned, recognizing that look of despondency and the feeling that went along with it. He hated the fact that she was experiencing this type of anguish and the isolation it could bring. He understood it all too well. Right now, she was still in shock. Her whole world had just been ripped apart now that Gretta was gone. Only time would mend it, and even then, it would still hurt.

"Sweetheart, I know you might not feel like eating, but please try," he begged.

With a heavy sigh, she finally consented. "Ok, I'll try." she uttered in a small voice while her back was still to him.

Signaling to the flight attendant, he gave her a few instructions and sent her off. He knew Keturah would likely not eat anything that the stewardess brought back, but he was going to try to get something in her stomach. She needed to keep her strength up. Blowing out a breath, he closed his eyes momentarily and massaged the bridge of his nose. She would need him now, more than ever, but was he up to the task? Trying to right a world that had been ripped apart with the loss of a loved one was beyond hard; sometimes it felt downright impossible; having to push yourself to go on, but not sure why you even want to. It was such a hard and difficult journey. He was surrounded by a host of friends and family, even when he didn't want to be. He had a company to run, a son to look after. But who did Keturah have?

She has you, Abraham

He sighed again. Their agreement was nine months to a year, tops. But already he could feel the door closing in on him. A part of him was already reaching out towards her, wanting them to be more than a temporary arrangement. It scared him more than he cared to admit. At first, he thought it was because they were intimate, but it was more than that. He could share and tell her things that he kept buried inside for so long. She was good to him and for him, and now that she needed him, how could he even consider bailing on her?

He shook his head as his heart filled with a renewed resolution. No, he wouldn't turn his back on her or let her go through this alone. After all, he was her husband. Maybe that's the reason he took charge of things when they got back home. Keturah looked completely worn out after accepting the endless condolences from church and family members.

She looked as if she would collapse, so he whisked her out of there and back in his private jet as soon as the funeral was over. Emory could handle things. Keturah needed rest, needed to be sheltered, protected and he was determined to be the one doing it. He was taking his wife away with him. He contacted her job to get her some time off, informing them that she would be interning with him the next six to seven weeks. Already knowing the board would agree; not that he gave them much choice. Keturah would have her time to heal and he'd have time to think about their next step.

***

Getting away was just what the doctor had ordered, Keturah thought, as she lazily drifted in and out of sleep; the warm breeze rocking her weary body into a restful state.

She and Abraham had now been away for three weeks. The board was awfully nice for allowing her the extended leave. She was sure Abraham had a lot to do with that. Whatever the case, she was glad.

Going home would be hard now that she had nothing to go home to. She knew this time with her husband was only temporary and would likely not last, although the more time they spent together, the harder it was for her to see them separate. Yes, she was clinging to him and he was being so wonderful in letting her do so. *If only this could last. If only he'd feel something for me. Maybe we could make this arrangement permanent.*

She was becoming obsessive and knew it, but couldn't help herself. Being alone in this world was too distasteful. She needed someone, something to love and to love her back. With Gretta, she had that. Now, she had nothing…unless. She rubbed her belly and hoped. She was a couple days late. Of course, it was too soon to tell- but still.

He'll hate you for tricking him! Her conscious screamed. Allowing the air to warm her brow, she allowed the negative thoughts to drown in the waves hitting the sandy shore.

He won't hate me; he may even be happy about it. Besides, I never tricked him. He came to me willingly, so he's just as much responsible as I am. Okay, that was likely farfetched. A baby was definitely not in his plans. He told her upfront that he wanted an uncomplicated arrangement between them. Now, it looks as if she had stirred up a mess of trouble for them both. Biting down on her lower lip, she wondered if she was doing the right thing. Something deep down said, probably not, but she chose to ignore that voice, too. She would not be alone, would not live without someone to love and be loved. To know that this time next year, she could be holding new life brought a smile to her lips. For the first time in weeks, she could feel hope again.

"Now that's a rare and beautiful thing," Abraham's tenor rang overhead.

Startled, she jerked upright and was met with a crushing kiss. Not wanting it to end, she clasped her fingers behind his neck and drew him closer, deepening the kiss.

Feeling lightheaded, she finally broke contact and stared into her husband's handsome face. It was funny how easy it was to refer to Abraham as husband. "And just what is so rare and beautiful?" she said smiling up at him.

Taking her face in his hands, he allowed his thumb to trace her full lips. "You smiling is a rare and beautiful thing, Mrs. Taylor," he plopped a kiss on her nose then sat down beside her. "So, what shall we do this evening? Dinner, dancing, or maybe something we can do in private?" He smiled suggestively, wiggling his eyebrows, "whatever your little heart desires."

Taking on a newfound boldness, Keturah smiled coyly, then jumped on his lap and kissed him with as much passion as she knew how, hoping to communicate exactly what she had in mind for the evening. Finally, letting him breathe, she nuzzled him under his neck with her nose.

"Something private it is," he chuckled, then chucked her under the chin. "Listen, I'll be gone the majority of the afternoon on for a business. But I promise, when I get back, I'm all yours. Okay?

"Promise?"

"Promise." He smiled, kissed her deeply, and then stood up, looking down at her, then at his watch. "You are definitely my weak- spot beautiful," he chuckled, and then jogged off.

She watched as he jogged away. She had every intention of enjoying her husband tonight and every night, as long as she could. She prayed he wouldn't be angry with her, but she was going to be a mother and he was going to be the father. Let the chips fall where they may.

***

"Dad?"

Surprised to hear Isaac's voice, Abraham immediately stopped and turned to see, not only his son, but Avery and a not-too-happy Emory exiting the elevator.

Requesting the receptionist to wait a moment, he walked back towards them with a smile. "What are you guys doing here?" he said, giving his son a hug, while extending a hand in greeting to the others.

"We need to talk," Emory said as a matter-of-fact tone. "Exactly, what is going on between you and Ket…."

Holding up his hand, he cut him off. "Em, can't this wait?" Abraham replied, already feeling an edge in his pitch. He knew Emory wanted answers about him and Keturah, but now was not the time.

"No, Dad, this can wait," Isaac stated while placing a newspaper in his hand.

Looking down at the headlines of the society pages, Abraham cringed. Wedding bells and mergers on the horizon for millionaire Abraham Taylor, who secretly eloped with longtime companion, Hagan Zarah. Apparently, someone was doing some snooping. He rubbed his forehead. If this rumor spread, it would put their current business venture at risk. He would need to squash these rumors immediately, but first he needed to know how much damage-control had to be done. "Has anyone else seen this?" He looked at the others with a frown.

"Just about everyone back home," Isaac said tersely, "the office has been filtering calls since the story came out. Many of our constituents are having a fit, the tabloids are having a field day, and all we can say is, no comment." He ran his fingers nervously through his thick curls. "What I want to know is, why are we the last people to know about this, Dad? We're your family."

"Excuse me, Mr. Taylor, but is everything alright?" the receptionist inquired.

"Yes. Yes, everything is fine. Please, just give us one more minute," Abraham requested with a smile, then turned back to the others. "Look let's shelve this discussion until the meeting is over. Afterwards, I will explain what's going on," he said quietly.

"Dad, this can't be shelved like everything else you put off. I've been trying to get in touch with you for two days. Hassan intends on throwing you a party tonight congratulating you on your new marriage," he said bluntly.

Abraham lifted his head and shut his eyes in silent prayer. *Lord help,* he thought, as Keturah's face flashed in his mind. The need for her to play the role of his wife in public was now at hand, regardless if they were ready or not. She was still very fragile emotionally, and wasn't ready for any public appearances. Not only that, she definitely wasn't ready to deal with his family.

He was all out of options on this one. Keturah was his wife and she would need to play that role, at least for the evening. "Isaac, this meeting is about to put *Canaan* into international waters. I appreciate you giving me the heads-up on this issue, but right now, we need to go into this meeting as a united front and show Hassan why *Canaan* is the right company for them to partner with. Everything else is secondary, including the lies in this rag. Now are you with me or not?"

"Of course, we're with you on this, Abraham. We have your back," Avery spoke up, laying a reaffirming hand on his friend's shoulder.

Blowing out a sigh, Isaac gave an affirmative nod as well.

Emory said nothing, but his look became more somber.

"Alright, let's do this." Abraham turned towards the receptionist, who smiled, then led them to a set of rich mahogany doors. Swinging them open into what looked like a waiting area, she immediately led them to another set of doors.

Quickly slipping her head inside, then back out, smiling at them she stepped aside. "You can go right in, Mr. Taylor, the rest of your party is already seated and waiting for you."

"The rest of our party?" Isaac murmured behind his father. "Who else is coming?"

Abraham was too deep in thought about Keturah, to pay attention to what Isaac had said. He cracked his neck and squared his shoulders as he cleared his thoughts. The only way this deal would be successful was if his head was in the game. He wouldn't allow this venture to fall apart. It was too important to his plans for *Canaan Enterprises* becoming global.

He was Abraham Taylor, successful entrepreneur, because God made him that way. *Canaan* was going international starting now, and God help anyone who was trying to stand in the way. Putting his game-face on, he walked in and stopped dead in his tracks, as a set of cobalt blue eyes, much like his own, glared back at him.

Their host had entered the room, greeting everyone, but Abraham had not noticed. His eyes were glued to Ishmael, his eldest son. His arms-ached with the desire to reach out and hug him, but he refrained.

"Abraham, my friend, it has been too long," Hassin Zarah said in his deep baritone voice.

Shaken out of a fog of memories assaulting him, Abraham finally turned his head to his host, "Hassin it's always a pleasure." He greeted the man with a firm handshake and pat on the back. "How is your wife, Darma?"

"That woman will be the death of me one day, I swear," Hassan gave an exasperated sigh, while shaking his graying head. "She is the reason for the slight schedule conflict we are having today."

"Schedule conflict?" Abraham frowned.

"Yes, my administrative assistant has taken ill and Darma has been helping out. Unfortunately, a misunderstanding occurred when reading my appointment book, she mistakenly confirmed this meeting twice."

"Oh, I see," realizing the mistake that must have happened. "Since I'm sure you recognize your own son, I'll forego the introductions. Truly, I could just strangle my wife for this," Hassan said nervously, as he moved past Abraham and entered the room.

"You're not the only one," Abraham thought. How bitter - sweet this reunion was. He hadn't laid eyes on his son in years, and now that he finally had, it was as business rivals and not family, like he always wanted. It was enough to make his stomach turn, he thought as he heard murmuring from behind him. Until that moment he'd forgotten his companions.

"This is just great," Isaac said, irritation riddling his voice.

"Everyone, just take a moment and breathe!" Avery said evenly. "This was unexpected, but there's no need to panic."

So many pent-up emotions were taking place in Abraham, he could hardly think clearly. Both men stood immobile, until his nephew Lot moved into his line of vision. It was only then that Abe even realized Lot was actually in the room.

"Hi, Uncle Abe. It's good to see you again," Lot Taylor said quietly. "Well, this business-meeting is turning out to be more like a family reunion. Ishmael, come say, "Hi," to the family."

As if shaken out of his fog, Ishmael slowly approached his dad and stuck out his hand. "Dad, good to see you," looking over his father's shoulder he nodded to the others, "Well, I guess to say this is a surprise is an understatement."

"So true," Abraham spoke up as he gave Lot a firm handshake, and then turned to Ishmael to do the same. Taking a deep swallow to contain his emotions, he smiled and spoke in kind. "It's good to see you also…son."

CHAPTER NINETEEN

"It would've been nice for a heads-up regarding dear old dad's appearance at the meeting today," Ishmael gave his mom an accusing glare before tossing his keys on the coffee table and flopping down on the brown leather sofa.

"Hey, you weren't raised in a zoo. Take your feet off the couch." After he begrudgingly complied, she continued. "Thank you. Now, how does your father look?" Hagan inquired, never looking up from her magazine.

Ishmael stared disbelievingly at his mom then rolled his eyes and cursed under his breath, "What difference does that make mom? You should've told me he was going to be there!"

"What makes you think I knew? I'm not your father's keeper," she stated calmly while flipping the pages of the magazine, then lazily tossed it aside to look at her son with a slight smirk poised on her lips.

"You knew. You know just about every move he makes, now, more than ever, since his witch of a wife died."

"Now, Ishmael. That's no way to speak of the dead, even if it is true." She gave a conspirator smile that he returned. "Now, how does your daddy look? Hmmm? Is his little heartbroken I hope?"

Huffing out a sigh seeing his mother was not going to be deterred from her train of thought, he swung his feet off the couch, retreated to the bar and poured himself a drink. "Want one?" At her nod, he poured her a glass and walked to where she was seated. "He looks tired," Ishmael remarked nonchalantly to his mom, and took another sip from his glass.

Although his dad's appearance that afternoon completely startled him, he only hoped he recovered well. *The man always did rattle me.* Ishmael thought back to when he was a kid, his dad had a way of seeing right through him. His dad had a sixth sense or something, and knew whenever he was about to do something dishonest, which was most of the time. Some way, somehow, the man always found out. It was likely his little brother Isaac, the little mama's boy, who told everything he did or didn't do. Which reminded him, he could have done without seeing him today, too. With renewed disgust, he finished his drink and went back to the bar and poured himself another.

"So, I guess seeing your father really got to you?" Hagan pressed

"Nothing gets to me when it comes to doing business," he lied! Turning from his mother, he poured more bourbon into his tumbler and took a long drink to help steady his nerves. He had his agenda all set. He had planned to be the first one to attack his competition, showing the weaknesses of their company, and showing his savvy and knowledge regarding international regulations. His presentation would have been flawless and before the meeting ended, he planned on securing the account. But everything went out the window as soon as his dad, along with his entourage, walked in the room.

His dad had a commanding presence about him that normally had most businessmen quaking in their shoes, him included. He only wished he could command that type of respect in the business world that his father did. When the senior Taylor surveyed the room that afternoon, everyone stiffened. *Canaan Enterprises* was known for its business ethics and he had to admit, there wasn't a chink in their armor and there was no one in the room that would try and fault them. Then his eyes connected with his dad's, few words were spoken; they acknowledged each other and then his Uncle Hassan ushered him to the front table.

For one, solitary moment, Ishmael thought he saw something in his old man's eye…was it regret, a father's pride, or just indifference, he didn't know. He was a teenager when he left his father's home for good, vowing to make his father regret the day that he had chosen Isaac over him. He didn't need his father's guidance, blessing or his money. As far as he was concerned, he could keep it. But looking into the wisdom of his dad's eyes made him feel the same ole void. *This is all her fault. She was the one who caused me and Dad to be estranged!* He accused within himself. If it hadn't been for her, he'd be in his rightful place as the next CEO. *Dimwitted woman, I'm glad she died*, he said to himself.

"What's troubling you son? You have a strange look about you."

"Nothing." He said finishing his drink. "I just wish I would've been properly informed that he was going to be there. That way, I could've done my homework and studied the Canaan. Besides, when did dad decide to bring *Canaan Enterprises* into the international market?" Ishmael grumbled.

"Since I told Hassan that I felt it would be a good idea for him to consider making investments in the West. After all, he planned on doing this sometime soon. So, I convinced him to do it now, rather than later. He thought it was a good idea and I dropped some names of businesses that would be able to meet his needs," she shrugged and held out her glass towards him. "Be a dear, and freshen this up for me."

"If you have that much influence over Uncle Hassan, why didn't you tell him to just do business with me, and we could've skipped all this," he said, his voice level raising a few decibels. "His account added to my company's portfolio would've been a real asset."

"Ishmael, how often have I told you, you think too small? Your company's portfolio is nothing compared to you being CEO of *Canaan International."* She waved her hand in a grandiose gesture and leaned back in the cushion of her loveseat, smiling at her son.

"Mom, please don't take this the wrong way, but have you been drinking something stronger than this sherry? He said, while stepping forward and taking her glass, as he quickly laid the back of his hand to her head, checking to see if she had a fever.

She swatted his hand away, "I'm being serious Ishmael!"

"And so am I, Mother! I have as much chance of being the next CEO of *Canaan Enterprises* as an ice cube has in hell."

"Oh, Mael. Stop being so dramatic," she chided, while taking the drink he had refreshed for her, out of his hand.

"I'm being realistic, not dramatic. Dad has been grooming Isaac to take over for him, since the day he drew his first breath; and nothing is going to change that."

"We'll see son. We'll see." She sat back and took another sip of her drink as Ishmael looked at her with a frown.

"What are you planning, Mother?" he said, as curiosity slowly crept into his eyes.

"You sound as if I'm some evil mastermind; planning the demise of some poor, innocent undeserving soul," she quipped.

"Now, who's being over dramatic? Look, Mom. I'm fine with my company. We might not have the recognition that Canaan has, but we'll get there and I won't need Dad's influence to get the respect I deserve." He frowned as he thought back on how comfortable his baby-brother looked when asked to speak on their company's objectives and projected profits that could be gained this quarter. He hated to admit it, but even he was impressed.

"That Canaan Enterprise is part of your inheritance. Not only that, but you would've benefited greatly from Abraham's guidance in the business world."

"But Jamar was a great stepfather and he taught me well in the...."

"That's not the point," Hagan snapped, swinging her feet off the chaise lounge. "It was Abraham's responsibility to father you, not Jamar's. You are doing well enough; that much is true. But still, if your father hadn't allowed that woman to throw us into the street like some stray dogs, you'd have had the support and respect you desire now," Hagan finished, her voice shaking with open hostility.

Throwing up his hands, Ishmael conceded to his mom's tirade. "Okay, Mom. You're right. Everything you said is absolutely, spot-on. But what good does it do me now?" he tried reasoning with her.

Never in a million years did he think he'd be partly defending his father, but something about seeing his dad and missing him more than he realized, got to him today.

"Mom, I'm my own man now. Yeah Dad coulda, shoulda done a lot of things, but the fact is, he didn't. I'm going to make it my own way and on my own terms. And, I plan on letting nothing, including Abraham Taylor, get in my way."

Hagan held her peace. She looked at her son with great pride, remembering back to when Sarah first put her and Ishmael out. She had no idea what to do or where to go. She only had the little stash of money Abraham was able to give her, right before the cab came to get them. Everything she and Ishmael owned fit in two travel suitcases. She was broke, unemployed, and only had the skills gained by being Sarah's personal assistant, which actually made her no better than a maidservant. At least, that was the way Sarah had treated her.

No one really knew the ugly side that Sarah had, but Hagan knew. No one but she and close family knew how Sarah had played with Abraham's heart and threatened to remain in the presence of one of Abraham's business rivals, just to ruffle Abraham's feathers. But Sarah hadn't expected Abraham to leave her there. And who was the one that comforted him when she was gone. Hagan.

She and Abraham shared a son and many tender moments before, during, and after her pregnancy; and Sarah new it and hated her for it. She remembered every cruel remark and when Sarah finally did conceive the son she had desperately wanted and couldn't have. She made Hagan's life a living hell. Hagan began to rub her temples with the tips of her fingers, as memories of her troubled past came rushing, full-force at her.

"Mother, are you alright?" Ishmael said softly. The agitation in his voice and posture was now replaced with that of concern.

Hagan looked up at him and gave him a wobbly smile, but the turmoil and tears in her stormy hazel eyes told another story, of anguish not happiness. On seeing his mother's tears, Ishmael rushed to her side. Dropping to the floor, he grabbed both of her hands in his and patted them tenderly, hoping to somehow calm the rising storm he saw brewing within her.

"Mom, please stop crying. Please, you know I hate it when you cry."

His mom's tears made him hate Sarah all over again. Abraham's failure to be a real father to him would likely be something he'd have to deal with for a lifetime. But what that conniving two-faced witch did to his mom, he would never forgive. Sarah was dead now and would never be held accountable for her misgivings towards them; at least not on this side of the Earth. But, Isaac. He was a different story all together. Isaac was definitely going to get a taste of his wrath. He'd make sure of it.

However, before doing that, he wanted to make sure his mom was back home. She'd hear about the details later. With a plan in mind, he made a suggestion. "Hey, Mom, why don't we just pack up and go home. We can catch an afternoon flight and be home before midnight."

"Oh, stop fussing over me, Mael. I'm fine. I just have to remember that it's never a good idea for me to take a walk down memory lane. You know good and well, that those memories always get me into trouble." She laughed at her own joke, which got a roll of her son's eyes, making her smile all the more. *Good, he's calming down. I can't let the past get to me. I have plans for my son and his future and, by god, Abraham is going to make it happen for us. My son will not be cheated out of his birthright, and now that Sarah is dead, retribution will be made to us.*

Going home wasn't an option; she would stay until every detail of her long-awaited plan was in place.

"Besides, we can't leave. I have dinner plans," she said, taking her hands from him and softly patting his right cheek before standing and going to a wall-mirror hanging in the hall foyer of their suite; and began repairing the damage her tears had done to her makeup.

Frowning, he looked at his mother, "What plans?"

Hagan turned around looked at him with expressed surprise on her face, as if she were shocked that he'd even have to ask, "With your father, of course!"

"You're just full of surprises, aren't you?"

"It's good for a mother to still be able to keep her son on his toes every now and then. Oh, and don't forget to tell that fiancée of yours that she will also need to be in attendance."

"She has a name you know!" Ishmael said agitated. "I wish you would accept the fact that Marlana Simone will soon be Mrs. Marlana Taylor. The sooner you do, the better for us all."

"Her becoming the next Mrs. Taylor is still questionable if you ask me. Really, Mael. She poses for one of those girly magazines. What's the one? *Hustler?*"

"She is a fashion model for *Victoria's Secret,* Mom, and you know it," he gave an exasperated sigh.

"With the next-to-nothing she has on in those magazines, it won't be a *secret* for long," Hagan rolled her eyes.

Needing his mother off his future bride's case, he decided to drop a little news he overheard his father saying to Hassan. "Well, you're right about one thing you said, Marlana might not be the *next* Mrs. Taylor."

"Glad you haven't lost all reason. Now, what about Noella Riza? She comes from a good family and has a wonderful upbringing," Hagan said.

"And has the face of a goat," Ishmael retorted.

"Now, Ishmael. Really!"

"Drop it, Mom. I'm in love with Marlana and I won't be persuaded otherwise." He gave his mom his, I-mean-business glare, before continuing. "What I was referring to actually, was Dad."

Hagan twisted around to look at her son." What do you mean?" she demanded, walking back towards him, and giving him *her* answer-me-right-now-young-man look that always had a way of making him come clean.

"Well, I overheard him speaking to Hassin. Apparently, he needed to talk to his family before springing his marriage proposal. He said something about you, but I couldn't hear the rest of it," he said, watching his mother's face light up with glee.

"This is it!" She clapped her hands in excitement. "He's going to ask me to marry him. I knew he'd finally cave!" Hagan hugged herself excitedly, then ran to her purse and grabbed her phone. "I have so much to do. I can't possibly get the country club on such short notice for our engagement party, but it won't hurt to try."

"Whoa, whoa, hold the phone. Wait a minute, Mom," he put a restraining hand on her arm to keep her from dialing only God knew who. "Here you go jumping to conclusions *again*. How can you be sure that he's going to pop the question?" Ishmael raised a skeptical brow.

"He called me before you got home. When I told him, I was here with you, he asked if I could come over, that he had something he wanted to talk to me about. What else could it be?" She gave him an incredulous look before returning to her dialing.

"Mom, all I'm saying is…be careful. You and Dad have been here before. Remember, it didn't work out then…"

Hagan quickly interjected, "*Then*, Sarah was in the picture. Now, there's only me. It's my time. It's *our* time. Everything we lost, we're getting back with interest, Son. I promise," Hagan said, her hand gently caressing her son's face then she returned her attention back to her phone.

Not wanting to be the rain on his mom's parade, he stepped back and let her do her planning. Walking back to the wet-bar, he refreshed his drink and downed it, and poured himself another. He was going to need to be good and toasted to be in a room with his mom and dad and the train-wreck that was sure to come of this evening.

CHAPTER TWENTY

A frantic call from Abraham early that afternoon still had Keturah's head reeling, as she walked in the door of their loft; her arms loaded down with shopping bags from every pricey boutique on the island.

Abraham's family was in town, and a party was being thrown in their honor to celebrate their not-so-secret marriage and, according to Abraham, she had to look the part.

Giving her full access to his credit cards and his personal driver, his last words were to spare no expense. It was a shopping spree like none other. She was ushered from one extravagant boutique to another. Of course, she had to text him a picture of her purchases. If they weren't elaborate enough, he'd speak to the salesperson directly.

Finally, his personal assistant took over and arranged for her to have the works done at the most exclusive stores on the island. At some point, she was no longer given the option of seeing the price-tag, to keep her protesting at bay. But it was their stop at the jewelry store that practically gave her a coronary.

The jewelry placed on her ring-finger was the biggest diamond she'd ever seen. Additionally, she was given a matching bracelet and diamond necklace that weighed a ton, and would likely cost her five years' salary, and then some.

"I- I can't wear that! Its way, too big and expensive and what if I lose it?" she shrieked.

Her protests fell on deaf ears, as the jeweler and Abraham's assistant, Emily, completely ignored her as they went about the business of picking out other items, they thought were appropriate for the occasion.

Soon, the cell-phone was returned to her by an overly enthused jeweler. "Emily wants to speak with you, Madame," he said in a cheesy accent, handing her the cell.

"Yes?" Keturah said into the receiver trying to hide her annoyance.

"I realize this must be difficult for you, but do try and understand: you are now the wife of one of the country's most prominent men. You can't go around looking as if he plucked you off a street corner."

If there was one thing Keturah couldn't stand, it was someone talking down to her. Even though Emily was saying it in a pleasant voice, she could still detect her condescending tone.

"I *do* realize that I need to dress for the occasion, Emily. It's just that this is only for one evening, and I don't think it necessary to break Mr. Tay..., my husband's checkbook."

"Umm. Well, Mrs. Taylor, I am following my employer's instructions. So, you might want to have this discussion with him. Alright? Now, you'll need to get moving. I've scheduled you for a three thirty appointment at the salon," she said dismissively, then hung up.

Feeling like a reprimanded child, Keturah turned to leave after receiving instructions from the jeweler of when they would arrive to deliver her purchases. The jeweler following close behind her, stopped to talk to the driver to secure the address.

She clutched her arms around her stomach and rocked. She wasn't used to all this. She had always believed that the wealthy were nothing more than spoiled snobs who were full of themselves. Always taking things to the extreme; doing things over the top to prove to the next person that they were better. Was she now one of them?

A buzz had her searching for her cell. "Whew!" She was glad it was him and not Emily. "Hey, Abe."

"Hey, Baby. I'm really sorry about all this. I know this is hard, with everything that you're going through. But please work with me on this. It will soon be over, and then maybe we can still have our special plans for tonight."

She definitely wasn't in the mood for celebrating, but the idea of being with Abraham was all too appealing. "You remember what you said, that you never go back on a promise?"

"I did say that, didn't I? Well, Mrs. Taylor, I guess I'll have to make good on my word." His voice dropped seductively low.

"Yes, darling. You do," she smiled as she heard the phone click off. Her heart fluttered with anticipation of what their evening would hold.

***

He had done countless takeovers and mergers with men who could intimidate Attalla-the-Hun, and not once would he back down. But, meeting with Hagan to tell her he had married someone else had him sweating bullets. He hadn't expected to see her today, but once Ishmael had informed him that she was with him, what choice did he have? He had every intention of telling her, but in a way that wouldn't necessarily jeopardize his fragile relationship with Ishmael. Seeing his eldest today was like ointment to a blistering burn. When Hassan suggested that they partner up on the project, he could've hugged the man. Despite both of his sons' protests, he was thrilled to have them both at his side.

Then there was Keturah. She was a wrinkle that he didn't know how to straighten out. He thought he'd have her back in the states before this meeting happened. He had no idea that his family would join him here. Hassan knew they were married and honeymooning, but his immediate family had no idea what had taken place. He was only glad he was able to pull Hassan to the side and request his friend to keep everything a secret until he had the opportunity to tell everyone.

When Ishmael casually mentioned that Hagan was with him, he had no choice but to tell her as well. He only prayed she would take it well, and hopefully not make a scene. Glancing at his watch, he saw the time was drawing near. The family would be there by four, and Hagan would arrive at...well apparently, it would be after three now.

Thankfully, he was able to convince Keturah to go out and do a little more shopping. The doorbell caused him to stop his excessive pacing. "God, help me do this," he said absently, as he turned to see Hagan walking behind the butler and looking as if she could've just stepped off the cover of *Vogue*.

"Abe, sweetheart, I've missed you so much." She held out her arms to embrace him.

This was definitely going to be more difficult than he thought. But time was against him. He'd need to be delicate; compassionate but quick. "It's good to see you too, Hagan." He returned the hug and gave her a brief peck on the cheek.

"Did you miss me terribly, darling? I know I've missed you." She nuzzled his nose affectionately as she continued, "I heard you saw Ishmael today at the meeting. Can you believe he's a man now? Oh, Abe. He's so much like you. Sometimes, if I close my eyes, I can't tell if it's him or you in the room. He so much wants you to be proud of him; of what he's accomplished."

Words escaped him as he swallowed several times to stay his emotions. "It was wonderful seeing him. I just wish..." he thought to himself, I *could've been there to watch him grow up into the man he is today*. But said out loud, "it was under different circumstances. I'd much rather meet on neutral ground, than against each other over a business deal."

"True, but if this is what it takes to bring the Taylor men back together, then I'm glad." She smiled and sat down on the loveseat, patting the other seat-cushion, so Abraham could take his place by her side.

"I pray what happens here today will be the start of wonderful things to come. Don't you, darling?" She said softly, a hint of intimacy inflected in her voice.

Abraham could feel sweat beading on his forehead. He needed to say what he needed to say, before Hagan had them walking down the aisle. "Listen, Hagan. There's something I need to talk to you about, before my family gets here. There is something you need to know," Abraham hesitated. There was no easy way to tell anyone that you ran away and got married. He knew Hagan wanted to be the next, Mrs. Taylor, but that would have been a mistake he wasn't willing to make. "I don't know how to put this, so I guess I'll just say it."

"Oh, sweetheart! You don't have to say anything more, my answer is yes. Yes!" she shouted, throwing her arms around a surprised Abraham's neck, then moved close and kissed him with an intensity that she knew they both felt. A gasp from behind them drew them apart abruptly.

"Keturah! I . . .!" Abraham stood quickly; stammering, not knowing what to say, but feeling guilty at being caught. He needed to say something, "I didn't know you had come back from the store."

Keturah looked at him first, then to Hagan and back to Abraham. "That's evident," she said in an even tone.

"Sweetheart, who is this? No, wait. Isn't this Emory's little niece? Why is she here?" Hagan looked her up and down, as if she was less than nothing.

"Yes, Abraham. Why am I here?" Keturah smiled sweetly, liking the fact it was making Abraham squirm a little. Their marriage might be in name only, but she still had feelings and right now, it didn't feel good seeing her husband passionately kissing someone else.

"Well uh, she's an intern that is doing a report on our family, as well as documentation of the project," Abraham winced at Keturah's look.

She said nothing, but he could tell she was hurt by the lie. He hated down-playing things between them, but he wasn't ready to get into the real reason Keturah was with him at the loft.

"Well, if she's the help, then she needs to act like it and dress more like an intern and less like some hormonal twenty-year old on spring break. She also needs to know her place. What intern calls the CEO of the company by his first name? It's Mr. Taylor to you Miss, and I'm his fiancée, Ms. Zarah."

"Hagan!" Abraham said in alarm.

"Hagan, nothing. It is completely inappropriate and unacceptable for her to call you by your first name and to be so scantily dressed in front of you. As your fiancée, I won't stand for it." Hagan protested.

"My apologies to you, Mr. Taylor and Ms. Zarah. I'll go to my room and change," Keturah said in a clipped tone. She swirled around and marched to her room without another word.

Abraham sighed in resignation of the new conflict already brewing with Keturah. But that would have to wait. From the sound of the doorbell, he knew he had another battle on the horizon, when he heard his Aunt Sari's high-pitched voice. *God, why is she here?* He caught himself before he let the words slip out of his mouth.

Indeed, lying was bad business, but despite himself, he kept digging himself deeper and deeper. Now that the web had been spun, he saw no other choice but to play this charade out for the benefit of his family. He had to see this through to the end. Hagan was still in his embrace as the old woman rounded the corner before the butler could announce her.

"How could you, Abe? How could you get married to…to that?" Sari pointed an accusatory finger at Hagan. "… and not have the decency to tell your own flesh and blood?"

"Yeah, Dad, like I said before, you should've at least informed us," Isaac said, sounding irritated as he looked at Hagan. "How'd the press get wind of this?" He wondered out-loud. He had been so careful. Making sure that they went to a private notary to sign the marriage certificate, then flying out of town on the private jet, so no one would suspect anything.

"Oh, please, darling. You're one of the most eligible bachelors in the country. Of course, people would be interested in a high-profile engagement. Especially, the one we're going to have." Hagan practically allowed the words to drip off her red-coated lips. The look of disdain she received from his family, only made her smile widen, as she tossed her head back as if she had won a gold medal.

"Look, everyone. I wasn't trying to hurt you or keep you in the dark; it just happened suddenly and..." Abraham sighed dejectedly. This was getting out of hand. How was he ever going to repair the relationship with his family if he didn't start being honest. He was leading everyone on by not telling them he, in fact, was married to Keturah; a woman practically the same age as his son's fiancée. *Arghh, what a mess!* Abraham thought.

"Abraham, this is the most irresponsible thing you've done since getting her pregnant in the first place. If you and Sarah would have just listened, this would not even be an issue," Sari fumed.

"Abraham, darling, I hate to spoil this little family get-together, but I have so many things to do before we have our little gathering to announce our engagement tonight. I have the caterers to call and a couple of people to invite over, so they can share in our happiness. Of course, Ishmael will be here, and that will give you time to get acquainted with his fiancée, Marlana Simone."

"Wait. Ishmael is engaged?" Abraham asked.

"Yes, isn't it wonderful? Oh, maybe we could have a duel announcement to celebrate.

Oh, that would be marvelous, wouldn't it?" Stepping up, she gave Abraham another long dramatic kiss. As she floated out of the room, all sets of eyes glaring at her back; except for one pair of dark, stormy, grey eyes glaring directly at Abraham. He hadn't even realized Keturah had come back in the room. He quickly walked Hagan out.

"Hagan, we really need to discuss some things. Please don't do anything until I call you," already knowing she was going to anyhow.

Leaning on the closed door for support, he dropped his head. He had definitely fallen into a hornet's nest. "Father, forgive me for this deceit. Show me the way out," he prayed softly.

He who practices lies shall not dwell within my house. He who speaks falsehood shall not maintain his position before me.

He sighed within himself and said, "It's time to come clean." Walking back to the room where his family stood waiting, he thought of how to break the news to them. Avery was the first to speak as he approached the room.

"Ok, Abe. What's really going on? Are you truly going to marry Hagan?"

"Absolutely, not!" Abraham stated.

"Whoa, wait a minute. So, you're not engaged?" Isaac stated, sounding both surprised and relieved.

"Thank God for that! At least we know you haven't gone completely crazy. You know full-well, all Hagan wants is to get her grubby little hands on Isaac's inheritance," Sari said, holding her head in her hands and turning, only to jump at the sight of Keturah. "Good lord! Why in the world are you here?" she demanded of Keturah.

"That's not the issue, Aunt Sari. Hagan is," Avery chimed in.

"I want to know why Keturah Birch is here, in this house and I want to know right now!" Sari demanded loudly, over everyone and stomping her foot like an overgrown child. "She's certainly not part of this family; therefore, why is she here?" Sari was like a pit-bull with a bone: she wasn't going to let go.

Here's your opportunity to come clean. The Holy Spirit whispered.

This served the perfect chance to be honest with his family and validate his new bride, as he knew he should. Looking at Keturah, who stood silently waiting for him to do just that; instead, Abraham chickened out. Not because he was afraid of what his family thought, but for another reason. He wanted to meet Ishmael's fiancée, wanted to feel the unity he had craved since Sarah's death. He looked at Keturah and prayed both she and God would be forgiving and understanding. "Keturah is doing an assignment for me as an internist," he said in a low voice, while dropping his gaze from her; not wanting to see the disappointment registering in her eyes.

"Well, if that's the case, she doesn't need to be here while we're having a private *family* conversation. Now, does she?" Sari practically hissed. "This conversation is for family only, not the hired help. So, go!" Sari barked her orders.

"Aunt Sari, is that tone really necessary?" Abraham chided, but before he could say anything more in her defense, Keturah had left the room.

"It's bad enough that your past transgressions are slapping you in the face, but now you've brought Kedron's indiscretion into the picture as well. Son, when are you going to learn that not every mistake can be fixed?"

"What are you saying, Aunt Sari? That Keturah and Ishmael are mistakes?" he challenged. "Those *mistakes,* as you call them, are people. They bear our names and we're responsible for them. You can't push them aside, just because you don't want them around."

"Spare me the "father's code of ethics for their bastard children" speech. I've heard it for twenty-seven years. Women, like that girl's mom and Hagan, worm their way into a man's family and spread their poison, until every, single member of the family has been infected. It's bad enough that you bring Hagan, a woman Sarah had to throw out to protect Isaac, but now you bring my husband's illegitimate child into the circle of this family; and yes, I know everything seems innocent now, but did you think of the importance of protecting Isaac? She'll be the very one to befriend Rebecca and drive a knife in her back the minute she's not looking."

Sari clapped her hands, causing a wide-eyed Rebecca to jump a little and cling to Isaac's arm protectively.

"Aunt Sari, I know you mean well, but please stop. You're getting all worked up over nothing." Abraham tried to reassure her but she didn't look convinced. He had to make a decision. From where things stood, it really didn't matter what route he took: his family would likely deem him insane for ever getting involved with Hagan again or simply incompetent for marrying a woman he was twenty-five years her senior. When considering his options, he could kind their point. Breathing in deeply, he covered his face with his hands and drawing them back over his head. For now, he would just reassure them that he wasn't getting married to Hagan. Once that was done, he'd need to speak to what he knew would be a very angry Hagan, before she contacted caterers and the press, which would only give further embarrassment to an already tumultuous situation.

Then there was Keturah. By the look she gave him, he wondered if she hadn't already packed her bags and heading stateside. Then, there was God, to whom he'd need to repent. It seemed like the list was steadily growing, as he thought of how furious Emory would be when he found out that he had married Keturah allegedly in name only, but had then consummated it during their secret honeymoon.

A tap on his shoulder brought him out of his thoughts. He was standing in the room alone with Avery.

"Look, I told everyone to give you a minute."

"Thanks!" Abraham went to the wet bar and was about to pour himself a drink, but thought better of it. He needed to have a clear head.

"Look, Abraham. I don't think you're crazy. Hagan's beautiful, and I get that. But after all the hell she has put you and Sarah through over the years...I-I just don't understand it."

"Trust me; I haven't forgotten any of it. But this is a chance for me to have both my sons in the same room together. Not as competitors, but as family. Can't you understand that?" he implored.

"Yes, I understand. But why does Hagan believe that you two are getting married?" Avery went behind the bar to pour himself something stronger than the water Abraham was holding.

"I never proposed to Hagan. She just assumed that I was going to, that it was the direction our relationship was headed. In all actuality, I called her over here to tell her that marriage wasn't on the table for us."

"Then, why is she still under the illusion that you two are getting married?"

"Because my family and friends have lousy timing. I was just about to tell her when everyone walked in," Abraham watched his friend hang his head and pinch the bridge of his nose.

"I tried to tell Aunt Sari to slow down, but when she heard the reports of your so-called engagement, she was heated; mainly because she wouldn't be able to wiggle Naidean Pickette in your face as a candidate for the next, Mrs. Taylor." he snickered as Abraham rolled his eyes.

"Please tell me you're not serious. Man is that the reason she's always batting those false eyelashes of hers at me?" looking at his friend as Avery nodded his head in confirmation. Abraham placed his glass on the bar, "Give me what you're drinking," he said wearily.

"Well, I guess the good thing is that you're not marrying Hagan. The bad thing is that you'll have Naidean to contend with," Avery chuckled good-naturedly.

He needed to come clean and Avery was as good a person as any to start with. "Avery, pour yourself another drink and have a seat. There's a little bit more to this story that I have yet to tell you."

Chapter Twenty-One

Thank God for credit cards! Keturah thought, on the way to the airport. She had already lost Gretta. All she had left was her sense of pride in who Gretta had raised her to be. No matter how much she wanted to be part of Abraham's life, she'd refused to allow those women to strip her of it. Besides, if Abraham was too embarrassed to tell everyone that she was his new wife, maybe this whole thing was a mistake. She had just stood in line for the security checkpoint, when her cell began blaring. Looking at the caller ID, she glared at the phone as she clicked over. "Hello, Mr. Taylor. How may I help you?" she said with no inflection in her tone. She knew he'd call, but there was nothing he was going to say to convince her to stay.

"Keturah, I know you're upset, but please let me explain."

"Mr. Taylor, I'm just an employee, no need to explain anything to me," she said tight-lipped, as she moved up in line.

"Okay. Look, I get it. I messed up and you have every right to be upset, but please try and understand."

"I'm sorry, Mr. Taylor, but I have to check my bags. So, I'm going to have to go."

"Keturah, I beg you, please stay. I have straightened everything out with my family, I told them the truth."

"And what about the woman you were kissing, hmmm? Oh, what's her name? Oh, yes. Hagan, your fiancée; did you straighten everything out with her?" Keturah snapped, not sure why the image of him kissing Hagan made her so mad.

Shifting her weight from one foot to the other, she waited for his answer. It was bad enough that Abraham didn't acknowledge her as his wife, but to allow Hagan to demean her like that was another.

Hired help! Wow, was that how he saw her? *Lord, I never should've done this. If only Gretta were still here.* There was no need to go in that direction; wishing the past away was useless. Maybe she shouldn't be upset. Her and Abraham's arrangement was…? She didn't know how to label it, now that they had been intimate, and not just once.

During those times, she felt closer to him; as if maybe the marriage could last longer than the year they'd agreed upon; but then to see him kissing Hagan, then dismiss her as if she was nothing but an employee, tore her up inside.

"Keturah."

A hand on her shoulder made her jump and turn around. "Abraham? What are you doing…why are you…you're here!?" she said, confused.

"I'm sorry. I didn't mean to startle you."

"But how…how did you know I was here?"

"The driver. He told me," he said simply.

Seeing she hadn't yet checked-in with the TSA, he motioned her to step to the side. "Listen, Keturah. Can we talk?"

"My flight will be leaving and I have to get through security," she was saying, but moving out of line at the same time.

"Keturah, I don't want you to go. Hassan is throwing a party tonight celebrating our marriage. How can I be there without you?"

"So, this is about your business deal?" she scrunched her face up in disbelief. She knew Abraham was tenacious when it came to business, but to be this insensitive made her feel as if the man she'd idolized for years didn't deserve all the worship. *Lord how could I have been so wrong about him?* Maybe she was wrong in wanting this relationship to last. Maybe she should just cut her losses and run.

Shaking her head, she picked up her things and stepped back in line. This conversation was pointless. She was about to move forward when a hand stopped her again.

"I know what you're thinking and you're wrong. This is not just about business. I really felt convicted about how you were treated today, and I need to make things right. I always teach my mentees that honesty is the best policy. God reminded me of that today, and I'm truly sorry for how I allowed Aunt Sari and Hagan to speak to you. This might be a short-term marriage, but I still took vows to honor you, and while we're married, I'm going to do my best to keep that vow.

There he is...there's the man I wanted to stay married to, she thought, smiling up at him as tears shimmered in the corners of her eyes.

"I'm not sorry that we got married. I'm just sorry how I've handled things so far. I want a chance to make it up to you, and I can't think of a better way than escorting my beautiful, new bride on my arm at the celebration of our union."

***

Keturah was going to be late for her own party, but really didn't care. She took one, last look at herself in the full-length mirror and sighed. Abraham insisted that she wear a floor-length, navy-blue gown, with rhinestones on the bodice and trailing down her back.

Her up-do hairstyle made her neck look long and elegant with the diamond necklace gracefully encircling it; the matching earrings and a diamond bracelet complementing her attire. Without a doubt, she knew that she looked good; even mature, and just the type of woman people would expect to be seen accompanying a man such as Abraham Taylor.

This isn't you. She heard a small voice inside her head say. She shook her head. Maybe it wasn't who she was this afternoon, but it's who Abraham expected her to be tonight.

Yes, Sari's remarks hurt, as did Hagan's. But this wasn't about them. It was about her husband who said he needed her by his side tonight. She looked at her reflection again. How could she deny him such a simple request?

But he lied to you! He told his family you where nothing more than his intern. And, that woman he was kissing; Hagan. What about her? Are they still seeing each other? He let her dismiss you like you were nothing...a servant. A dark thought taunted.

Gripping the marble counter, she closed her eyes to the voices inside her head. The words hurt, but the truth in them was overwhelming. It was the same words that drove her to the airport that afternoon. But it was the gentleness in his voice when he called, that drew her back. Abraham had been a rock for her, and her only comfort the last couple of weeks, since Gretta had died. He took care of everything, which was beyond nice. For once, she didn't have to be responsible for everything. It was wonderful to be able to kick back and enjoy life unencumbered for a while, it felt liberating. In fact, now that she was free from everyday worries, she located what she really wanted in life. It came to her their first day on the island: not only did she want his baby to love, she wanted the love of her husband also. So, if dressing up and playing nice with his family was what it took, then she was about to give the performance of a lifetime!

Smiling at herself and full of resolve, she turned and exited the ladies' room and ran smack into a young woman who seemed vaguely familiar to her. She couldn't place her, until a young man who looked so much like her husband was close behind. All eyes seemed to lock on each other simultaneously.

"So, you're the one," Isaac stated, irritation clearly in his voice.

"Zac, don't start. You promised," the young woman's voice rose in warning.

"Me? Becca, honey, I'm not starting anything," he said defensively, then pointed a hand at Keturah, "This mess Dad is in is all her doing," he spat out.

Keturah winced as if he had slapped her face. *Well I guess getting the family to like me is out,* she thought silently. *Why was he acting so hostile towards her? She hadn't done anything but stayed, at Abraham's request.*

"Zac, you don't know what happened between the two of them and you shouldn't jump to conclusions," Rebecca tried to reason.

"I'll tell you what, Keturah Birch or Jaymes, whoever the heck you say you are. If you think you're going to get another dime out of my dad, you're mistaken. I won't allow any two-bit hustler from the street, coerce anyone in my family," he said, pointing an accusatory finger in her face like she was beneath him.

"Isaac!"

A stern male voice from behind had them all turning around to see Abraham's quick approach. The look on his face made Keturah step back. She recognized that anger; had seen it up close and personal when he had awakened in her hotel room. She didn't want to face it again.

"I know your mother and I raised you better than this. So, I suggest you act like it," he said tersely. "Like it or not, this is my wife and you will respect her as such. Is that understood, boy?" Abraham stood toe to toe with his son, staring him down like a boxer facing his opponent. Isaac's silence didn't go over well as Abraham took a threatening step towards his son, "I said, is that understood?" He gave a low growl.

Keturah could feel the hairs on her arms stand on-end, as she watched the exchange between the two Taylor men. Looking across from her, she saw the woman she now recognized as Isaac's fiancée, Rebecca, clutch her neck, fearing for her betrothed's safety.

"Abraham…Isaac!   Stop this foolishness immediately!" Sari demanded as she approached them.

Keturah's stomach flopped as Sari made a bee-line towards the men, but not before giving her the once-over; a look of disapproval evident on her face.   Several other people, including her Uncle Emory, who she had no idea was there, were coming forward.

"Have you two lost your God-given senses?   What in the blazes is wrong with you?" she reprimanded the men, as if they were preschoolers.

"Aunt Sari, all I was trying to do was make sure that this…"   Isaac immediately swallowed as his Dad gave him a warning glare. "All I want is to make sure our family is free from any type of scandal," Isaac finished as he allowed his eyes to rest on Keturah with his last word.

"There is no scandal to speak of.   Keturah and I were married over a month ago, and she married me at my request. That's all any of you needed to know," Abraham stated, coming to her side and placing a protective arm around her shoulder.

Feeling his warmth made her nuzzle closer to him, then the image of him and Hagan kissing buzzed in her thoughts like a pesky fly. Even before she could erase the memory of the woman in her husband's arms, the real thing emerged from the crowd.

"Well, well if it isn't the newlyweds. Let me be the first to give my condolences, umm, I mean congratulations to you and the new, Mrs. Taylor." Hagan's voice rang over everyone.

Feeling Abraham's body stiffen, Keturah braced herself, already knowing that some type of snippy remark was about to come their way.

Looking up at her husband, she noted the direction of his gaze, and turned to see who he was reacting to. She was startled to see a man who was every bit his height and build and remarkably-looked like him.

He was standing by a young woman who had beautiful, hazel-brown eyes and looked of Indian descent. They both cut her an assessing gaze; the man's eyes lingered on her a little longer than what she felt necessary. Feeling uncomfortable, she nuzzled as close as she could to Abraham. She wanted to forget this whole sordid mess and get out of town, like she had planned on doing a few hours ago. Why hadn't she listened?

"Mother, the Helms family wants to wish us well, let's go." He said holding out his hand to his mother, Hagan.

After glaring at Abraham for another moment, she then acquiesced, "You're right, Ishmael. I'm sorry. I won't let anything, including your father's poor judgment, spoil your and Marlana's engagement party tonight.

"Wait!" Abraham spoke, hurriedly walking away from Keturah as he rushed after them.

Keturah immediately felt the loss of his heat and missed it. Like a baby cub left to fend for itself, while surrounded by a pack of hyena, she stepped back, as all eyes turned to watch Abraham's retreating form. This was her chance to escape and she'd better be wise and take it. But, before she could, she felt an arm surround her shoulder.

"Come on, Tourie. Let's go outside for some air," a warm tenor said overhead.

Looking up, tears sprang to her eyes as a comforting shoulder-hug came from her uncle. "Oh, Uncle Em," was all she managed to say before her voice broke.

Ushering her away from the crowd, he led her to a balcony outside the reception area, for some much-needed fresh air. Taking her to a private spot, he allowed her to rest on his chest as she unleashed her penned-up emotions.

"It's okay, Tourie. Shh, don't cry. I'm here," he patted her on the back, as he rocked her in his arms like he did when she was little. "I'm so sorry about all of this, honey; and I promise, I won't allow them to gang-up on you again."

"I just wanted to help Gretta..." she managed to say through her sobs. "He said it would be only for a couple of months, or maybe a year. He'd help me take care of Gretta's bills. I didn't think things would turn out like this," she continued to cry.

"Don't worry, honey. When we get back to the states, we'll simply have it annulled. And then we'll put this entire nightmare behind us."

"We can't have it annulled," *And I don't want it annulled either, I want to remain Abraham's wife.* She thought to herself.

"Of course, you can. From what you told me, it was in name only. So, there shouldn't be any problems," he said, in a matter-of- fact way. "You'll fly out with me in the morning, and you can stay with me and your aunt for a little while."

"That won't be necessary," Abraham's voice cut through curtly. "Thanks for your concern, Emory. But, Keturah and I will be flying back to the states together in the morning."

Startled, they both jerked their heads up towards Abraham. Somehow, the look he gave her almost made her feel guilty; as if she was doing something other than having a conversation with her uncle.

"I think Keturah needs to be with me," Emory challenged. "As her uncle, I appreciate your concern. But, as her husband, I will decide what's in the best interest for my wife, Emory."

She could feel the air surrounding them tense. She didn't want any more fighting; not tonight. She also needed to make a decisive choice as to who she was going to be. Already knowing where her heart truly lay, she turned to Emory, "Thank you, Uncle Emory, for listening, but I'll be returning to the states with my husband tomorrow," she said with a shy smile at Abraham, who then extended his hand towards her. Stepping out of her uncle's arms, and taking hold of her husband's hand in that moment, she felt as if she had truly become Mrs. Abraham Taylor.

CHAPTER TWENTY-TWO

Excitement swelled in her chest, as Keturah stepped off the elevator and onto the polished redwood floors of the executive suites, where her husband's office was located. Up until now, she hadn't seen where he worked, and admittedly was curious.

"Wow!" Keturah's mouth hung open as she saw the elaborately decorated hallway.

It was evident that no expense was spared when designing his executive office suite; she could only imagine what his home looked like. The thought made her pause, as she realized that they had been married a little over six weeks now, yet she still had not set foot in his home.

After the fiasco that occurred in the Caribbean, while flying back to the states, they had a long talk and had finally come to an understanding that things could go a little further than the year they originally agreed on.

However, as things were, whenever he'd come to see her, it was either at her apartment or he'd have her meet him somewhere out-of-the-way. She knew, for a fact, other married people didn't act this way, but she was willing to put up with it if, in the end, staying married to him was the ultimate prize.

With that thought firmly planted in her head, she turned the corner and stopped dead in her tracks. Mounted high, on what had to be an accent wall, was an enormous portrait of the Taylor family greeting her. She first noticed Sarah's piercing grey eyes, which seemed to stab at one's soul, next was Abraham's gentle inviting smile, then her eyes traveled to Isaac's image. Standing next to his mother made Keturah see where he got his high cheekbones and steely gaze. He was strikingly handsome, but he still had nothing on his father. Abraham's classic rugged good looks could make a nun take a second look! *And he's all mine.* She smiled inwardly. *For now.*

That thought chilled her and made her want to run in the opposite direction, but that was foolish. Besides, it was too late for that, she thought rubbing a hand over her flat stomach. She could be carrying his child, and if so, their lives would always be intertwined. Taking a breath and squaring her shoulders, she looked back at the family posing in that picture. Moving a little closer, she read the inscription on the bottom of the picture,

My pride, my joy, my love always. ~Abraham

It was so sweet. She never got a chance to see that side of him. But sometimes, after they had been intimate, he would say things that warmed her heart. "What a romantic heart you have Abe. I pray you've saved room in there for me," she had just finished saying the words, when a voice behind her spoke.

"Don't hold your breath, honey," Sari muttered.

Startled, Keturah swung around to look into the disapproving glare of her step mother Sari Jaymes. "I, um, I," at a loss for what to say to the woman, she fumbled over her words.

Looking her up and down, Sari gave a disapproving shake of her head. "Abe, Abe, hmmm, what a mess you have made for me," she sighed. "The next time you're summoned to this office, please try and wear something more appropriate. After all, if you're going to try and play the part of a woman with class, do everyone a favor and at least dress the part," she said distastefully, as she again, assessed Keturah from head to toe. Then, with a roll of her eyes, she twisted her lips into a snarl before speaking again, "Let's go, ladies. We need to get this meeting started."

It was only then that Keturah realized Sari was not alone, but had her daughter, Tippany, Rebekah, and a couple of other women who she didn't know, but by the smirks on their faces, she knew that they concurred with Sari that she was beneath Abraham's caliber.

Keturah always prided herself in being able to see the good in everyone and never charged hatefulness to anyone, but this woman put the 'H' in hateful. And, she was good at it. How her dad could ever be married to a woman like her was beyond comprehension, and from what she gathered, her children were just like her. Just then, Tippany reached out, linked arms with her, and pulled her along.

"Don't let Sari Sourpuss get to you," she whispered. *Okay, Lord. Maybe all of the woman's children aren't so bad.* Giving a nervous smile, she allowed herself to be pulled forward. "I hope you don't allow Mother's bad attitude to make you look at the rest of us in a negative way," Tippany offered.

Shrugging her shoulders, Keturah lowered her gaze. "I think God wants us to see the good in everyone, but with some, it's more of a challenge than with others," Keturah confessed.

With an unladylike snort, Tippany laughed. "You ain't never lied!" She chuckled again, causing Keturah to relax a little and laugh as well.

"Tippany, this is no time for you to be engaged with inconsequential things," Sari said.

Keturah knew immediately, that she was the *thing* that Sari was referring to, as did everyone else. To her surprise, Tippany spoke up in her defense.

"I think making sure the CEO's new bride feels at home in his company is definitely not inconsequential, Mother."

"And I agree," came Abraham's deep tenor.

Sari doesn't have to like my choice in a wife, but she will respect her, Abraham thought, as he gave Sari a challenging glare. After which, she gave him one right back. She was a tough old bird and he was certain that she likely didn't have a caring bone in her dried-up body, but had more than enough spunk and attitude, to keep him hopping.

While still in the Caribbean, he had stressed his point for Sari to ease up, and give his new wife some slack; especially, seeing that Keturah was Sari's late husband's daughter; which made Sari her stepmom. *Well, that went over like a lead balloon,* he thought remembering Sari's words.

"Kedron's bastard is nothing to me."

Her coldness made him cringe. He was only glad that Keturah had already left the room. They had a not-so pleasant chat afterwards that still had his head reeling.

Finally, he pulled out the only trump card he had in his arsenal. Just the mention of scandal had her shut her big mouth. And he would use it, if necessary. She must have read it in his face, for suddenly her eyes dropped. Abraham, up by two; Sari, zilch.

It was the pull on his arms that caused his focus to leave his Aunt Sari and look down. Those eyes, those sparkling diamonds encased in such a lovely face. "Hi, sweetheart," he said softly, caught off guard at how much she reminded him of Sarah.

"Hi, Abe" she breathed, while standing on tiptoes to kiss him. "I've missed you."

"Don't tell me, Baby, show..." he caught himself. What was he doing? So often he'd say that phrase to Sarah. *Don't tell me Baby, show me.*

Yes, he wanted his relationship with Keturah to look authentic before his employees, but he was taking things too far.

"Show you what?" Keturah asked, a small smile on her face, as if she was aware of what he was going to say next.

"Show me what you've been up to these past couple of days without me," he said in controlled voice. Seeing the confusion, then disappointment in her brow, he kissed her gently on the forehead.

"That'll have to wait. I've called her here for a reason. Do whatever else, on your own time," Sari barked.

Aunt Sari had always been abrasive with everyone, including him. But to do so in front of his staff; this time, she'd pushed him too far.

"On the contrary, Sari, since this is my company, I decide what takes precedent and what doesn't. So, for whatever reason you need my wife, it will take place after she leaves my office. Is that clear?" he said curtly, before extending his hand towards his wife, which she immediately took.

"Well, in that case, your holiness, take all the time you need. After all, we're just your hired help!" Sari reared back at him in challenge.

The tension in the foyer was tangible. He had always backed down, not wanting to disrupt the peace within the office, but Abe had had enough of her nastiness and refused to allow her to get away with it a moment longer.

"I suggest if you want to continue being employed here, Aunt Sari, you'd better watch your tone with me." He could feel himself taking a step towards her direction, when a soft touch on his arm distracted him. Keturah's pleading eyes came into view.

"Come on, Honey. It's okay. Why don't you show me your office?" she asked quietly.

Other employees had already scattered, as the commotion in the foyer had intensified. Only Isaac and Avery had come out of their offices to see what was happening. But, he didn't care. He was tired of being questioned. Today, he was going to squash it and them, if he had to.

"What has gotten into you, Abraham?" Sari said quietly, looking at him in astonishment.

Yes, what has gotten into you? A still, quiet voice within him inquired.

It was as if her voice spoke to him. Looking up, his eyes immediately locked with the portrait of Sarah's. They seemed to come to life and were glaring at him. He needed to get out of there fast. "Keturah, go with Sari and then stop by my office when you're through," he said abruptly, before walking away, leaving everyone, including Keturah, standing there in wonderment.

"Lord, what's happening to me?" he spoke out, in the privacy of his office, while trying to relax the tension building in his shoulders.

It bothered him that he'd lost control of himself in front of his staff. He had always prided himself on remaining level-headed, no matter how intense a negotiation or disagreement got.

He always wanted his staff to feel they worked in a stress-free environment; it was good for morale and it helped retain good employees. But lately, he hated coming to work, and he knew that he was the cause for the mounting tension in the workplace. Just last week, he snapped at Avery and Isaac for some offhanded remark that normally wouldn't have caught his radar.

Lord, why are you so distant? The deafening of sound of silence greeted his ears. *Had the Lord forsaken him as well?* The open communication he had enjoyed with God over the years had taken a severe beating the last couple of months. A war had begun brewing in his heart, since seeing Ishmael.

He saw his eldest son, all grown up, in business for himself and now engaged to be married. Yet, Abe knew, as his father, he hadn't done a single thing to help him, and it really hurt. Sending Ishmael away, all those years ago, was the only time he remembered God siding with Sarah; the only time he felt in his heart, that he'd made a huge mistake.

Looking at the portrait of him and Sarah hanging over his mantel, his jaw clenched, as the same anger began encroaching on him. He had forgiven her years ago, had even seen the wisdom in separating his boys, but it didn't stop the hurt. It didn't stop the heaviness in his heart, knowing he had another son of whose life he wasn't a part. He didn't dwell on past mistakes or live with a lot of regret, but Ishmael's absence was the one thing that made him wonder, *what if?*

A tap on his office door made his thoughts snap back to the present. He really wasn't ready for a confrontation with anyone, but he needed to get his head out of the clouds and deal with the reality at hand, "Come in," he commanded from his desk.

"Wow, your office is amazing!"

At the sound of Keturah's voice, Abraham's head snapped up and a hint of a smile began touching the corners of his lips. What was it about this woman that seemed to instantaneously lighten his mood? Getting up, he moved towards her, "I forgot you hadn't been in here yet," he said casually, as he took her hands and pulled her in for a quick kiss that he allowed to linger.

"So, this is where you do all your magic." Her eyes twinkled as she twirled her arms around in the air like a fairy with a magic wand. "Tell me, oh great and powerful one, what do you have stirring on the horizon today?"

"Nothing very elaborate, my dear. The best that I can do is conjuring us up some lunch," he smiled, reaching for his office phone.

Placing a quick hand over his, she tilted her head until she was in his line of vision and then pouted, "Aww, such a waste of your mighty powers on such an insignificant task. Maybe with the right incentive…" she placed a soft kiss on his chin, then on his cheek and then closer to the side of his mouth, "maybe you might conjure up enough strength to think of something else," she said laughing as his eyebrows shot up acknowledging her intentions.

"Keturah Taylor, you are a naughty one. What am I going to do with you?" he said, as he got up from his seated position and walked away from her. He went to his office door, looked back at her, smiled, and locked it.

"A skilled businessman like yourself, who's handled hundreds of mergers, I'm sure you'll figure out something," she sighed contentedly, as he encased her waist in his strong arms and kissed her deeply.

An hour later, they lay in each other's arms, looking at the skyline in peaceable silence.

"I'm going to have to visit your office more often. I like your lunch options," she giggled.

"You are a distraction I could definitely get used to. Mind you, I'd never get anything done, and the company would likely go under, but I'd definitely be in a good mood," he chuckled.

"You are in a better mood, Abe? You had me a little worried earlier. I hate it when you get so worked-up," she said with concern in her eyes.

"Don't worry about me. You're the one I'm concerned about."

"Why?" she said perplexed.

"Why?" he gave her an incredulous look, "because of Aunt Sari's attitude towards you. She doesn't have to like the fact that we're married, but she sure better respect the fact you're my wife and treat you courteously; especially in front of my staff," he said, raising his voice.

"Abe, I've come to accept the fact that Sari Jaymes will never accept me. In her eyes, I'll always be nothing more than Kedron's bast...."

"Don't say it, Keturah. Don't you dare say it," Abraham said tersely, placing his hand to her lips, "that is not what you are. You are fearfully and wonderful made. God made no mistake when he created you." He held her tightly in his embrace, as if trying to channel strength into her frame.

He hated that word…bastard. Sari had used it more than once when referring to Ishmael. It was an ugly word. He remembered once, in the heat of an argument, Sarah had called Ishmael that: it was the first and last time. Never had he thought of his beautiful wife as ugly, until that moment. Normally, they never parted angry - until that day. It took a long time before things were right between them. He even suspected that it was part of the reason she was so desperate to have another child; to replace the one she had him send away. He rubbed his eyes. So much pain could have been avoided if he would've accepted God's plan.

"Abraham, I know you mean well, but Sari will never see me in any other way. My mother had an affair with her husband. She interfered in their marriage. I can't imagine the hurt that must have caused. Then they had me, a constant reminder of the betrayal," Keturah took a deep breath and let it out slowly shaking her head in sorrow. "It's not a thing a woman gets over quickly; if ever."

"You don't know Sari Jaymes like I do. She probably drove your dad to it, she can be a very…" Abraham searched for the words he wanted to say without being too harsh, "…difficult person," he stated, while feeling that no word could adequately describe his Sarah's favorite aunt. Yet, in her defense, she had taken good care of Sarah and Isaac, any time he went out of town on business.

He knew Kedron and Sari's relationship was different and that his involvement with other women was well-known. They had a complex union.

"My father made vows to stay true to one woman and he should've kept his word. It wasn't right for him to look for love or affection outside of his marriage. He made a covenant before God and his wife; he should not have broken it," Keturah huffed as she fumbled to button up her shirt.

"There was more to it than that, Keturah," Abraham said abruptly as he stood up, straightening out his own shirt and tucking the tails in his pants. He needed this conversation to end, before his own guilt got the better of him.

"No. When people make a commitment before God, they need to stick it out, to work it out, for better or worse. I realize Sari is difficult, downright mean at times, but was she always like that? Maybe, if my dad would have remained faithful; no matter what, things would be different."

"Keturah, you're an idealist and I admire that. But, Honey, real life has a way of challenging those values. And honestly, they don't always make it in the real world," he said bluntly.

"I realize you think I'm young and naive, but Abraham, did you ever stop and think about the ripple effect of my dad's sin? How his indiscretion has impacted so many others? Sin starts off tiny, but it grows up and becomes an ugly, destructive monster."

Keturah had no idea, but her words were hitting home in a major way. He never liked playing out what could have, should have or would have happened if he'd just stood his ground to Sarah's proposition; told her, no, he wouldn't sleep with Hagan and they would trust God for a child or remain childless.

Looking back, he remembered the expression on Sarah's face when he finally conceded and told her he'd do what she asked. It wasn't one of sheer delight. No, thinking back, her face looked pained. At the time, he attributed it to the strain of the whole situation surrounding her infertile condition. But now, thinking back, could it have been because he had let her down?

What woman really wants her husband to sleep with another woman? He thought.

"Abraham, did you hear what I said?

A small hand was on his shoulder, as his mind drifted back to the present. "I'm sorry, Keturah, I…forgot I had a meeting to attend this afternoon and I'm already running behind. Why don't we shelve this discussion for another time, okay?"

He kissed her quickly, before she could respond. Grabbing his suit coat and briefcase, he headed towards the door.

"Will I see you tonight?" she asked in a small voice.

"Can't really say, I'll call you," he turned to look back at her and ironically, she was standing right in front of his mantle where Sarah's portrait hung. It was unnerving how they both were looking at him with the same hurt, noticeable within their gazes.

He exited the door feeling the shame of disappointing both of his wives.

***

"I've been dealing with Abraham with kid's gloves out of respect for my Sarah. But if he thinks that now that she's dead and gone, that he's going to let his hormones overtake his good sense and let that little tramp muscle-in on my territory, he's in for one rude awaking."

Sari Jaymes twisted in the backseat of the limo as her driver took her downtown. She wouldn't be outdone by that little hussy. It burned her to no end, that as hard as she worked to keep Kedron's indiscretions at bay that now instead of enjoying the fruits of her labor, she had to be dealing with his screw-ups.

"Kedron, Abraham and especially Emory are all conspiring against me and I'm won't have it." She smacked her hand on the leather seat. A snicker from the opposite side made her turn.

"Look at the great and mighty Sari Jaymes, already scheming on how to set things in her favor, no matter who she has to climb over to do it," came the sarcastic remark from her daughter, Tippany, who had been relatively quiet until now.

Sari gave her daughter a dismissive look and turned her head again towards the window.

"Mother, did it ever occur to you that maybe you shouldn't interfere in other people's lives without their permission? I mean everyone has the right to live the way they please."

Tippany knew that pleading with her was useless, but she owed it to the memory of Sarah to at least try. Nothing but silence came from the other side of the car; it was as if there was an abyss separating them, instead of a foot of leather seating. She and her mom rarely agreed on anything these days, but she wanted her relationship with her mom to get better. When Sarah was alive, her mom didn't pay much attention to her. She found herself doing all types of crazy things, even eloping at nineteen, to get her mom's attention. Sari had someone pay-off her husband and Tippany found herself being collected and sent out of the country to a private girls' school until she turned twenty-two. By the time she'd returned, Sarah was so sick Tippany didn't have time to act out...didn't want to. Now that her mother's prodigy was gone, suddenly she gained her mom's attention; but for all the wrong reasons.

Never in a million years did she believe her mom would try and marry her off to one of her business associates in order to gain more influence in a town she practically owned. But she had. When she found out, she was disgusted and told her mom. Tippany closed her eyes as the memory of her mom's callous words resounded in her ears, "I have invested in your education, sent you to the best finishing schools in the country. All for what? So you can throw yourself at the first man who looks at you and says you're pretty? Please! I've picked a man for you who has the right political affiliations and social connections. It's time you start contributing to this family."

Sari banged her hand on the seat cushion, to gain her daughter's attention. "Tippany! Lord, sometimes I wonder if you're a Jaymes at all, with your foolish sentiments."

Sari cut her eyes at her daughter; a look of sheer disgust masking her features. "You sit there trying to lecture me about interfering in others' lives, but there wasn't a day you didn't benefit from my so-called interference. Kedron's little princess, you were such a spoiled child. Now my Sarah, she was a real lady. Under my tutelage she optimized what a true Jaymes could become. She had everything because she listened to me. Followed my instructions and look at where she is today."

"Oh, please, Mother! Sarah is dead because of your constant interference." Before she could finish her sentence, a open hand slammed into her cheek. Stunned, Tippany held her hand to the side of her stinging face, shock that her mom had raised her hand and slapped her.

"Shut up! Shut your lying mouth right now!" Sari bellowed. "Sarah was everything to me. Everything! She was like my own child more than you ever were," she glared at Tippany. "She had everything, including the love of her man, and if she would have just listened, nothing could have stopped us!" Sari said with bitterness in her voice that she could not disguise.

Still holding her hand to her stinging cheek, Tippany took a long, hard look at the aging matriarch. Deep embedded lines marked the contours of her mother's face.

Her mother sat there with loathing in her eyes, but she long ceased from being any type of mother figure to Tippany. For years, Tippany kept the peace for her father's sake, but now with him gone...there was no need to continue the farce. Any relationship she hoped to develop with her mom was pointless. She felt sorry for the woman who had made every day of her life miserable, from sun up to sun down. Looking at her now, she felt sadness that Sari Jaymes was destined to die bitter and alone.

"You never appreciated the lengths that I stooped to keep you from being trash like Keturah, to keep her and that whore of a mother away from what rightfully belongs to us. You should be glad I spared you from that type of life and kept you living as well

as you do. Just where do you think you'd be for that matter? Where would any of you be if I had not made things happen to protect what rightfully belonged to us?

"What are you talking about?" Tippany gave a hard stare at her mom.

"You owe me, Tippany. Just remember that. Cream always rises to the top, and if you don't start getting on board with this family, you're going to find yourself in the gutter, just like Keturah.

CHAPTER TWENTY-THREE

"Ouch!" Keturah flinched as she stubbed her toe on the concrete walkway. She was doing her best to keep up with her husband and his business associates, but she was having a time of it. Maybe wearing four-inch stilettos wasn't the best walking gear she could have come up with, but they sure looked cute with her outfit, not that Abraham had taken much notice. His mind had been on this project for weeks. She could have strutted around buck-naked the entire time and he wouldn't have noticed.

Letting out a frustrated sigh, she continued to lag behind. In all fairness to Abraham, he told her from the start that it wouldn't be a pleasure trip; that the project was at a critical point and he wouldn't be good company for her. "He could at least slow down," she muttered, as she slowed her pace even more when her heel hit an uneven part of the side walk. When she finally looked up, she had lost sight of him in a sea of heads.

"He's gone...he left me. He probably doesn't even know that I'm not with him!" she fumed. *Wow! So, this is marriage*, Keturah thought despondently. Just thinking of all the times, she and her girlfriends had wasted on the phone talking about their favorite subject, "When I get married." What a laugh!

"Boy, wait until they find out that once you get married, you still have more sex in your head than you do in bed," Keturah chuckled to herself about how delusional they had been about what really goes on in marriage.

She used to hate when her married friends would tell her, *"Giiiirlll! If you knew what I knew, you'd thank God, you're still single. Because, honey, when you get married it's more than a notion."* Keturah always thought those dumb bunnies were obviously not doing something right.

"Guess who the dumb bunny is now?" she mumbled to herself, trying to gaze through the sea of faces, to catch a glimpse of the one face she had come to love. Although right now, she was deeply angry that he suggested walking to the restaurant. "It's only a couple of blocks," she mimicked. Then, there it was; his closed shaven salt and pepper head just a few feet away. Heaving a sigh of relief, Keturah smiled despite her aching feet. She was not lost; Abraham was a few feet ahead of her, still caught up in business- talk with his sons and other colleagues, as they maneuvered their way through the crowded street. Boy, it seemed like everyone was out today.

Chicago was not only the windy city, but a crowded one too. Keturah held on tight to her small clutch that matched the shoes that were punishing her feet every step she took on the hard pavement. Looking up to make sure Abraham was still in sight, Keturah felt her heel suddenly twist beneath her, causing her to stumble forward. Her stockinged foot now lay bare on the cold, hard, grimy ground.

"Jesus, keep me near the cross," Keturah muttered, as she looked around for her shoe, while being jostled by the crowd.

"There it is!" she shouted, as she hobbled her way over to her missing shoe, only to find to her dismay, that the heel was firmly wedged in-between the bars of a heating grate. Keturah sighed heavily. She should have stayed in the hotel. No, she shouldn't have insisted that Abraham bring her in the first place. It was her own dumb insecurities that made her want to be here, when he clearly told her that basically, she'd only be in the way.

The ground was getting cold and although the coldness to her throbbing foot felt good in the beginning, it was now beginning to go numb. She needed to retrieve her shoe and catch up to Abraham and company. She felt like a fish out of water in the big city. Abraham loved this. It was like an adrenaline rush; it made him come alive, her, not so much.

Keturah, bending down, examined the plight of her poor shoe. She pulled the shoe up slightly, attempting to release the heel with minimal damage, but with no luck. After her fifth attempt with no success, Keturah knew she would have to break her precious heel to get the shoe unstuck. That wasn't so bad, at least it could be fixed. Getting back to the hotel; however, that was going to be more of a challenge.

Please God, let Abraham be coming back down the street, Keturah pleaded silently, as she stood up to look for the one face in all of Chicago she knew. But that was not to be. Keturah's heart dropped, "He's probably at the restaurant by now," Keturah said tersely, as she sighed aloud, dreading having to break her heel but even more, walking back to the hotel with only the sheerest of nylon protecting her feet. The thought was enough to make her cry, which no one would notice since the wind-chilled air was causing her eyes to water anyway.

"Women need to learn how to wear sensible shoes," a male voice spoke from behind her.

Startled, Keturah quickly turned towards the voice, surprised to find Parson smiling down at her.

"Parson, what are you doing here?" Never in a million years had she expected to run into him.

Looking at her predicament, he shook his head and chuckled, "My dear, you do find yourself in the oddest dilemmas."

"Oh, hush up and help me get my shoe out of this grate," she fussed good-naturedly, while trying to balance herself on one foot. He had appeared out of nowhere, but God knows she was glad to see him!

"Well, since you asked so nicely," he gave her an assessing gaze, then shook his head and looked down at her stuck shoe. "You've got this thing wedged in there pretty good. I don't think it's going to come out without breaking the heel," he reasoned.

"But these are my most comfortable heels and they go with everything," she whined.

"I don't think the grate cares!" he groused, while trying to jiggle the heel loose.

A popping sound indicated that indeed, the heel broke and dropped off down into the grate, as the rest of the shoe came free.

Lifting the broken shoe, he looked at it, then at her and shrugged his shoulders, "Sorry," he said, handing it over.

Looking at the battered shoe she huffed, "Now, what am I going to do?" she said, holding on to Parson's arm while still trying to maintain her balance. "I don't know where Aaa...uhh, where my uncle went and I don't want to walk back to the hotel in my bare feet on the cold cement." Before she could say another word, she felt her feet leaving the ground, "Ohh, my goodness, Parson...w-what are you doing!"

"You mean to tell me your uncle left you here like this?" he said forcefully, as he swung her up in his arms.

"He didn't know my heel got stuck in this old stupid grate. He was walking ahead of me and I couldn't keep up," she did her best to defend her *uncle* who was in fact Abraham, but it sounded weak; even to her.

"Well, to show you that chivalry isn't dead, I'll carry you back to your hotel. So where are you staying?" He smiled, amused at her mortified look.

"Parson, put me down this instant!" she insisted, trying not to meet the curious glances of onlookers. "Seriously, Parson, put me down."

"Do you really want me to put your delicate feet on this mucus infested sidewalk? God only knows what types of body fluids are lurking on this ground, but if you feel that that thin pantyhose, you're wearing are enough of a barrier between your feet and the pavement, then I'll...." he teased, while pretending to place her on her feet.

"No, Parson. Wait!" Keturah squawked, "Okay, point taken." she wrinkled her nose, looking at the soiled sidewalk.

"You sure?"

"Positive!" she smirked at him.

"Then, let us proceed, my lady. Where to?" he said in an English accent and proceeded to carry her down the sidewalk, to the smiles of onlookers.

"To the Ritz Hilton my good man," she chuckled. "Oh, this is so embarrassing. I don't know how I keep getting myself in these crazy situations."

"The Ritz? Well ain't we fancy," his eyebrows arched. "Anyway Keturah, crazy just seems to be able to find you," he chuckled, as she swatted him on his arm. "Hey, you never answered my question. What are you doing here?"

Not sure it was wise to reveal her marriage to Abraham just yet, she decided to keep that information to herself. "Oh, my uncle and some of his associates had some business to attend to, so I decided to tag along. I was going to fly back home this afternoon, after we had lunch." It wasn't a complete lie, but it wasn't the truth either. In the worst way, she wanted to tell Parson everything. But right now, Abraham wanted to keep a low profile. She wasn't a gold-digger like his family had said and she hadn't sought out Abraham; it was quite the opposite.

"Hey, why don't you come to the charity ball tonight? We could make some connections; maybe even raise a few bucks for the school?" he said enthusiastically.

"I can't!" she stated quickly, "I have to catch my flight back home." Finally, something she didn't have to lie about.

"I drove up here, I can drive you back," Parson said easily.

"But I've already checked out of my room. I-I won't have a place to stay." She said frantically.

"No worries. I have an adjoining suite. I'm sure, I can stay with Townsend for the night, and you can stay in my room," he said in a matter of fact tone. "It's settled then. We'll drive back in the morning; give us a chance to catch up on things," he said, as the sliding glass doors of the hotel opened and he walked inside, still carrying her in his arms. "Why don't you grab another pair of shoes and we'll go shopping for a gown."

"Parson, I don't know about this? Maybe I should just grab my bags and go home," she hesitated. Part of her really wanted to stay.

"You know, I'm not going to let you go until you agree. And if I have to throw you over my shoulder, it will be quite a scene," he jested, juggling her in his arms.

"Parson! Parson, don't you dare! Alright, I'll go! Now, put me down," she stifled a laugh as she felt her feet hitting the floor. "I'll need to go to the concierge's desk and get my bags."

"Well, get to getting, woman. It's going to take a lot of work to get you looking good enough to accompany a man of my status."

Shaking her head, she hobbled to the concierge's desk, unaware of several pairs of eyes watching her retreating form.

***

"You make me wish that there was more than friendship going on between us, Ms. Birch," Parson grinned as he twirled her once more on the dance floor. Keturah smiled up at him as they swayed to the music.

So far, the night was going off without a hitch. Parson had introduced her to anyone who was of influence or importance. She had made several promising contacts and should've felt great, but she just couldn't shake this feeling that someone was watching her.

Feeling increasingly uneasy as the night stretched on, she decided to fake a headache and leave early. So, with plan in mind, she went in search of Parson. Before she could find him though, a hand touched her shoulder.

"May I have this dance?"

Startled by the oddly familiar male tenor behind her, she turned around and immediately her heartbeat quickened as blue eyes like her husband's, bore into hers. At a loss for what to say to Abraham's eldest son, she just stared back at him.

"Shall we dance Mrs. Taylor, or should I call you, Mom?" he said in a patronizing tone.

"W-well, I guess we can dance... and you can call me Keturah," she stammered, as he pulled her into his arms.

They swayed to the music in silence, for what seemed like forever. This was just as well, because she didn't know what to say to her step-son.

"So, you're my new step mom. Interesting," he said giving her an appraising look. Where'd they say Dad found you? College campus? Freshman dorm or something or other?" he chuckled.

Catching the condescending tone in his voice, she bristled. She refused to be the butt of anyone's joke. "Thank you for the lovely dance, Mr. Taylor. Have a nice evening." She gave a forced smile and walked off the dance floor, looking for Parson.

"I wouldn't go out that way, Mom. Dad has had his eye on you all night, and I can tell you he's not a happy man: seeing you here, looking the way you do, dancing with all these men, so soon after the honeymoon," he said, a hint of sarcasm in his voice.

Seeing herself through Ishmael's eyes made her feel dirty and exposed; as if she was some type of seductress and not doing her job as a fundraiser for her school. Folding her arms around her waist to shield herself from his intense gaze, she walked towards the balcony for some much- needed fresh air.

When warm hands touched her shoulders, Keturah jumped, alarmed. She turned around, just in time to see Ishmael advancing. At the same time, a young woman stepped out of the shadows.

"Ishmael! What are you doing and who is *she*?" an olive complexioned woman, with bronze-colored, angry eyes and a thick Mediterranean accent spoke, her long, raven black hair hanging in shiny waves to her waist. Her full mouth turned down into a frown. She quickly placed a possessive hand on Ishmael's arm and gave her a hard glare.

"Now, now, retract your claws, love. I was just greeting my new step-mother." he said, placing his arm around the woman. He gave a playful tweak to her nose. "Mrs. Keturah Taylor, may I introduce to you to my fiancée, Marlana Simone. Darling, this is Keturah Taylor, our new stepmom," he said with a smirk.

Apparently, his fiancée caught his demeaning tone, because her face relaxed and her gaze suddenly turned from angry to contemptuous.

"Stop teasing me, Mael. Why, she doesn't look much older that my baby sister, Tallya. Seriously, who is this woman?" she gave a demure laugh, as she snuggled into his shoulder. With her nose, she nuzzled the lobe of his ear.

They were trying to humiliate her and it was working. She felt like she was in an alley-fight, trying to defend her identity and was losing badly. She'd had enough; when she found Parson, she wouldn't have to fake a headache. Without a word, she turned to go, then stopped suddenly, as Isaac blocked her path.

"Wow, been in the country for less than an hour and big brother's already trying to move in on another man's wife. Typical, like mother, like son," Isaac charged.

All eyes turned, just in time to see Isaac and Rebecca come into view. Abraham and Sari were trailing behind.

"What in heaven's name is she doing here, Abraham?" Sari demanded. "I thought you sent her home this afternoon. This event was to show a united front for the Taylors and not to showcase your indiscretions."

"Well, well, will you look at this? The gang's all here: the favorite son and his beauty queen, not to mention, his wet nurse. Still changing my little brother's diapers, I see, Ms. Jaymes," Ishmael taunted.

"You're one to talk. Everyone knows you and your mother are practically joined at the hip," Isaac rebutted.

As the brother's bickered at each other, Keturah found herself backing away into the shadows, until she could disappear through another door. She had a mounting headache and all she could think of was getting out of there and going home, which is exactly what she planned on doing, even if she had to rent a car and drive the entire way back to North Carolina by herself. Besides, she had a lot to think about, including the fact that Abraham had lied to her saying he was sending her home because he was leaving that afternoon on another business trip. "Wow all of this just to keep me from tarnishing his family's precious reputation" she muttered while hitting her thigh in frustration. With clutch in hand she marched towards the main entrance of the party when a firm hand on her arm restrained her.

"Leaving so soon dearest?" Abraham asked.

She wouldn't turn around, didn't want to see the look on his face. "I have a headache, Abraham. So yes, I'm leaving," she said in a shaky voice.

"Oh, what a shame. You seemed to have so much energy for everyone else you danced with tonight. What? You don't have any steam left to dance with your hubby?"

His voice was pleasant enough, but Keturah could detect the malice laced in his tone.

"Quite frankly, Mr. Taylor, from what it sounds like, you never intended to dance with me in the first place, seeing that I wasn't supposed to be here," she said through gritted teeth. "Apparently a half-Jaymes isn't good enough to be seen with the likes of the Taylor clan. God forbid, I do anything more to tarnish your impeccable name," she said maliciously.

"Anything more! Sweetheart I think you've done quite enough," he said nastily. "It was bad enough to watch your boyfriend carry you in his arms through the streets of Chicago this afternoon, but then to see you here, dressed up in a revealing gown, parading yourself around the dance floor and propositioning men for money for your so-called job; that takes the cake."

The force of his words felt like a physical slap to the face, causing her to step back. Swallowing hard to keep from lashing out further, as well as keep the tears at bay, she lowered her eyes from his steely gaze.

"Fundraising for my department's scholarship program *is* my job." She said calmly willing herself not to cry. "I wasn't born with a silver spoon in my mouth like your children were. And I didn't have a dad who gave a crap about me, so I had to work and get scholarships to make it in school, Mr. Taylor. So, when I can come to events like this to raise money for the scholarship program, so some other fatherless child can go to school, I will do it, even if it makes me look to you like a whore."

"Keturah…I didn't…"

She held her hand up to stop him. "As for tarnishing your name and embarrassing your family, I will not trouble you anymore. Since Gretta is dead anyway, there is no need for you to burden yourself with Kedron's bastard any longer." She pulled off the ring, grabbed Abraham's hand and slammed it into his palm.

"Goodbye, *Mr. Taylor*. I hope your next arrangement will prove to be more to your liking." She twirled around and would have plowed into Parson, if it wasn't for Abraham's firm grip on her wrist.

"Mr. Taylor, it's good to see you again. I guess everyone is out tonight," Parson said, with a hint of uneasiness. Although his words were directed to Abraham, his eyes gave Keturah a questioning stare. When she didn't meet his gaze, he continued, "Well, I see you've found the most beautiful girl in the room. Even though she's my date, I haven't been able to get more than one dance with her the entire evening," he joked. "So how 'bout it Keturah, shall we dance?"

Keturah shut her eyes, wishing the floor would open and swallow her whole. Abraham stood there saying nothing, but he still had a firm grip on her.

Why didn't I just get on that plane this afternoon and go home! She thought, rubbing her temple with her free hand.

"Keturah are you alright?" Parson stepped towards her in concern. "Do you need to go back to the room?"

"To whose room exactly, are you referring?" Abraham finally spoke up anger evident as he looked at her.

Parson looked first to her, then to Abraham, then back at her again. "Keturah, what's going on? Am I interrupting something?"

"Just the brewing of a lovers' quarrel between the newlyweds," came Ishmael's sarcastic voice from behind, as he and the rest of the family came into view.

"Newlyweds?" Parson gushed.

"Parson... I...ahh," Keturah was at a loss for words. So many thoughts were swimming in her brain, but she didn't know how to explain this.

"Yes, newlyweds. Keturah and I were recently married, Mr. Parson," Abraham said in a controlled voice. "I'm not sure what arrangements you've made with my wife for this evening, but I'll be handling things from here on in. Now, if you'll excuse us, my wife has a headache, so she'll be turning in for the evening," he said, side-stepping Parson, with Keturah
in tow.

CHAPTER TWENTY-FOUR

He hadn't said another word to her as they left the ball room, or during the ride up in the private elevator. Surprised when he led her into his one-bedroom suite, Keturah paused at the door's entrance, while he went in, preoccupied with his phone conversation with Avery.

Her heartbeat sped up as her eyes focused on the king-sized bed in the middle of the room. Did he expect them to sleep together? She hoped not. She was tired of this charade. Things had become too complex between them.

Tonight, he did a Jekyll and Hyde on her, all in the same moment. One minute he was ashamed of her. The next, he acted like a jealous husband. The smart thing to do was to put some space between them. Seeing him end his phone call, she spoke, "Listen, Abraham. I'll stay someplace else." There, it was said.

"Like in Parson's room?" he jabbed as he pulled his suit jacket off.

Rubbing her eye sockets hard, she snatched her hands from her face and held her arms wide. "For Pete's sakes, Abraham, Parson is not, nor has he ever been, my boyfriend. And I wasn't going to be staying in his room. He had a suite with two separate rooms. He was going to stay in the room with another co-worker."

He wasn't paying attention to her, but she felt compelled to continue. "You know what. Believe whatever you want. I can get my own room!" she said arbitrarily, as she folded her arms over her chest.

"Take off your dress," he ordered, casually unbuttoning his white shirt and kicking off his shoes near the chair where he had already discarded his tuxedo jacket.

"WHAT!" Keturah's eyes bucked as she stared at him in disbelief at what he'd just asked her to do.

Looking at her over his shoulder, as he headed for the bathroom he shot back, "Stop being so dramatic, Keturah," he said walking into the bathroom leaving the door open. "It's not as if I haven't seen you before, besides hospitality is coming up to dry-clean my things. They might as well do yours."

"But I don't have anything to wear besides this dress," she said, keeping it to herself that her suitcases were likely in Parson's suite. God knows she didn't want to open that can of worms.

"Here, put this on," he said tossing her a silky piece of fabric as he came out of the bathroom dressed in running gear.

She looked at the item; it was a medium length, beautiful, green, silky nightie like she had seen in one of the boutiques the other day. She could tell by the look and feel of it that it was costly. What bothered her was why he had it.

I bet it's for Hagan. After all, Ishmael is here and normally she's not that far behind. Maybe that's why he wanted me to go home early, so he could rendezvous with her.

As images of him kissing her surfaced, her anger was rekindled. "I won't wear this," she protested, throwing it on the bed.

"Why not?" he challenged.

"I won't wear another woman's gift," she said hotly, while crossing her arms over her chest, as his eyes bore into hers.

Giving a mirthless laugh, he cocked his head to the side and looked at her intently. "So, let me get this straight: you have no problem wearing a gown that your boyfriend buys you. Yet, you protest about a nightie I saw you admiring in the store? I purchased it yesterday as a present for you." He raised an eyebrow at her.

"Oh, I didn't know you bought it for me," she said quietly, feeling foolish for her accusation.

"Who else would I buy it for, Keturah?"

Hagan's image slowly faded from her mind as she dislodged the thought. There was enough friction between them without adding her into the mix. Seeking to disperse the mounting tension in the room, she decided to call a truce. "Look, Abraham, we know all too well that you and me in a hotel room don't always bring out the best in each other. Let me just go and get another room," she said wearily.

His approach was slow but steady, his intent unclear. Backing up until she felt the end of the mattress hitting the backs of her legs, Keturah held her breath; not sure what she should do. Would he try and kiss her, maybe even make love to her? Better question was, if he tried, would she attempt to stop him?

She knew why her heart was hammering in her chest, understood why her mouth had gone dry as awareness of him and his total maleness was sending her senses into a tailspin. Closing her eyes, she knew the moment his essence invaded her personal space. Why did her pretend husband have such an effect on her?

"From what I recall, Mrs. Taylor, the last time I had you in a hotel room, you didn't seem to mind it at all," his voice had dropped to a husky whisper, his nose within inches of hers. His masculine scent mingled with his spicy cologne, caused her to lean into him like a magnet to metal. His hooded eyelids kept traveling to her nose, then to her eyes and finally remained trained on her lips. Something in her stomach quivered. She didn't understand why she struggled to resist this man so. With the vast age difference between them she thought it would be easy to stave off any advances he might make.

What she was feeling right now was nothing like what she felt in high school, or even what she thought she felt for Parson at one time. This was different. She was operating on a whole different level. It would be so easy to lean in and touch his lips with hers. His cologne was intoxicating and she felt herself becoming inebriated by it.

This is crazy! Why hold back, kiss him! Her mind screamed, after all he was her husband. Why should she hold back what comes naturally to a man and his wife? With that thought in mind, she decided to do it. She was going to take the plunge and let him know she wanted his affection. After all that had transpired between them, the hateful words, the accusations; yet, still she wanted him, wanted to be the one to initiate this intimate dance they'd been cultivating over the last couple of weeks.

She might not have his love, but tonight she would have him, and that would be enough. Standing on her tiptoes, she placed her hands on his chest to steady herself, memorized where his lips were; she closed her eyes to savor a tender kiss…a kiss that never came. Popping an eye open to see what happened, she was mortified to see a smirk on his lips.

"All I want from you tonight is that dress, Mrs. Taylor," he said, barely able to restrain the humor in his voice. Before she could protest, he quickly turned her around and unfastened the hook around her neck, undid the zipper and watched the silk material cascade down around her ankles. "Say what you want Keturah, but if I can so much as glance at you and you're willing to fall in my arms, I'd hate to think about what could have happened if you had stayed in Parson's suite tonight."

Furious at what he'd implied, but more hurt by his rejection, she kicked her shoes off, grabbed them and the dress and hurled it at his laughing head.

"Now, now, Tourie, you're too old to have temper-tantrums; but then again, maybe not," he chuckled as he bent down to pick up the dress and carried it out of the bedroom.

She rushed to the door and slammed it behind him. Insensitive jerk! She wanted to yell out, but she kept it inside. Turning around, she looked for something she could throw or tear, but the only thing her eyes landed on was the nightie.

It was too beautiful to take out her vengeance on. She needed to do something, anything, to let him know his behavior towards her wasn't okay. After all, the arrangement was a mutual thing. Plopping down on the bed, she plotted her revenge. Shutting her eyes, she thought of all the ways she could get back at him for so easily dismissing her affection. She allowed her mind to wander as she fell into a fitful night's sleep.

***

The intensifying heat in his calves, only served to make him press on even harder. The steady rhythm from the treadmill's motor was his music. The pounding of his *Nikes* on the belt, kept him in rhythm. He needed the noise to drown out his thoughts of Keturah and Abraham married.

"Keturah is married!" Parson muttered. It was a fact, not some rumor or idle office gossip, but fact. He had heard rumors around that she was seeing an older man, but the older man was always him. People had deemed them an item a long time ago, so it wasn't anything to get excited about. No one mentioned that it was someone different, but it really didn't matter because he knew she had it bad for him; or so he thought. Abraham Taylor was old enough to be her father, for pity's sake. How could she marry him? Was she a gold-digger! No, she wasn't like that. Then, maybe for the sex!

The thought made him nearly break his finger jabbing the button to increase his speed on the treadmill. Keturah having sex…with him! The thought made him want to hurl his evening meal. The man was practically sixty-years old, wasn't he? What was she thinking? Panting harder now that he'd increased his speed, he thought of how much time he wasted pursuing his last love-interest. She was so not worth his time.

Knowing that Keturah was still holding a torch for him, he decided to play the field a little longer. After all, he always thought Keturah would be waiting in the wings when he decided to settle down.

Now, he wished he had taken her feelings into consideration. *If she would've just talked to me, I could've talked her into marrying me.* He thought, feeling out-of-sorts, and now tenser than ever. Hitting the *stop* button, he pulled his towel from the arm of the treadmill and buried his sweaty face in it. This wasn't working. He needed fresh air. Maybe a walk outside would do him some good.

Turning around, he stopped dead, shocked to see Abraham and another man lifting weights. *God, get me out of here, quick.* He was in no mood to talk with anyone, especially not this man. They hadn't spotted him, so he decided to slide out as quietly as possible, because at that moment, if he got into a confrontation, he'd say something he and the university might live to regret. As if fate would have it, Abraham looked up and caught his eye before he could get to the exit.

"Carlton Parson, isn't it?"

Crap! Putting on a fake smile he stopped, "Mr. Taylor," he responded with a wave of his hand.

"Got a minute?" Abraham asked.

Watching the man stand up, he didn't look like any sixty-year-old he'd ever seen. Abe had donned a black sweatshirt and matching workout shorts that fit him to a tee. Both his arms and legs looked massive, and there wasn't a piece of flab anywhere on his body. He had to admit, the man was in great shape and his physique was impressive at any age. "Sure, what can I do for you, Mr. Taylor?

"You can explain to me the relationship between you and my wife."

Wow! That was direct. Parson thought but said to Abraham, "I don't think I understand what you mean," He said hesitantly, wishing he could dodge his question.

"Then, let me be clear. Are you dating my wife?" he stood facing Parson steely-eyed, without cracking a smile.

Very direct, indeed. "No, Mr. Taylor, I'm not. Keturah is my colleague. That's all," Parson began feeling his own tension mounting and tried to remain calm.

"Really?"

"Really!" Parson stated, a little too forcefully.

"So, you normally carry all your colleagues through the streets of Chicago in your arms or refer to them as dates on work related events?" he challenged.

"No, not usually," Parson stated, a hint of sarcasm in his tone. Abraham was pushing his buttons big-time, and for some reason, Parson had a feeling Abraham knew it.

"So, Keturah is the exception? Which leads me back to the original question: what exactly is your relationship with my wife?" He said folding his massive arms.

"Let me make *myself* clear, Mr. Taylor. What I mean is that normally, my colleagues don't get the heel of their shoe stuck in a street grate, and since whoever was with her, left her there stranded, I thought it was the polite thing to do to assist. When Keturah's heel broke, I thought, instead of letting her walk barefoot on the nasty streets, I would carry her back to the hotel. Now, to answer your second question, I've always considered Keturah like a kid sister to me," *Forgive me Lord, for lying.* We're always joking around at these events about being each other's date to keep unwanted admirers at bay. As you already know, your wife is a very beautiful woman and when men become too interested or friendly, I'm always her designated date. Keturah doesn't know how attractive she is and when guys approach her, she doesn't always know how to turn them down. So, to keep her out of uncomfortable situations, I'm her buffer," Parson said in a cool tone.

"Well Parson, I appreciate your concern for *my* wife's welfare, but your services are no longer required. If she needs protection, I'll hire bodyguards. If she needs to be carried anywhere, my driver will be the one to do it, and if she needs a low-cut dress, I'll be the one to purchase it. Are we clear?"

Parson knew this was a power-play and if funding for the department project wasn't riding on this, he would say a few choice words to the high and mighty Abraham Taylor. But for now, he would take the low road.

Swallowing the lump tightening in his throat, he looked Abraham squarely in the eyes, "As you said, Mr. Taylor, she is *your* wife." Parson fisted his hands to his side. "It's getting late and I have a long drive ahead of me tomorrow. If there's nothing else, I'll be leaving. Have a nice evening," he said in a tight voice, then turned and opened the door and stepped out; not waiting for a reply. Forget waiting for morning. He was so steamed, he wouldn't be sleeping any time soon so, he might as well pack his things and head out now. Hopefully, the cool air would calm his raging thoughts and hormones.

***

It was nearly three in the morning when Keturah heard the bedroom door open. She shut her eyes tightly, as she pretended to be sound asleep. Soon, she felt the mattress dip under his weight as he lay down beside her.

"Keturah?"

She remained silent and became steamed when she heard him chuckle, then sigh before speaking again.

"Keturah, I know you're awake because you're not snoring."

She quickly flipped around with that remark, "I do not snore!" she said emphatically, before flopping back on her other side.

"How do you know if you snore or not if you're asleep?" he raised a questioning brow at her.

"I don't snore!" she said snappily.

"Fine, you don't snore! Can you please turn around so I can talk to your face, and not the back of your head?"

"I can hear you."

"Yeah, I know, but I'd still like to look at your beautiful face when I'm talking to you." He placed his hand on her shoulder, loving the way her skin sent a jolt of electricity down his arm. Resisting this woman was not in the plan tonight.

"You think I'm beautiful?" she said in a small voice. That got him smiling. One thing he liked about Keturah was her

innocence and unawareness of her own charm. It was maddening and endearing at the same time. It's what made him go all crazy, when Parson started invading what he considered, private territory. He had learned the hard way that not protecting his wife could cost him.

Case in point, was the time he allowed Sarah to stay overseas too long with one of his business associates, who ended up trying to seduce her. It was also during that time, when he got Hagan pregnant.

Shaking his head, he gazed at the back of Keturah's head and began to stroke her long hair. He would never allow Keturah to be exposed to another man's charms; he didn't care how harmless things between her and Parson seemed to be. Clearing his mind and throat, he spoke, "Of course, I think you're beautiful. So, does any man with eyes in his head."

"What's beautiful about me?" she said, flipping on her back and staring at the ceiling.

He was amazed that she didn't know how lovely she was, but that was no surprise. She didn't have anyone to lavish love on her; tell her from a man's perspective how desirable she was. Kedron hadn't built her up. He wasn't around to do much of anything. Emory was likely too busy building his successful career to make a dent in the distorted self-image she was suffering from. That left him.

"Well, you have gorgeous eyes, and the longest eyelashes I've ever seen," he moved his head closer to hers and spoke in her ear. "Then you have this long, ink-black hair that smells like Jasmine. And I can't get enough of your velvety soft, kissable skin." Kissing her shoulder, then her neck, then the tip of her nose; now that she was looking at him, he finished, "and then there's your mouth, with lips so soft that I lose all concentration when you smile at me." She gave him a shy smile as he closed in for a kiss. If he said he hadn't intended to make love to Keturah, he would've been lying. In fact, it was his intention to bend her to his will; to possess her so deeply that no other man could ever take his place. She was his for the next six to nine months and he was going to enjoy every minute of it. He'd think about the consequences of his actions later, but for now, he was content in holding onto his woman all night, he determined while searching for the straps of her nightie and pulled them off her shoulders, as she eagerly responded to his kisses. Just before dawn, as they lay in each other's arms, spent; he heard her soft voice speak.

"I love you, Abraham. I love you so very much," she sighed with contentment.
Shutting his eyes, he could feel his pulse speed up with excitement, and then plummet in despair, now he had to face the consequences of his actions.

She loved him, but he could never love her back. His heart beat only for Sarah, and with her gone, there was only a hole left where his heart used to be. Trying to explain this would be next to impossible, so, he wouldn't. He would do what he was best at doing. He'd leave town on business and only pray her foolish notion of loving him would soon fade with his extended absence.

Chapter Twenty-Five

Waking up alone in her hotel room, wasn't the way she thought her morning would begin. For starters, she expected to wake up to a very exhausted but extremely satisfied husband. She was crushed to discover he was gone. He left her wedding ring on top of a note on the night stand on her side of the bed, but the letter was so vague, she didn't know where he was or when he intended on returning. Her suitcase was in the foyer of their suite, along with a plane ticket that had her flying out later that evening. *He's truly gone,* she thought.

After such a wonderful, magical night, he up and left without even saying goodbye? It was only nine in the morning; maybe she could still catch a ride with Parson. At least the long drive home would give her a chance to explain, if that were possible, her relationship with Abraham. Dialing his room number and waiting for his response, she got nothing. She thought to herself, *maybe he's checking out. I better run down and see if I can catch him.*

Dressing quickly, she pulled on a pair of jeans and a semi-wrinkled shirt and made a mad dash for the elevator. Once on his floor, she ran quickly to his room, only to see maid-service coming out of his door. *I'm too late!* she thought, but decided to ask the maid anyway.

"Did the gentleman in this room check out already?" she asked.

"Yes, Ma'am. He has."

"Thank you," Keturah said dejectedly.

He left without telling me. Wow, he must really be mad. No Abraham, no Parson, she was alone, with no one to talk to. "God, I have you but, I'd really like someone to sit down and talk with," she confessed. Sighing, she made her way towards the elevators, her eyes focused on the carpet.

"Keturah?"

A vaguely familiar female voice called from behind causing her to jump, while turning towards the voice.

"Tippany? Oh, hi! How are you?" Her sister was the last person she wanted to see. She always acted so standoffish to her, especially when her mom was around. *Oh, Lord, please don't let Sari be lurking in the shadows somewhere,* Keturah thought, looking behind the girl's shoulder for a trace of the gray-haired sour-puss. This weekend had been a total bust, to add her nastiness to the mix right now, would totally crush her.

"Don't worry. Mother left with the rest of them early this morning," Tippany said in a jovial tone.

Stunned that the woman had just read her mind, she gave a nervous laugh and relaxed a little, "I didn't remember seeing you last night, I wasn't aware that you were here."

"Well, the entire family saw you last night, our brothers included and boy, did you have everyone up in arms," Tippany said, but held no malice in her voice. She sounded glad.

Cocking her head to the side, Keturah looked at her sister's candor, and friendliness, and was puzzled, "You and your mom don't always see eye-to-eye, do you." she phrased it as more of a statement than question.

"Ha! Make that, most of the time. In fact, most of the time, we're at each other's throats," Tippany laughed.

"You're definitely not what I expected," Keturah confessed, relieved. "I thought you were so...." thinking better of her choice of words, she paused. "Well, let's just say I'm pleasantly surprised."

"Oh, come on Sis, you can say it. You thought I was a snot-nosed snob, like the rest of the Jaymes clan," she said unashamedly.

"Okay. Well, yes. I guess that was the first impression I got from you," Keturah said hesitantly, not sure where her sister was coming from.

"Good. I still have a good poker-face, even with you," she smiled, revealing straight, cosmetically whitened teeth. "When I found out you had married, ole Abe, I didn't know if I was going to be able to trust you or not. So, I had to put on my "Jaymes-face" while you were around Mother. But now that I see you care as little for her as I do, I guess I feel free to act like myself," she said.

"You don't care for your mom?" Keturah said surprised.
"Does anybody?"

That got Keturah laughing a little bit. Never in a million years would she have thought she'd find and ally in her half-sister.

"Listen, Sis, never judge a book by its cover, and don't take things at face-value, because that face will always turn around and surprise you."

Keturah's eyes went wide, "Who taught you that saying?"

"It doesn't matter; Just something I picked up somewhere. Why do you ask?"

She shrugged her shoulders, "It was something my Gretta always said to me. I always thought she had cornered the market on quirky sayings," Keturah said, a faraway look in her eyes.

"Yeah, grandmothers are funny like that," Tippany said, a hint of nostalgia in her own voice. "Well, anyway, what are your plans?"

She had no plans. She was stuck in Chicago until 6'oclock with nothing to do, but look at the scenery outside her hotel suite windows. The only dress-down clothes she had were the jeans and t-shirt on her back. "I guess I'll go to my room and order room service. Maybe watch a little TV, until it's time for me to catch my flight home."

"No, seriously, what are you really going to do?" Tippany stated with a deadpan look on her face. When Keturah gave no response, she rolled her eyes and sucked her teeth. "Listen, you're my big sis. If anyone should know how to have a wild and crazy time, it's you. But, if I must be the one to teach you how to have a good time when the cat's away, so be it," she laughed and grabbed Keturah's arm, pulling her in the opposite direction. "Prepare yourself, girlfriend. We are about to have the best time ever!"

"Whoa, wait a minute. I can't go out dressed like this, and I don't have...." Keturah hated to admit she was running low on cash, the university only paid her once a month and even that money was earmarked for certain overdue expenses. She might as well be honest, "I don't have a lot of money on me. So, I think it's best if I go back to my room."

"Keturah, you are a Taylor. Your husband is one of the richest men in America. Of course, you have money," Tippany flipped her hand as if what Keturah had just said was the craziest thing in the world. "Now since this is Sunday, why don't we start things off with going to church? That way, we get in God's good graces."

"I can't go dressed like this!" Keturah protested.

"Maybe not to Abe's old stuffy church, but you'll fit right in at the church I'm about to take you to," Tippany said with confidence. "Girl, I can't even see how you can stand going to the Evangelical Holier-Than-Even-God Church," Tippany bucked and rolled her eyes.

That caused Keturah to laugh out loud, "I've never been to Abraham's church," she confessed.

"Well, believe me when I tell you, you ain't missed a thing, not a single solitary thing," Tippany said again, taking Keturah by the arm. "Where we are about to go doesn't just *say* Jesus is alive, but shows it."

Keturah hadn't been to a lively, charismatic church, in a long time. Not since her undergrad days. She loved the freedom of the little storefront nondenominational church she used to attend back then. So, when she, Tippany along with Rebecca, who seemed nervous to enter the loud, wailing storefront, walked up to the doors, immediately, Keturah felt at home.

Lord you're welcome in this place, Holy Spirit have your way.

As the familiar tune greeted her ears, Keturah found herself leaving the other two women behind and going straight to the altar to worship her first love. It had been a long time; only Keturah hadn't known it until she felt the presence of God rush over her like a mighty wind and settle on her just like the hug of a long-lost friend. Tears she could not explain immediately fell from her face, as she felt herself being ushered into the presence of the Lord.

The worship leader took them right into the song, "I Love You Lord Today." All concerns about Abraham, Parson and the loss of Gretta were vanquished in that moment. All that was left was her and God, as the song shifted to, "Jesus, You're the Center of My Joy."

How could she have forgotten this feeling of wholeness and completeness that God's comfort always brings? Why did she allow her fears and doubts to overwhelm her, knowing who was always on her side? Worship was high that morning, and as Keturah felt herself being drawn deeper into His presence, her natural tendency to dance before the Lord broke out, and before she knew it, she was dancing and twirling before her king, unashamed. She danced and sang praise to God until she had exhausted herself and kneeled at the altar. She could have laid there all day, soaking up God's presence, but knew she had to go back and be seated, knowing that the service was transitioning from praise and worship to the announcements.

She had no idea where Tippany and Rebecca were, all she wanted was to sit as close to the altar as possible. Moving away to take a seat, she noticed a gray-haired woman approaching her. Taking her by the hand and smiling, she hugged Keturah. At that moment, Keturah had not realized how much she missed being hugged by a grandmother figure.

Keturah's mind snapped back to the present, as she felt the woman's embrace lessen. Pulling back so she could look in Keturah's face, she spoke, "God bless you baby girl. You looked so beautiful, dancing this morning. All I could see was your elegant form while babies danced around your feet, and your husband stood back smiling, watching you worship and praise God."

"Thank you," Keturah said, a little confused at what the woman was saying. She didn't see any children around her and Abraham certainly wasn't there. Besides, how did she know she was married? Keturah still hadn't placed Abraham's ring back on her finger, even though he left it and asked her to wear it.

The woman with the watery, brown eyes wasn't finished talking as she looked keenly at Keturah once more before speaking.

"Listen, honey, you stop all this fussing and worrying about your husband. God is still molding you two together. He can make miracles out of your mess-ups. Continue to dance before your first husband, and he'll cause your second husband to fall in line. You hear me? Honor your first love, and one day, your second love will be honoring you," she said with an extra squeeze of Keturah's shoulders. With that said the woman let her go and hobbled back to her seat, while chills ran up and down Keturah's spine as she tried to process what was spoken to her.

Suddenly, she was flanked on both sides by Tippany and a wide-eyed Rebecca.

"This is like no other church I've ever been in," Rebecca said.

"Yeah, I know. It's awesome!" Tippany squealed.

As if God wanted to put his two cents in; the choir stood and began to sing, "Our God is Awesome."

Keturah concurred, God truly is awesome.

**

The next week went by like a blur. Instead of going home on her Chicago flight, she, Tippany and Rebecca, did a girls' week that ended by them flying down to Jamaica for an impromptu bachelorette party.

Keturah never had what she considered close girlfriends, because she didn't have a lot of time on her hands when she was a kid or while in college. She had to make the grades or work to stay in school, so this was like having a crash course in wild and unabashed fun.

They had their own private suite and were enjoying the night-life of the city. She had never gone to so many places in such a brief time. They had gone to Vegas, then flown to LA., flew back to Atlanta to go to a premiere, then it was off to Jamaica.

She had always dreamed of what it was like to live in the fast-lane and to have no worries. This week was only a taste of what that life was like.

The bachelorette party was wonderful. The ladies started first thing in the morning with a full spa treatment, followed by an afternoon of shopping. The evening was promised to be full of dinner, dancing and drama, as Tippany described it.

It was nearly mid-night when the Karaoke began and both Rebecca and Tippany dragged Keturah up front to sing. Feeling rather silly and a little sexy too, thanks to her new wardrobe, she decided to sing her favorite love song and dedicated it to Rebecca, who she surprisingly, had grown rather fond of over the past few days.

It was amazing how getting away from Sari made people loosen up. She closed her eyes and began to sing *Miracles*, by Whitney Houston. She hadn't realized how lost in the song she had gotten until she finished and opened her eyes to a standing ovation. The crowd cheered, asking for an encore. Keturah smiled and looked in the direction of her friends, only they weren't smiling at her as others were. It only took a raise of her eyes to see why. Two sets of glaciers- blue eyes were staring back at her, but only one set was smiling. Ishmael, she didn't really care about, it was the other set that had her trying to swallow the lump in her throat.

"Abraham!" She couldn't sing anything else even if she tried. Bowing once more to her audience, she made her way through the crowd to her table. She saw Tippany's frown as Sari was standing nearby lecturing her. Rebecca sat like a stone statue with wide eyes again. Abraham didn't speak at all, only held out his hand towards her. Keturah took it, noticing its coolness or maybe that was emanating from his eyes. She couldn't tell. *What a way to end a perfect evening,* she thought, as she obediently followed her husband's lead.

They had come to a secluded spot, and by that time, Keturah was ready to face the music. However, this time, ole Abe would be in for a little surprise. If he was angry, she was more so. He was so flippant when it came to her feelings. She had just told him she loved him, which she was sure he'd heard, but his response was to get up in the wee hours of the morning and leave. She hadn't heard from him the entire week, and now he shows up out of the blue. *Well, he won't get off easily,* she thought, rubbing her arms to combat the chill in the night air.

"Are you cold?"

Jumping a little, not realizing he was close behind her; she steadied her heart. "A little, but I'll be…" before she could finish, she felt his strong arms encase her from behind.

Pulling her to him, her back now rested on his chest; his body heat immediately warming her while sending shock waves to her senses. His cologne was overpowering, his touch, electrifying. Her reasoning at that point, already lost. The cat had caught his mouse and she felt helpless to defend herself against him.

"Sing for me, Tourie," he whispered, his command in her ear then bit her earlobe playfully, before kissing it.

All anger from last week's events quickly faded. All she could think of was him, and wanting to desperately please him. She'd give and do anything to keep him with her, make him love her.

"What do you want me to sing? Her voice was barely above a whisper. How she would manage to sing anything would be a mystery.

"Do you know *Unforgettable*, by Nat King Cole?"

"You mean, Natalie Cole?"

Chuckling, he nodded, knowing that the true composer of the song was the woman's father, they swayed to the rhythm of the song as she sang it.

CHAPTER TWENTY-SIX

What game was he playing? she wondered, as she lay against him, feeling the rise and fall of his breath against her back. When she first laid eyes on him while on stage, he seemed a little lost.

His formidable stance somehow lacked its usual luster. She was sure he was going to have a fit and lecture her about her performance and how, as his wife, her behavior in public had to be above reproach. At least that was the lecture Sari was giving Tippany and Rebecca. Once she came off the platform and reached their table, Abe took her hand, and without hesitation, kept them walking towards the beach.

They walked for some time. He hadn't said anything and neither did she. There seemed to be peace in the silence, so she allowed it to linger between them. She was so deep in thought that when he stopped, she hadn't noticed. Turning her around, she readied herself for a lecture, now that they were out of ear-shot from everyone; but the lecture never came. "Sing to me, Tourie," was all he said. In the night air, they swayed to the music and it was as if time had somehow stopped, and they were the only two people on the planet. After some time, he whispered, "Let's get out of here."

It was the only prompting she needed from him. Taking his hand, they turned back towards the hotel and headed back to her suite. He made no pretense about desiring her. And once they were alone, he showed her more passion than she had ever known. It was this side of Abraham that she loved and wanted to be loved by. But her beautiful night soon turned into horror as she heard him mumble in his sleep.

"I love you, Sarah," Abraham muttered before drifting off to sleep.

Sarah. Once again, he was thinking of her. Keturah curled herself into a ball and silently cried in her pillow. *You can't conquer what you won't confront!*

She blotted her eyes with the sheets as one of Gretta's old sayings kept echoing in her head. If her and Abraham were ever going to have a chance, she had to understand this hold Sarah had over him.

Shifting in bed so she could watch her husband sleep, she determined in that moment that even if she had to tie him to the bed, they were going to talk about Sarah, she determined as she drifted off to sleep.

Keturah awoke, feeling Abraham's arms wrapped around her waist. Abraham rarely stayed with her after being intimate, and there were so many things she wanted to know about him and his life with Sarah. Another opportunity might not present itself for some time, *It was now or never*, Keturah thought so taking a deep breath, she spoke.

"Abraham?"

"Hmmm?"

She hesitated. He was still groggy with sleep. Maybe she could work it to her advantage. If she started off with small questions, maybe she could draw him in to answering the bigger ones. "What's it like being so successful?"

He hunched the shoulder her head was resting on. "Like anything else, it's work," he said in monotone yawning.

"But is it just work? I mean, didn't you and Sarah enjoy building Canaan together?" she smiled inwardly, triumphant at the fact that she could slip Sarah's name into the conversation.

"I suppose we had our moments," he said without elaborating.

Seeing the need to be more direct if she was going to get anywhere fast, she continued, "When I was in your office the first time and saw that beautiful mural of your family, it seems that you have had a lot of happy moments. You both seemed so vibrant and full of life, like you were ready to conquer the world."

He made no reply, but she, for some reason knew he was listening, so she pressed on. "It must have been hard losing someone like that, someone you know is in your corner, supporting you no matter what. That type of love.... it's a powerful thing to have, then lose." He remained quiet for so long, she thought he must have fallen asleep. She was just about to snuggle closer to him and go back to sleep herself, when he spoke.

"I still miss her...." he said quietly.

It was a start, she thought inwardly. Maybe she should leave well enough alone. The last thing she wanted to do was poke the bear or, in Abraham's case, poke the grizzly, but her curiosity couldn't be quenched.

She proceeded cautiously, "I think we always miss the people who knew us best," she smiled, turning her face against his chest. "I miss hearing Gretta's voice. I keep trying to remember every detail of our last conversation; playing it back again and again, in my mind. Trying to remember each inflection of hers, or how each word sounded coming out of her mouth."

"Yeah, Sarah had such great facial expressions. I knew exactly what she was feeling before a word would be said, especially when she was upset with me," he chuckled a little.

Keturah found herself enjoying how the rumble jostled her head back and forth, "Did she get upset with you a lot?"

"Is water wet?" he said with humor. "I remember one time; I took Isaac out on a safari with me. It was his first time hunting big game. Of course, Sarah didn't want me to take him because he was still relatively young. Reluctantly, she let him go, with a warning that I better bring him back safe and sound, or else. Anyway, once we got there, we somehow became separated from our guide. Next thing I knew, I heard Isaac screaming. I ran towards his voice and when he came into view, a huge African Buffalo was charging him.

Keturah lifted her head off his shoulder and gazed wide eyes into his. "Oh my God, Abraham! What did you do?"

"I said a quick prayer, asking God to either let me hit Isaac, or kill the buffalo. I took aim with my rifle and shot. The fact that Isaac is still here is a testament that God answers prayer."

"Wow! What did Sarah say when you told her?"

"It wasn't so much what she said, as it was what she did."

Confusion graced her face and she asked the logical question, "What did she do?"

Moving her head off his shoulder, he took her hand and guided it to his bare forearm. "You feel that?" Seeing her nod, he allowed her to feel three other distinct scars on his bicep and hand.

"What is it?" She asked rather softly trying to keep the giggle out of her voice.

"That nights evening dinner served on hot china," he laughed, "I think I would've rather faced another angry buffalo than to deal with Sarah's fury."

After they finished laughing, Keturah spoke up, "Why didn't you just not tell her? I mean Isaac didn't get hurt. It could've been your secret."

"I know. But at the time, I was trying to teach Isaac that when you mess up, you fess up; to be responsible means that you have to take the good and bad."

She was in silent awe of her husband. This was the type of man she wanted for her children. "Isaac and Ishmael were so lucky to have you as their dad," she said softly, not aware that she'd spoken out loud.

He sighed as he stroked her other arm, "Keturah, I know it must have been hard for you not having Kedron around. But just because he wasn't there, didn't mean he wasn't concerned about you."

She jerked herself upright and pulled the covers over her chest, wrapping her arms around her knees, she rocked back and forth trying to tap down her raging emotions, "Please don't, Abraham. Don't defend him," she said, swiping at the moisture that fell on her cheeks.

"Keturah, I'm not trying to defend him. I'm just saying he cared."

"No, he didn't!" she insisted. How can you say that when he was never there for me? Maybe if I had a father like you, things would have been different. You were there for your kids. You didn't shirk your responsibilities and act as if one of your sons didn't exist. So please, spare me the, "he cared" speech, when he never showed it." She turned towards him, only to be confused by what looked to be guilt on his face.

"Keturah, you don't know the whole story. It's complicated."

"Abraham, my mom was taken away from me when I was only three years old, and my dad never came for me. He was the only parent I had and he never even acknowledged me. Thank God, for Gretta and Uncle Emory.

If it hadn't been for them, I probably would have ended up in foster care. Gretta always said that when my father and mother forsake me, the Lord would take me up. But it hurts to know the people who should love you and care for you don't."

Abraham laid back and covered his eyes for a moment. When he finally drew his hands down over his face, it bore a somber expression. Propping himself on his elbows, not really looking at her, but beyond her he said, "Kedron and I are a lot alike, Keturah." When she tried to protest, he quickly held up a silencing hand. "I didn't raise Ishmael and I wasn't the loving father you think me to be. The day I saw you at the lake house with your mom, I was there with Ishmael. Things in my house were becoming explosive. There was so much animosity between Sarah and Hagan, it began to affect my boys. That day at the lake house, I was trying to connect with Ishmael, just like Kedron was trying to do with you. I don't know how Sari and Sarah found out about it, but all hell broke loose when they did. I was given an ultimatum, just like your dad was: Our wives and families or our mistresses. We both made the choice to stay with our families. That was the last day Kedron saw you, and the last I saw Ishmael, for several years."

Keturah shook her head, no. It couldn't be true. Ever since she was a teenager, she promised herself she wouldn't get involved with a man who was like her father. She had been so careful about the guys she dated. If they even smelled like a playboy, she'd lose interest. Yet, if what Abraham just confessed was true, all her efforts were in vain. She did all that, only to end up with a man exactly like her father. Angry at herself and now at Abraham for deceiving her, she lashed out.

"But, how could you just walk away from your own flesh and blood like that, without so much as a thought?"

"I made a choice, Keturah. So, did your dad. No matter what choice we made, someone was going to be unhappy; someone was going to be without their father. I can't speak for your dad, but I had to do what I felt God was directing me to do, and that was to stay and work things out with my wife and our son."

"But, what about Ishmael? Did you ever stop to think what his life would be like without his father?" she yelled as tears filled her eyes.

"I entrusted him to God's care, to protect him; to be the father to him that I couldn't."

"But, didn't you care how that would make you look in his eyes? Didn't you care that he would feel abandoned by you?" Keturah pressed.

"Tourie, I've learned some time ago, not to place anyone on a pedestal. Humans make mistakes. It's part of our nature. The only perfect being is God. He's the only one who won't fail you."

"So that's it," Keturah gave a humorless laugh. "Kids like me and Ishmael should just accept the fact that we're products of our parents' bad choices; mistakes to be thrown in God's hands, so our fathers don't have to be bothered."

"Keturah, that's not what I meant."

She held up a hand to stop him from talking. The more he tried to explain, the worse she felt. In her mind, there was no good reason for anyone to abandon their child. It was way, too easy to throw the responsibility on others. While he and Kedron took their favorite kids on safaris and vacations overseas, she and Ishmael had to do their best to scratch out a living. Maybe Abraham and her father did trust God to take care of them, but somehow, that felt like the easy way out. Keturah threw the covers off and quickly scrambled out of bed, just being near him made her angry. "I take it you're here on business for a couple days?" she asked, putting on her robe; not looking at him.

"Well, yes, I am. I have several business meetings and some other public appearances to do with the family," he said slowly.

"So, guess my being here wasn't part of the plan," his silence gave her, her answer. "Then, I guess I'll go pack my things and go." Keturah said crossly, while stalking towards the bathroom.

Chapter Twenty-Seven

Most married couples had their share of squabbles; from how to divvy -up chores, to who was going to pay what and when: typical marital stuff. But the rich don't bother arguing about stuff like that. As a matter of fact, rich couples likely had to schedule their disagreements through their husband's secretaries, Keturah thought as she fumed, still waiting on hold, for Abraham's assistant to place her call through. Okay, she got it. She wasn't on anyone's favorite list right now. Yes, their marriage came as a shock to his company, and with the help of dear ole. Sari Jaymes, the witch, now the entire company had heard of how this young, conniving temptress had trapped poor ole Abe into a loveless marriage to extort money from him. And, because he was still so grief-stricken over his beloved Sarah, he had fallen into her clutches.

The thought caused her to slam the phone down extra-hard. Pacing back and forth in her little office space where she had been hiding out for most of the day, for a moment she thought to just march herself right over to his office, kick in the door and demand he fire his assistant and anyone else who didn't respect her as his wife. But, if she did that, he'd have to fire his sons, and then himself. She sighed while gripping the sides of her arms, inadvertently giving herself a tight squeeze.

Walking to her desk, Keturah again glanced at the offending newspaper article and began to fume all over again. Since the story broke about their marriage, her life had become insane. News reporters were outside of her apartment, that morning and a couple of other times, she could have sworn she had seen photographers snapping her picture.

Didn't people have better things to do? She was not the gold-digger they had made her out to be. She hadn't received any money or taken one, red cent from Abraham, since they had married. As for her being a seductress, that was absurd. Abraham was the only man she had ever been with and their first time was when they were married; however, not according to the tabloids.

Someone must have seen him coming out of her hotel room the first night they met, because they had it listed as one of their many seedy rendezvous. The only statement Abraham made was, "no comment." No comment! Why didn't he straighten things out before they got to this point? She told him not being honest was a recipe for disaster and so far, her prediction was spot-on.

A shrill sound on her desk alerted her to her cell ringing. Picking it up, she glanced at the caller ID and became incensed. Placing a hand on her hip, she was set to give her husband an earful.

"Yes?" she spoke in a clipped voice, hoping he could hear the chill in her tone.

"I have five minutes, what do you need?"

His abruptness pushed her over the edge, "What do you mean, what do I need, Abraham? Have you seen the articles in the tabloids about us? What they are saying is simply not true. What are you going to do about this?" she questioned.

"Keturah, I have better things to do with my time than read some trashy tabloids," he said, irritated. "Now, what is it that you called me about?"

"Don't you care that these people have belied our name?" she practically yelled.

"Keturah, time is money for me and I don't have time to waste with this nonsense. Now, what do you want?" he stated, exasperated.

"Apparently, nothing. I'm so sorry for wasting your precious time, Mr. Taylor." Keturah hung up. "Oh, that man," she growled as she started pacing again.

This might not be a big deal for him, but it was to her. Maybe his circle of friends didn't read the "tabloid trash" as he called it, but her circle of friends did and by the looks she was receiving from her co-workers and some of the other school personnel, they had read the article. "So much for doing a good deed," she muttered while flopping in her chair, wondering why in the world she put herself in this kind of situation in the first place.

"How did you think things would turn out when you hid the truth and embraced a lie?" The Holy Spirit whispered.

Squirming in her chair, she wrapped her arms around her middle, still feeling somewhat miffed, but more convicted than anything. She should've never gone and done this in the first place, especially when Abraham suggested they keep secrets.

But you didn't lie, exactly, and Abraham was the one who didn't divulge the whole truth. Besides, you married him for a good reason, you couldn't risk Gretta's health, and she really did need surgery, Keturah reasoned within herself.

Oh, this was such a big mess and apparently, Abraham wasn't going to be a help. She was tired of hiding out in her office. Sending the office secretary, a quick email stating that she was leaving early, she opened the back door and was ready to bolt, but ran straight into Parson.

"Oh, hi, Parson. I didn't see you standing there," she said in a rushed voice, unable to bring her gaze to his. It had been two weeks since the fundraiser in Chicago. She was so ashamed that she had been caught in a lie, she couldn't bear facing him, so resorted to avoiding him like the plague.

"Apparently, you haven't seen much of anything. Oh, except for Abraham Taylor, Ms. Birch, or are you going by Mrs. Taylor now?" Parson raised an eyebrow at her as he placed another tabloid in her hand.

Taking it, she quickly glanced over the headlines and felt her heart sink, as she looked at the headshot of her and Abraham in Chicago, with an inflammatory caption stating, "cradle-robber or gold-digger? You decide."

"Parson, let me explain." Hesitating, Keturah bit her lower lip, realizing she really couldn't explain all this. There had been so many lies that had been told, she couldn't keep them straight. She didn't like lying. It was stressing her out and putting a strain on her relationship with God and her friends. It would end now, "Parson, the truth is that I can't explain this mess." She heaved a cleansing sigh. They were the first truthful words she had said since this whole ordeal started. "I want to, no, I need to be honest with you."

"I'd appreciate the truth, Keturah. But first, tell me, are you in any kind of trouble?" his eyebrows furrowed, his face full of concern.

That was Parson for you, always concerned about his friends. She already knew before she shared the sordid details of her first encounter with Abraham to their quick ceremony, that he wouldn't judge or criticize her. He knew that her love for Gretta knew no ends and she would've married an ogre if it meant Gretta was going to get better.

They were standing in front of her car, when she finally finished telling him everything. She watched him as he paced back and forth, stroking his neatly trimmed goatee.

"And you say this bogus marriage is only to last for nine to twelve months?" he looked at her intently.

She slowly nodded yes.

"And you believe that's all he's after? A name-only marriage for appearances' sake, nothing else?" he pushed

Narrowing her eyes, she looked at him inquisitively. "Like I said, he just wants to be married until this business deal goes through."

"From what I've heard, marriage doesn't make a man's life simpler at all. It complicates things," he chuckled, rubbing his hand across his head.

"Spoken like a true, forever-bachelor," Keturah said, rolling her eyes. If Parson would not have been so skittish when it came to relationships, she imagined they might have married and this whole ordeal with Abraham would never have happened.

"It's not that I've never considered marriage, it's just that..."

"You like your singleness more. Why be tied down to one female when you can feast your eyes on the multitudes?" Keturah knew she was being spiteful with her words, but Parson was notorious for flirting and playing the field; but it wasn't right. He was messing around with women's hearts. Making promises with his mouth, he knew full well in his heart, he had no intention to keep.

He shook his head, "No, that's not it, and believe it or not, I don't play the field as much as you and others think I do."

Lifting his hands to stave off her retort, he continued, "Keturah, it's nice to be wanted and even nicer to be appreciated. And yes, I often do feel that appreciation from the women I go out with, at first. Much like you, I too, have things that I'm asking God to send me in a wife; qualities that I feel are invaluable. I want someone who's not after my money or my status. I want someone who genuinely cares about me. So yes, I go on a lot of first dates, but truthfully, it doesn't go much further than that."

Curious now, Keturah leaned back on her car, "Why not? Are you seriously trying to tell me, of all the first dates you've had, not one of those women, interested you in the least?"

"What I'm saying is you, of all people, should now understand how awful it feels to be part of someone else's agenda without your needs being considered. Most women I've dated had a plan set and are looking for a guy to fill the "husband" slot. They want the stigma of their singleness erased, but do they really want marriage? I can't tell," he said with a shoulder shrug. "They're so independent and focused on their careers or the lifestyles they want you to create for them. Oh, and by the way, on my numerous first dates, I'm not always the one who is giving the brush off. Y'all do an excellent job of that yourselves."

Keturah folded her arms across her chest, as heat rose in her cheeks. Apparently, this conversation was long overdue and seeing that she had nothing to lose, she was going to have her say, "We have no choice. What should we do, sit around and wait, hope and pray that you guys will finally stop playing games? Men act as if women are Venus fly-traps, just waiting for the chance to snag you, and then suck the life out of you. Yet still, here you come, buzzing around us with no intentions of doing much more than buzzing."

Keturah didn't know when the conversation turned from Parson, to Abraham, to ultimately, her dad; but it did. They all seemed so much alike. They wanted you to notice them, but not get to clingy. Typical males.

"We're all not alike Keturah," he had slipped his hand under her chin and lifted her head until her eyes contacted with his. "You're going to have to let the past go."

He took his thumb and swiped at the lone tear rolling on her cheek. "Oh, and to answer your other question, yes, there was a woman I had dated and I was thinking very strongly of marrying, but she ran off and married someone else." He paused for a long time, looking raptly at her before continuing, "So, I guess it's back to the drawing-board for me."

Stunned into silence, Keturah gave him a wide-eyed stare. This was the most serious conversation she had ever had with Parson. Maybe she had underestimated him, well, most guys, in fact. But what puzzled her more was his last statement, was the married woman he referred to her?

CHAPTER TWENTY-EIGHT

"Look, Dad, it's not that we are trying to pry into your personal life, but you have to admit, this…this marriage took place quite suddenly and then to find out that your new bride is a younger cousin to Mom," Isaac rubbed his forehead, trying to process everything, "well, frankly, it makes things look bad," he finished, not quite able to look his dad in the eye.

"That's stating things mildly," Sari said tersely. "Now, look, Abraham. I think we all realized that one day you would remarry. Actually, Sarah made me promise that you would get on with your life once she was gone." Seeing him about to interject, she moved on quickly, "But, I'm sure she didn't have this little girl you married in mind."

"That little girl, as you call her, has a name, as a matter of fact, your husband was the one who gave it to her," Emory spoke up harshly. Sari looked at him distastefully and narrowed her eyes.

"Look, Aunt Sari. Her name is Mrs. Keturah Birch-Taylor. Roll it around on your tongue a couple of times to get used it, but don't call her anything different," Abraham said testily glaring his aunt down until she conceded by turning her head. "Besides, I make my own decisions and who I have decided to marry is no one's concern but my own."

"That's where you're wrong," Sari stated, slamming her hand forcefully on the conference room table. "Since your marriage has gone public, the company's stock has dropped. People want to know that the head of a multi-million-dollar company is playing with a full deck. And to be frank, your behavior at the launch of the *Sarah Foundation* was deplorable.

First, you brought Hagan with you, then got so drunk Avery had to practically carry you out of there. And if that wasn't bad enough, you were seen leaving the same hotel Keturah was in, and now this quickie-marriage to her? I don't know about the rest of you, but that doesn't sound stable to me," Sari said, looking around the table where Isaac, Avery and Emory sat. "Maybe you should consider retiring a little early and passing the reigns over to Isaac now."

"Now, hold on, that's taking things too far Sari!" Avery nearly shouted.

"You're way out of line, Sari," Emory spoke up at the same time.

"No Aunt Sari, absolutely not I'm in no way ready to fill my dad's shoes in this company and we all know that," Isaac said unsteadily. "Look, we're all still grieving over Mom. Everyone shows grief in unusual ways. Mom's death left a great hole in all of us. You can't expect Dad to be perfect in handling his feelings."

"Yeah, I'm still grieving, but you don't see me jumping the broom and marrying the first yahoo that passes by," Sari bellowed.

"That's because you're too busy flying it, to jump over it!" Emory rebuffed, while Avery snickered.

"Emory, you don't want to go there with me. I'll tell you that right now," Sari leaned forward pointing her boney finger towards him.

"Everyone, please...please. One crisis at a time," Isaac charged.

Crisis! When did his life become a crisis? Abraham thought while looking at the feuding board members who had called him at the last minute to do an emergency meeting. The topic: his relationship with Keturah.

It was laughable. Only he wasn't in a laughing mood. He understood they wanted to know what was going on with him, only he didn't really know. His plan was to walk away from Keturah by summer's end. Intimacy occurring between them was never in the plan, but when it happened, he couldn't deny he enjoyed it and wanted it all the time, which was the reason he had stayed away for so long. He missed her terribly. He hated how they parted their last night in Jamaica. He, in fact, was developing feelings for her.

"I love you Abraham."

He shut his eyes, hearing Keturah's declaration of love for him. His heart belonged to one woman, and she was gone, never to return. He wasn't planning on loving anyone else but Sarah. Yet, something about Tourie's love for him stirred his heart. Could he be falling for her, too?

Sometimes, when he was out of town and alone in his bedroom, it wasn't Sarah's face he was seeing or Sarah's face that made him smile or filled him with desire. His family was right on one count: this thing with Keturah was getting out of hand and impacting the business.

He needed to get away to get his head on straight. He was working with Ishmael on a portion of the project overseas. Maybe that's where he needed to concentrate his efforts, and let Isaac play a larger role in the company state side. He would give him a trial-run, at least until Isaac married Rebecca, then he would come back in during their honeymoon. If things went well, maybe he would consider retiring early.

Keturah's face drifted into his mind. Shaking his head clear, he knew it was time to make his decision. "Everyone, I think Sari has a point. I haven't been the best example and that has negatively impacted the company. That's my fault. I think taking a step back isn't a bad idea. Isaac, you're more than capable of running this company."

"But, Dad, you and Mom built this company from the ground up. It's your legacy. You belong here," Isaac protested.

"No, son. We built this company for you. You're our legacy. I'll always be here for you, but it's time you begin making your own mark."

"Dad, please this is not what this meeting was about. I never wanted you to leave the company...we're just worried about you that's all?" Isaac pleaded.

"Son...you can do this. I have faith in you, now it's time you had faith in yourself. I have always leaned on God to help in times of trouble, doubt and fear. Its time you exercise your faith in him. Watch what he'll do." Abraham stated.

"Abraham, are you sure you want to do this?" Avery asked.

Taking in a deep sigh and feeling lighter than he had in weeks, He gave his friend a smile. "Yeah, I'm sure."

CHAPTER TWENTY-NINE

Keturah sat on the park bench looking at everything yet nothing. She didn't know whether to laugh or cry, now that God had granted her request. In six months, she would be a mother. She wanted to jump for joy, but couldn't. There was a sour note to her song of joy. Abraham. What would he think of her joyous news?

"He will probably have a coronary, no doubt," she muttered, hating the fact that she would likely be the only one to see this as a good thing.

Why does everything have to be so complicated between us, Lord? Why is it so difficult for him to love me?

She heard the words somewhere in the abyss of her mind, but couldn't pinpoint where, exactly. She knew she didn't have a right to ask him for his love. After all, that wasn't part of the agreement.

She had already fallen for her husband. Yet, she knew he would not love her in return.

Well I guess you're more like your mother than you thought.

The ugly thought pierced her soul. She had vowed to herself never to end up like her mom; pregnant and alone. At least, to her credit, she was married to the father of her child. But still, she wasn't loved and their baby wouldn't be either. Keturah swiped at the tear trekking down her cheek.

"I will not be my mother and my child will not be seen or treated as a millionaire's mistake," she said pointedly, protectively holding her belly.

What if Abraham wants this child, wants to have the opportunity to start over and raise a family. Will you take that away from him? Will you deny him the right to be a father to his child?

That question seemed to come from outside herself. Looking up at the heavens, she closed her eyes hoping to hear His voice again, but there was nothing. Leaving her to wonder, *Was God in this? Did he have a future laid out for them both? Together?* "Lord, what should I do? Should I call and tell him? He does have a right to know." Hinging on what to do, she reached into her purse, fumbling for her phone when it began ringing. "Uncle Emory?" she noted on the caller ID. "Hey, Uncle Em. How are you?" she asked, hoping to clear her head of her jumbled thoughts.

"Tourie, are you busy? I need you to come to my house as soon as possible," he said adamantly.

"Okay. What's going on?"

"I can't talk about it right now, but I really need to see you. It's urgent."

"Okay, well I just finished with my doctor's appointment. I can meet you at the house in forty-five minutes."

"Perfect, see you then," he clicked off abruptly.

An uneasy feeling began surging through her belly, but she wasn't about to give in to it. Her uncle sounded angry and she had a pretty good idea at whom. He wasn't happy about the arrangement that she and Abraham and made, but thought after the marriage announcement, he would be better about things. But, from the sound of his voice, trouble seemed to be on the horizon again.

"Lord, help!" she looked up, before getting off the bench and moving towards her car.

***

"Here's to you, Abraham. Not only have you managed to screw me over, but you've messed up Keturah's life in the process," Emory raised his glass in salute to the picture of him, Kedron and Abraham on his mantel, then downed the amber-colored liquor in one, quick gulp.

Slamming the glassware on the mantel, he heard a distinct crack and two feminine gasps from behind. Turning, he saw his wife and Keturah standing behind him.

"Emory, whatever is the matter with you?" his wife Adele asked, perturbed at his last statement.

Turning from both women, he placed his hand back on the cracked glass and tossed it in the trash can. "Anyone besides me want a drink?" he asked sourly.

"No, I don't want anything," Keturah remarked, as did his wife.

"Well, I sure do. And by the time I'm finished talking, the both of you will likely want one, too," he said, already at the wet bar pouring himself another drink. With a glass in one hand, he waved to the nearby couch with his other, "Keturah, Adele, have a seat. We need to talk."

"Emory, what exactly is this about?" Adele gave an impatient grunt.

"It's over, Adele. My political career is over before it even got started. I'm through."

"What on earth are you talking about? We've just started putting out fliers regarding your election for governor. Anyway, it's too early to tell anything, right now."

Holding his hand up, his wife immediately quieted, "I'm not getting the Taylor/Jaymes backing."

"And, why on earth not?" Adele's green eyes blazed as she immediately stood to her feet; both hands on her hips, nostrils flaring. "You've been good to Abraham, always stood by his side. He can always count on you. So, why wouldn't he give you his support?"

"Because, my darling, he won't be there to give it," Emory said in a more subdued tone as he downed his second drink then turned to Keturah, whose eyes went wide with his words. "I'm sorry to be the one to break the news to you, Baby, but he's leaving the country and turning everything over to Isaac. He says it's only temporary but, I don't know."

Keturah sat very still without saying a word, which only made him more nervous. "Didn't I tell you to be on guard with him? Boy, I sure wish I would've stopped him from marrying you. This whole situation is nothing but one, big disaster."

"Emory, please!" Adele gave him a look to hush up, as she went to Keturah's side.

"Aww, honey. I'm sorry, Keturah. I didn't mean to make a tough situation worse but, I just wish you would've talked to me about Gretta's needs before you got involved with Abraham." He rubbed his forehead then allowed his hand to ease to the back of his neck where the tension was building. "I knew he was grieving his wife and a person in grief doesn't always make the best decisions."

"Well, look. No actual harm was done," Adele reasoned. "So, you'll get the marriage annulled quicker than expected and Keturah can resume her normal life. Emory, the Taylor/Jaymes support is not the only show in town. You have plenty of followers who know your character and commitment to this state; they know you'll make a good governor."

That was his Adele, always looking at the positive in the worst of circumstances. She truly deserved to be in the governor's mansion compared to Malcom Jaymes and his wife Shannon, who weren't much more than carbon-copies of their mother Sari.

"I guess you're right, Dear. I still have a fighting chance."

Keturah sat mute as her uncle and aunt discussed new sources of support to make up for the loss of the Taylors. She would have gladly taken the drink her uncle offered her, if she had not discovered she was pregnant. Abraham was leaving her. She wanted to fall apart right then, and there. Yet, somehow, she kept it together. Numbly, she listened to her aunt and uncle, as they planned their next move. All the time wondering, how to put her shattered life back together.

CHAPTER THIRTY

It was only his persistent knocking that finally got her up off the sofa and moving towards her front door. Keturah was in no mood for company. Standing on her toes, she looked out the peephole. With relief and aggravation, she pulled open her front door. "What?" Keturah said unenthusiastically to Parson.

"Well, hello to you, too," he said sarcastically, pushing past her and coming into her foyer, without an invitation. "I've been calling you, and texting you for the last couple of days, with no response. All I could get from the secretary was that you've called off for a couple days. Are you sick?" Parson asked, his brows knitted together in concern.

"Yes, I'm sick...sick of your gender, sick of being lied to and sick of living this lie. She thought in her head, but said to Parson, "I've been working from home the last couple of days, that's all. Is there something you want? Because I'm tired," she said, moving past him, not caring that her robe was hanging open, revealing the *Hello Kitty* nightshirt beneath.

"Yes, there's something I want, Keturah. I want to know what's really going on. There are rumors flying around left and right that Abraham Taylor has taken a leave of absence from *Canaan Enterprises,* leaving Isaac in charge, while he is overseas to set up a new company with his son Ishmael, who has openly converted to Islam. As it stands right now, our projects have been suspended indefinitely, by the board. After all, we are a Christian community college. Our department has already put a lot of capital up and now, with funds suspended from the board and the Taylors, our whole department is in an uproar and is looking for answers."

"Well, don't look at me. I've only stepped foot into *Canaan Enterprise* once in my life. I have nothing to do with Abraham's business affairs."

"Well, is there a way for me to reach him? Maybe a phone call can clear up this matter?"

Grabbing the side of her head with both hands, she vigorously began to rub her temples. She was the one with the least power. Yet, somehow, she was left holding the bag.

"Parson, I can't get in touch with him," she confessed, in a small voice. Doing her best to hold back the tears, she walked away, not caring if he followed or not. She was tired…sick and tired. She had morning sickness leaving her feeling shaky, weak, and too tired to deal with this mess.

"Of course, you can. He's your husband, for crying out loud! Tell him what's going on, or at least what you should tell the board, so our funding can be restored." Parson paced back and forth in the living room. "I mean, I wouldn't be so adamant about it if it was just me, but this is going to look bad on all of us."

"Parson, I can't."

"Keturah, didn't you hear what I just said? If this project falls through, it can crumble our department, putting all our jobs on the line; including funding for the kid's scholarship. You've got to contact him, Keturah. You've got to," he insisted.

Maybe it was the lack of sleep, or the endless worry, or the not knowing what to do next that brought her to her to a fit of unbridled rage, but whatever it was, she let it fully unravel on Parson. "I don't know where the *hell* he is Parson. I don't know. I haven't known for weeks. He hasn't called me or texted me. I don't even know if we're still married," she was hollered, while pounding and punching on his chest. "Our marriage was a sham!"

Somewhere between her babbling, she was leaning on Parson, holding the lapel of his suit as he hugged her tightly, rocking her back and forth as she sobbed.

"Keturah, honey, it's all right. It's going to be all right," he held her tighter.

"No, it won't be all right, Parson. Don't you understand? Things will never be all right for me again," she looked up with tears streaming down her face. "I love him. I really do love him, but he doesn't want me. So, he ran halfway across the world, just to get away from me," her voice cracked.

"Keturah, listen to me. So, he doesn't' love you, so what? If you ask me, he's a blind old fool to throw away a woman like you."

Shaking her head, she tried pulling her hands away from Parson's chest, but he still held them. Tipping her head up, he looked intently into her red eyes.

"He's not the only fool, Keturah. I've been an even bigger fool, for not chasing you down and marrying you when I had the chance. You gave me your love, and like an idiot, I threw it away. But, Keturah, if you'll give me a second chance, I'd like to make it up to you."

It was all too much for her to bear. Parson's declaration of love, on the heels of Abraham's abandonment, pushed her over the edge.

"Parson, I can't think right now, I can't do this with you. It's all too much. I need time to clear my head, time to think things through." She again, tried to pull away from him and this time, he let her go.

Running a hand through his curly locks, he stepped back, too and blew out a breath, "Look, Keturah. I'm sorry; I didn't come here with the intentions of revealing my feelings for you. It's just that..." he paused then threw up both hands. "I don't know, ever since you told me you were married, I can't help but think what could have been between us. I had no intentions of trying anything since you were married, but now..., I don't know. I just want a second chance with you, if you'll have me. I really think things could work out between us. I know you think you feel something for Abraham, but..."

"I'm pregnant Parson," she said with no emotion. Her fantasy world had been shattered a long time ago. She didn't feel the need to protect someone else's.

"What?" he turned towards her, with his eyes wide.

"I'm carrying Abraham's child."

"His child?!"

"Yes! So, do you still want to be a part of my world, Parson? Because in a few months, it's going to get pretty crowded."

Parson remained silent.

"Just like I thought," Keturah said. "Look, all I want right now is to get my life back; to make my world sane again. All I can offer you right now is friendship...nothing else."

Breathing out a heavy sigh Parson looked at her intently, before speaking. "Then friendship it is." He said spreading his arms wide towards her of which she immediately filled them.

CHAPTER THIRTY-ONE

"Mrs. Taylor, Ms. Jaymes, I'm glad both of you could meet with me on such short notice. It took some time tracking you both down, I had no idea you were both in the same city and already knew each other. I'm Attorney Larry Cart and I've been the guardian over your grandfather's estate." He said in a warm southern accent.

Keturah and Tiffany looked at each other then back at the attorney.

"I don't understand?" Keturah was the first to speak.

"Well I understand about the estate but what I don't understand is why our older brothers aren't not in attendance? Shouldn't they be here for this as well?" Tippany inquired.

"Older brothers?" Larry furrowed his brow at first, then, as if understanding took hold of him, his face brightened. "Oh, I'm sorry. I should've been clearer. I'm not talking about your paternal grandfather, but your maternal grandfather, Leonard Birch. It's his estate that you've inherited."

Keturah's hand covered her mouth in shock. Tippany was the only one who seemed to have more questions.

"Okay, well that's great for Keturah, but I still don't understand. Why I've been summoned here? Keturah and I are only half-sisters."

Now it was Larry's turn to frown. "According to my information Leonard Birch left his two granddaughters an inheritance worth million, and you, Ms. Jaymes, are one of the two."

"But that's impossible," she said in a small voice, the lawyer's words almost shocking her into silence. This had to be a mistake. She wasn't prepared to hear about this.

"Ms. Jaymes, there are copies of both of your original birth certificates and they will verify that you and Mrs. Taylor are full, biological sisters."

Covering her face with her hands, Tippany shook her head vehemently as tears sprang to her eyes, while her brain tried to comprehend the words that he had just spoken.

"This can't be true...it just can't be," she said in a whisper. For so long, she wished she had another mother; someone who loved her and cared and now she found out she did. It was just too overwhelming, as she clutched the armrest to her chair and felt a sob catch in her throat. As the tears flowed freely down her cheeks, she felt a hand on her shoulder. Looking up, she saw through watery eyes, Keturah smiling at her.

"I know this is quite a shock, Tippany. But I must say, for me, this is a wonderful surprise," Keturah smiled through her tears. "I always felt we had a special connection, and now I know why." Extending her arms out to her sister, Tippany quickly filled them. They hugged, cried, laughed and then did it all over again.

"Well, I feel as if you two are more excited about discovering your full-blooded sisters, than you are at the knowledge that you've both just inherited a fortune," Attorney Cart said with a little laugh, not sure how to handle the weeping women in his office. "Let me see what I can do to get you excited about how drastically your lives are going to change." For the next two hours, he went over every detail of their inheritance, including a lucrative land-developing business that they now co-owned.

***

"I can't believe this has happened," Keturah said, while sitting at a little Italian restaurant where she and Tippany decided to have lunch. "I only wish Gretta were still alive, so she could enjoy this with us."

"I wish I would've known her," Tippany said remorsefully. "I hate that I missed out on having a happy childhood, surrounded by people who actually loved me. Instead, I had to grow up with a controlling, bitter woman who made every day a living hell for me," Tippany stated, feeling angry at her mother.

Reaching over, Keturah placed her hand over Tippany's, "I realize things weren't easy for you, Sis, but at least you had one of our parents in your life. I didn't have either. I had to learn about Mom from Gretta and I knew nothing about Dad. Now, we both are finding out that we had a rich grandfather," Keturah let out a frustrated sigh. "He could have helped me and Gretta, especially the last few months of her life. I could've avoided so much misery, if he would've come forward sooner. I don't understand his decision to keep his distance," Keturah said.

"Things between you and Abe haven't changed?" Tippany took hold of Keturah's hand and gave it a squeeze.

Keturah just shook her head, knowing that there were no words she could really say that would make her feel any better about the current state of her marriage.

Mostly everyone in the area knew that he had left the country without her. Rumors of an affair with Hagen were already beginning to spread, as well as more unflattering comments about her driving him away. Because she was left behind, she was the one dealing with the whispers and sideway glances. Rubbing her eyes, she wished she could just disappear.

"Lord, I'm so tired!" she muttered.

"Keturah, you're not in this alone anymore. I'm here, I'm your real family and with the money we just inherited, we have the ability to start over, the both of us."

"Tippany, things are not that simple. I'm carrying Abraham's baby."

Tippany gasped, and then asked, "Does Abraham know?" Keturah shook her head no and replied, "Only you and my co-worker Parson know. I had intended to tell Abraham, but with his abrupt departure, I didn't get the chance."

"Well, that's his loss," Tippany said indignantly, "Abraham has made his choice. I fear it's not a good one, but a choice nonetheless. I don't mean to be insensitive to your feelings, but you're going to have to face the facts that your arrangement is over."

Keturah openly let the tears slide down her face, as she stated, "But, I'm pregnant. That should count for something."

"Keturah, sex and love aren't the same thing. Men can have sex all day long and will get up and not even remember your first name. Now Abraham, he is a good man. But he has needs like any other man. You filled a need; a void. Don't try to build romantic sentimental notions off that," Tippany said absently, as she played with her tossed salad.

Her words weren't harsh, but they rubbed a sore spot causing Keturah to fire back at her sister, "Tippany, don't you think I know that! I'm not stupid. I know he doesn't love me, I just thought that maybe…I don't know," she heaved out a sigh. "I wanted our child to have two parents that loved and cared about them. I wanted my child to grow up differently than I did."

"Keturah, who's to say you won't have that type of relationship? Maybe it won't be with Abraham, but didn't you say God would grant us the desires of our hearts if we trust in him?

Keturah sighed, she couldn't fight against the truth of the word of God no matter how impossible her situation looked.

"Look, my vacation starts tomorrow. Why don't you and I take some time away from here? We can go and tour our company, maybe even take a trip abroad." Tippany said, hopefulness ringing as she spoke.

Keturah sat silently for a moment, thinking of all the times she and Gretta talked about what they'd do if they had a million dollars. Well, now she had it and then some. The first thing on the list was always taking a nice long vacation and thinking about life. "Getting away from all of this doesn't sound like a bad idea to me," she gave her sister the first hint of a smile.

"Yes!" Tippany smiled and gave a fist pump in the air. "Okay, where to?"

"Wherever women with a lot of money and broken hearts go," Keturah said, attempting to sound upbeat.

"How about Paris?" she held out her wine glass to Keturah, who smiled, picked up her water glass and tapped it with her sister's.

"Paris, the city of romance, perfect!" Keturah gave a sarcastic chuckle.

"Hey, who knows who's out there waiting for two gorgeously eligible," she pointed to herself then pointed to Keturah, "And almost, eligible bachelorettes."

"I think falling in love, getting pregnant, and divorced, all in the same year is all I can stand," Keturah laughed out loud at how incredulous it all sounded, "I don't think I have room for anything else. But you, on the other hand, Sister, you're about due for a nice romance."

"I don't know about that, but God knows I'm going to enjoy looking."

They both cracked up at that and with plans in place, decided to enjoy the rest of their meal, compliments of Grandpa Birch.

CHAPTER THIRTY-TWO

Checking everything twice, Keturah placed her hands on her hips and looked around her bedroom. Everything was in place and all her bags were packed. She was ready for her adventure in Paris.

It took some time before she and Tippany could get everything squared away so they could leave, a month later she was ready for their adventure to Paris and looking forward to having some awesome sister-time.

So far, she hadn't heard from Abraham, and was constantly getting stonewalled by his secretary about his whereabouts. She had to accept that their marriage was over.

But this was no time to dwell on her failed arrangement, the driver that Tippany was sending to collect her would be there any moment, so she dragged her last bag down the steps to the front door.

Noticing how winded she'd become from doing such a small task, her mind was already in relocation mode as soon as she got back. She needed to find another place, preferably one without steps and in a good school district.

"What do you guys think about a three-bedroom condo?" she queried out loud, laying a hand on her growing belly. *Twins,* she shook her head, "I'm having twins." Blowing the hair out of her eyes, she leaned on the wall for support, as anxiety rolled over her.

Ever since she learned about the dynamic duo growing inside her, she had moments where she felt completely overjoyed, and then in the next moment, overwhelmed. The feeling of being overwhelmed always passed when she remembered where her true help came from.

She closed her eyes and gave a short prayer, "Lord, thank you for these babies, and thank you for giving me the future strength needed to raise them up to be mighty men or women of God. Thank you for our destiny," she whispered out loud as the doorbell rang. "The driver!" She quickly pushed away from the wall and walked to the door. Swinging it open wide, she was stunned to see Parson standing in the doorway.

"Hey, you," he greeted.

"Hey!" she smiled in return.

"Am I catching you at an inconvenient time," he gave her a questioning look as he motioned with his eyes towards her luggage.

"Well, yeah, I guess so. I'm on my way out of town. I actually thought you were my ride." She shrugged her shoulders, noticing how attractive Parson looked sporting his five o'clock shadow. *Lord, help me. I shouldn't be noticing things like that. Despite everything, I'm still a married woman,* she thought.

"You know, I'm more than willing to take you wherever you need to go," he offered.

"Thanks, but I have it covered," she smiled, thinking to herself how awkward things still felt between them. She wished things could be different, but she wasn't about to go down that road. Living with regret got you nowhere.

"Listen, the real reason I stopped by was because I owe you an apology. I said some things that I shouldn't have. I was angry and hurt, but I feel that I made things worse between us when I shared my feelings; and if there is one thing I don't want to do, it's to lose your friendship."

"Parson, I realize things are crazy right now. Truth is, I should've been honest with you from the very beginning. I..."

Parson raised his hand and shook his head to stop her from continuing. "The bottom line is that you're a married woman, and for me to try and talk about a relationship between us when you're already in one is just wrong. I won't lie, I do wish things were different, but I respect your vows and only want friendship from you; if you're willing to still be friends," he said, sticking out his hand towards her.

"Friends?" she looked at his hand, then remembered what her sister said last week, "God might have a good husband for you, but just not the one you picked for yourself." Parson was a good man and a wonderful friend, no matter what did or didn't happen between them. She knew he was someone she could always count on and didn't want to lose that. "Can't you do better than a handshake, friend?" she said sarcastically with a smirk on her lips this time as she opened her arms.

"Yeah, I guess that was lame, huh?" he laughed, moving forward and walking into her embrace.

A buzzing in her pocket caused them to separate. Smiling at him, she felt in her pocket to retrieve her phone. It was Tippany.

"Hey Tippy, the driver's not here yet, but as soon as he comes, we'll swing by and come get you," she said cheerfully.

"Tourie, the driver is going to be extremely late because guess who just came in the office," she whispered.

Keturah's hand gripped the phone. She didn't have to ask who it was; she already knew. Call it crazy, but she had a strange sense that he was close by.

"I know this isn't the best time, but if you want to talk with him face to face, maybe this is your chance."

It wasn't in the plan to see Abraham today. She was still relatively small, so her pregnancy could still be hidden, but she wasn't certain if keeping this information from him was right. Maybe she should just bring everything out in the open. Tell him she was expecting twins and if he didn't want to stay with her, so be it. He could just sign the divorce papers and be done. At least that way, she knew it was over.

Part of her was scared that that's exactly what he'd do. But what if he wouldn't divorce her only to remain tied to her for the sake of the children? That idea didn't sit well with her either. She wouldn't be destitute, no matter what, now that she had an inheritance. Nevertheless, she wanted her husband's love, not his sense of duty.

He deserves to know and you should be the one to tell him. The Spirit whispered.

She knew she needed to do the right thing. She owed it to her children and herself to at least try and reason with him one last time. With a renewed determination she agreed, "You're right Tippany, I need to settle things with Abraham. I'll be there as soon as I can." Clicking off, she turned around to see Parson had already started taking her belongings and settling them in the trunk of his car. "Lord, thank you for good friends," she said as she grabbed her coat.

***

Standing in his office, glaring at the picture of the happy couple smiling back at her, Keturah rolled her eyes at the portrait of Abraham and Sarah. "I wish you'd drop..." realizing what she was about to say, she hung her head in shame and repented. Feeling foolish for being jealous of a dead woman, she turned and tried to focus on something else. Her eyes landed on a picture of her husband in his younger years. "Wow, you were a handsome devil," Keturah smirked. There was no doubt where Ishmael and Isaac got their deadly handsome looks. No wonder their fiancées kept them on a short leash, she figured.

"If you guys look anything like your daddy and older brothers, I'm going to have to beat the girls off you with a stick," she smiled as a warm feeling spread over her body. Instinctively, her hand traveled over her small mound. In a few more months, her dream of motherhood would become a reality. The thought was both exciting, but disheartening since it seems her children would be fatherless.

"Why are we in this mess, Abraham?" she sighed, allowing her hand to move from her midsection, to her loose curls. Scrutinizing the other pictures that littered his desk and mantle on the opposite wall, she looked at all the people in Abraham's life who put the brilliant smile on his face. It was obvious that Sarah did, but so did both his sons. Two pictures that stood out were the ones he had posed with them together. He looked genuinely happy standing between his boys in a casual pose, while they were in Jamaica. The other was when he stood, toasting his sons on their upcoming nuptials. His family made him happy; gave him his strength. She quickly turned away, no longer able to take the rejection, as she had to finally acknowledge what the absence of any pictures of them together meant.

He doesn't love you and you'll never be part of his family. A dark thought spoke.

It was clear to her now, that after being together for almost five months, she was still, and would likely always be the outsider. The knowledge of that truth hurt. *If we only had more time,* she thought, but no, time was up. Stepping out of Abraham's office, she approached his secretary, "How much longer will my husband be?"

"Oh, I'm sorry Mrs. Taylor; I thought his administrative assistant inform you that Mr. Taylor was running terribly late for his afternoon appointments and couldn't meet with you," she explained.

"What?!" Keturah bit out. "You mean he left, knowing I was here waiting for him?!" Keturah tried to keep her voice level, but didn't quite make it. She didn't want to take her anger out on his secretary, but she couldn't believe what she was hearing. "Mrs. Taylor, please try and understand. Mr. Taylor's work-schedule makes tremendous demands on his time. He's always juggling three to four meetings; some of them clear across the country. Now, I'm sure missing you was a simple oversight and he..."

Keturah held up her hand. "Stop. Just stop. Please don't insult my intelligence by making excuses for my husband. He's the CEO of a multimillion-dollar company; he could have made time for me, if he wanted to. Anyway, it no longer matters." She dropped a weighty eight-and-a-half by eleven-inch envelope on the desk and pointed to it, "See that your boss gets that," Keturah said in a clipped tone, not giving his secretary a chance to respond, turning on her heels she marched out of the room making her way to the elevators; her back straight and head held high. She was tired of being second in Abraham's eyes; second to his dead wife, second when it came to his grown children and second when it came to this company. She had given it her best shot. She had bent over backwards to try and make things work between them, but marriage was a two-way street that needed two willing participants.

One thing was clear; she was the only willing party in this marriage and, as much as she loved Abraham and wanted things to work for the sake of their children, she had her pride and would never beg any man to love her.

She wouldn't waste another day trying to salvage their failed marriage. No, make that a failed arrangement. She waited impatiently by the elevator, and when the doors opened, she went in. She closed her eyes as the elevator began to fill with Abraham's employee's. She didn't worry about them recognizing her. Why would they, she had only been at the office once before. She was sure if she'd been Sarah, everyone would've fallen over themselves trying to speak.

Feeling anger and a touch of bitterness pushing its way to the surface, she breathed in deeply and let her breath out slowly, remembering that stress wasn't good for the twins. *God, I need you,* she thought, as the motion from the elevator made her legs feel wobbly. Deciding to take a moment, she shut out everything around her as she began to inwardly pray.

God, your word says, in all things give thanks. So, I thank you. I never thought this would be the way things would end between me and Abraham, but it is what it is. I was wrong about so many things and I know I must deal with this pain in my heart, but with you, I'm going to make it. She vowed just as the door open on her floor. Stepping off the elevator she made a beeline out of the office building doors and onto the sidewalk. Feeling the warmth of the sun on her face she smiled up into the sky and repeated in her heart her solemn vow. Keturah Birch will be second to none.

AUTHOR'S NOTES

Keturah, which in Hebrew means incensed, fragrance, or sacrifice, married the biblical patriarch Abraham shortly after his first wife Sarah died. Some commentators have noted Keturah to be one of the most important yet, overlooked persons in the biblical text being mentioned only in Genesis 25:1-6 and I Chronicles 1:32, 33. A complete portrait has not been painted of this phenomenal woman who by God's grace her lineage includes Africans, Arabs, and possibly Greeks.

I hope you enjoyed reading *Keturah the II* and invite you to read the upcoming sequel *Keturah II to None*, coming Fall 2020.

Your feedback is extremely valuable so if you enjoyed the story please consider writing a review at Amazon.com and feel free to connect with me on my webpage: www.vicstories.com or my Facebook page HerBet Publishing. I would love to hear from you, so please feel free to email me at vicstories17@gmail.com

Blessings,

Vickie

www.ingramcontent.com/pod-product-compliance
Lightning Source LLC
Chambersburg PA
CBHW051102030726
47504CB00006B/1753